The beast of Rannoch Moor

by
Mike Healey

A DCI John White and Elspeth Grant crime novel

The Beasts of Rannoch Moor

Dedication

For Tom, my son
Who is not always crazy about rich food but who *does* love a good yarn

Copyright

Mike Healey has asserted his rights under the Copyright, Designs and Patents Act, 1998 to be identified as author of all five works

All rights reserved. No part of this publication may be reproduced, stored in a retrieval system, or transmitted, in any form or by any means, electronic, mechanical, photocopying, recording, or otherwise, without the written prior permission of the author.

Disclaimer

This is a work of fiction.

While I have tried to place the action in actual locations, none of the characters are based on real people, nor indeed is the Rannoch Moor Hotel in my story based on any real hotel in or even near that part of Scotland.

My hotel is a complete invention.

Any resemblance to actual persons, living or dead, is entirely coincidental.

© Copyright 2013 Mike Healey

The beasts of Rannoch Moor

1
Thursday, 11th October

Rannoch Moor is a desolate spot in Scotland - not unlike the surface of the moon but a great deal wetter. Numerous small lochs and countless lochans dot the landscape. There are no indigenous trees on the moor itself - only a few stunted bushes or clusters of gorse clinging tenaciously to the rock, and the occasional ruin of a tree - twisted, dead, probably destroyed by lightening. There are cultivated forests to the north of Loch Laidon and below Loch Eigheach reservoir, through which the railway line runs going south, but otherwise the landscape is bare, bleak and magnificently beautiful. Here in winter, cold winds blow relentlessly - invariably bringing sleet or snow. The surrounding mountains are rugged and uninviting. Above it all, looming dark on the western horizon, Britain's tallest mountain - Ben Nevis and beyond that, the awesome scenery of Glen Coe.

In other words, Rannoch Moor is not somewhere you would want to be out at night, alone.

Charles Mitchell is a short, balding, somewhat overweight sixty-one-year-old marketing director dressed immaculately in brogue shoes, tweed jacket and plus fours. For the last twenty minutes he has been running across the moor below Dubh Lochan, pursued by three men with dogs. It is late evening and although the lights from the hotel are just visible behind him, it is growing dark very quickly. The sun, now sinking fast in the west, rims the mountains with a dull, red glow. Mitchell had cried for help the moment he realised that they were after him but his words had been instantly blown away by the wind, unheeded. Besides, there was no one there to heed his cries for help.

He is now running for his life.

His pursuers are some thirty yards behind him and closing. The dogs are straining at their leashes, snarling and gnashing their teeth. Saliva dribbles from their jaws and their demonic barking spreads across the moor like a thunderous curse.

Suddenly a shot rings out. The high velocity bullet hits Mitchell in the shoulder, spinning him round. He takes two or three more steps, backwards, then falls to the ground. He lies there, groaning in agony and clutching the gaping wound that was once his shoulder. Blood stains the grass and rock on which he now lies in agony.

'Stop this, you bastards. Stop! Why are you doing this? Why? What in God's name have I done to be treated like this?'

The men have now reached him. They are close enough for their dogs to snap at Mitchell's ankles. Their barking and ferocious growls make him momentarily forget the pain in his shoulder. He is now absolutely terrified.

Their leader - a lean, nut-brown ferret of a man holding the rifle - leans forward. His face is close to Mitchell's. He speaks in a quiet yet menacing manner.

'You have done nothing, wee man. Nothing! This is sport. We are the hunters and *you* are the hunted. Its as simple as that. Now get to your feet and run or I will let the dogs finish you off!'

Mitchell scrambled to his feet. He backed off a few yards then turned and ran away from the hunters as fast as he could. Although he was still losing blood, the pain in his shoulder had vanished - extinguished by absolute fear. Behind him, as he scrambled from rock to rock, he could hear the wild cries of the hunters, raucous and full of mockery, mingled with the ferocious barking of their dogs.

It was as Mitchell scrambled over an outcrop of rock, his body silhouetted against the lowering sky, that a second shot rang out. It struck him just below the knee. Although it was a glancing blow, his legs buckled beneath him and he fell to his knees.

By the time the huntsmen reached him a second time he lay sprawled on the ground, face down in an icy puddle.

Rough hands at once haul him up into a kneeling position.

He tries to speak, to plead for his life again but the barrel of a twelve-bore gun is immediately shoved close to his face and the trigger pulled. His head, blown to smithereens, is instantly reduced to bloody shards of bone smeared with brain tissue that end up in a gorse bush, some twenty feet away. For a bizarre moment or two his body remains upright, but then topples slowly sideways onto the blood-stained snow.

They then strip Mitchell naked and stuff his clothes and personal belongings - wallet, watch, keys - into a bag. By this time the dogs are in a wild frenzy and its is all that their keepers can do to keep them under control. Once Mitchell has been stripped, the dogs are released and begin to devour the body, tearing it limb from limb. It is a gruesome sight but the men seem to relish the process, sharing a dram or two as they watch their dogs gore themselves on the former client and guest.

Once the dogs have had their fill, the men drag what remains of the body and throw it into the nearest lochan. At first the torn and mutilated torso floats but when one of the ghillies wades into the water and places a large boulder on the dead man's lacerated chest, it slowly disappears out of sight beneath the dark, peaty water.

By the time dawn breaks over the wastes of Rannoch Moor, bringing ominous dark clouds and a real threat of snow, Mitchell's body has completely vanished, as have his hunters and their dogs. Calm descends once more upon the beautiful, stark, desolate moor.

Friday, 12th October

It has been a particularly busy week for Detective Chief Inspector John White. His CID team have finally wrapped up a case involving the death, under somewhat mysterious circumstances, of an old man found in bed in a small village called Muir of Ord, on the outskirts of Inverness.

The man had been dead for several days but because the electric blanket had been left on, his body had swollen enormously. When the police were finally summoned to his house by neighbours complaining of the dreadful smell, they were obliged to break down the door .

The smell was unbelievable. Even hardened paramedics recoiled from the body when forced to pour this bag of putrefying tissue into a plastic container. DCI White had actually witnessed this part of the process and had had great difficulty in retaining his breakfast. That night he washed his clothes to try and get rid of that smell but in the end threw them all into an incinerator. As it turned out, the autopsy proved that the man had died or natural causes but it was a death that White and his colleagues, not least the paramedics, will long remember.

It is, therefore, with some relief that Friday evening that John White turns his car into the drive of his cottage in Dunkeld, parks it in the garage and greets his wife in their kitchen. It is a cold October evening so that he is glad to then slip into his chair in front of a roaring wood-fire and accept the dry-martini cocktail Poppy handed him, accompanied by a gentle kiss on his cheek.

'Good God, John! What on earth is that smell?'

* * *

Charles Mitchell was not missed that weekend. When one guest enquired as to his whereabouts he was politely told that Mr Mitchell had checked out of the hotel on Thursday evening and had driven back to Durham 'on urgent business'. The guest, who only knew Mitchell slightly, thought no more of the matter. What was strange, however, was that Mitchell's suitcases were left in reception, next to the Porter's Lodge. They remained there for most of Friday. They were, it seemed. 'to be sent on'. True enough, they had vanished by that evening.

How they had been 'sent on' was something of a mystery; a mystery that was never solved since none of the guests were remotely interested. Least of all the late Charles Mitchell himself, now forgotten in some remote corner of Rannoch Moor.

Saturday, 13th October

John White and his wife Arabella have been married nearly eighteen years. Although there are no children, they are happy and content. They love each other and are not afraid to show it, even in public.

That evening they are dining in their favourite restaurant in Dunkeld - a small, family-run Italian restaurant.

Dunkeld is in Perthshire. It is where Beatrix Potter first learned all about mycology from the local postie, Charlie McIntosh. It was here too, one magical summer's day, that she wrote a letter to a young relative featuring four rabbits - Flopsy, Mopsy, Cottontail and Peter. The date was September, 1893 and that illustrated letter was the start of Beatrix Potter's future career as a writer, illustrator and storyteller.

The restaurant favoured by the Whites is situated in the 17th Century part of Dunkeld and within sight of the ruined cathedral. Their host that night is its owner, Mario Ghironi.

'Madame, I can recommend the grilled swordfish this evening, served with a fresh sauce of oregano, garlic and lemon.'

'Thank you, Mario. That sounds delicious. Darling?'

'Wow. There is so much to chose from. Pollo all cacciatora. What is that, Mario?'

'Cacciatore means hunter. It was, traditionally, a dish that the wife of the hunter gave him when he returned after a day's hunting. It is chicken, anchovies and olives cooked in a Chianti sauce with plumb tomatoes. It is served with cannelloni beans.'

'Fantastic!', said John. 'That's my choice, please.'

'Very well. May I recommend a Chianti? I have a very good one this month from Pontassieve. Perfect for that 'special occasion.'

'Yes. Thank you Mario.'

Mario left the table and went to place their order with his Chef - a young relative of his from Verona. Even the waiters are cousins. This really is a family-run business. Mario's wife is the only one not visible that evening. She occupies a tiny office at the back of the restaurant and rules the accounts with an iron fist. She is called Angelica.

'And what 'special occasion' might that be, John?', asked Poppy.

'Why, our eighteenth wedding anniversary, my darling. Had you forgotten?'

'Certainly not. I naturally assumed that you had, though. You did last year.'

'Yes. Well, not this time! What's more, I have a very special treat for you.'

'Treat? Oh goodie! Not another diamond, surely? New Porsche or is it a Aston Martin this time?'

'Stop teasing me. No, I have some leave due so I have booked us into a very smart hotel for an extended weekend, starting next Friday - to celebrate our eighteenth anniversary in style. Fine food and excellent fishing.'

'Wow! Where. Tuscany? Bahamas? Worthing?'

'No. Scotland's very own Rannoch Moor.'

Monday, 15th October

The hotel on Rannoch Moor has stables containing six horses.

These fine animals are available to guests, at a price, for their enjoyment and exercise.

The stables are housed behind the hotel, on three sides of an old, cobbled courtyard. It is here that Geraldine Capulet waits early this morning as the stable-lad saddles up a fine, chestnut mare for her use.

It had been snowing earlier that morning and a thin layer now covers the ground. However, the sun is out and it has all the appearance of a fine day but on Rannoch Moor the weather can change within minutes. Geraldine has been out riding most mornings since she arrived at the hotel last Wednesday. She is due back in Edinburgh in two days time. Despite the poor conditions underfoot, she is therefore determined to get in as much riding as she can. Her mare is a well mannered, steady animal and providing she sticks to the track the horse will cope comfortably with the thin layer of snow and occasional patches of ice.

Some children, belonging to staff at the hotel, are playing in the yard, throwing snowballs at each other and generally gadding about.

They are a scruffy lot, unkempt and rather dirty - as far as Geraldine can tell. She has seen most of them before. There are about seven very young children living on the estate and a handful of teenagers. It is unclear if any of them attend school for the nearest is some thirty-seven miles away at Kinloch Rannoch and Geraldine has never seen a school bus at the hotel or any sign, most weekday mornings, that these children are driven anywhere by their parents. Perhaps, thought Geraldine, they are taught at home but if so, there is little evidence that it is working for these children are not only dirty but wild and noisy. 'Little savages' is how most people who have encountered these urchins describe them.

It is when one of their snowballs lands close to her feet that Geraldine makes a snowball herself and throws it back in their direction. To her surprise it strikes one small, ugly child of about seven full in the face. Immediately, all five children stop what they are doing, stare malevolently at Geraldine then turn and run away, quickly vanishing somewhere behind the stables.

'She's ready, Miss.'

It is the stable lad. He leads the mare out onto the cobbles and hands the reins to Geraldine.

'I hope I didn't hurt him. I did not mean to hit him in the face!'

'Dinna fret, Miss. They're a wild lot. I canna stand them myself. Little buggers, pardon the expression, Miss.'

The stable lad, whose name is David, helps Geraldine into her saddle and watches her as she crosses the cobbled yard and moves out onto the service road behind the hotel. From there she heads towards the railway station, crosses the line at the small level-crossing and trots off towards the forest that follows the loch due west.

The clear skies have now vanished, replaced by dark grey clouds threatening more snow - such is the speed with which the weather changes on Rannoch Moor. Being an excellent horsewoman, she quickly gets the measure of her mare and the surface underfoot and sets off at a fair canter down the lane into a snowy, lunar landscape of ice-age rubble, large boulders and scrubby moor-land flecked with lurid, yellow gorse. She decides to skirt the southern edge of the forest and then double back in a broad circle of about five miles across open moorland - in time for lunch.

She has only gone a mile or two when suddenly, stepping out from behind a large rock, there appears the figure of young man - blowing hard on his bagpipes and making a racket that would startle a troll.

The mare, not expecting such an apparition or such an alarming sound in the middle of nowhere, immediately rears onto its hind legs, unseating its rider. It then takes off at a gallop, back towards the hotel - leaving Geraldine, momentarily winded and lying on the stony path.

It is then that three other McBanes appear - diminutive creatures with slightly bandy legs. One of them she immediately recognises - the ugly child whom she had inadvertently struck in the face with a snowball.

Geraldine lies on her back, groaning in agony from her fall. Nothing is broken, as far as she can tell, but she is badly winded. The three young McBanes move towards her cautiously. They are grinning and looking at each other expectedly. The teenager with the bagpipes looks on from a few yards away but makes no effort to assist the fallen rider or take part in what follows.

The last thing Geraldine sees before they bash in her skull are two weird children with pale skins and wild, blue eyes pinning her to the ground while a third, sitting on her chest, holds a large boulder high above her head.

* * *

No one missed Geraldine at supper that evening.

She had made no friends during her short stay at the Rannoch Moor Hotel. Indeed, several guests who had noted the well-dressed English woman, normally in expensive riding clothes often seated alone in the saloon bar or residents' lounge, had thought that she was somewhat stand-offish and had chosen therefore to ignore her.

No one either saw the chestnut mare return to its stable without its rider later that morning. Nor, indeed, did any of the guests see Geraldine's body in a black plastic body-bag being taken by a quad-bike and trailer to the large furnace behind the hotel - the furnace that seemed to be permanently lit and which supplied heat to the McBane's extensive hot-house. As far as any of the guests cared or were interested (none were), Geraldine Capulet had checked-out and had left unexpectedly - 'on urgent business'. That at least was the official line that the hotel now used (whenever necessary) to cover up and otherwise conceal her unexpected and horrific demise.

No one, however, could ignore Colonel Blunt.

Blunt by name, blunt by nature - a noisy, gregarious individual whom it is difficult to either disregard or avoid in public places. He is a former military man, now in his mid-fifties. He has a fine moustache yet is as bald as a coot. He also has a red nose and bleary eyes - clear indicators that the retired colonel is very fond of his whiskey. Indeed, he is drunk most evenings and invariably the last one to leave the hotel bar. He is, however, an experienced huntsman and an excellent shot and for that reason the professional Gamekeeper and ghillies attached to the hotel enjoy his company on the moor. He also tips well so that may also explain his popularity.

It is now Tuesday afternoon, the day after Geraldine Capulet's 'accident'. Since the snow has not returned, Colonel Blunt has been encouraged by Head Gamekeeper Jamie McBane to try once more to bag a deer or two. Although snow is still thick on the hills above the forest adjacent to Loch Laidon and the terrain there very rough, McBane is confident that the Colonel will enjoy some excellent sport that afternoon - before his brief stay on Rannoch Moor ends. Indeed, deer have been spotted leaving the shelter of the forests for higher ground only an hour or so ago.

'It is', Jamie McBane argues, 'now or never, colonel.'

Colonel Blunt is easily persuaded and after a largely liquid lunch he puts on his hunting jacket and plus-fours, checks his gun and meets Jamie at the entrance to the hotel.

* * *

The Rannoch Moor Hotel and Hunting Lodge occupies a very remote spot, slap in the middle of Rannoch Moor. It consists of a large, Victorian hotel or 'hunting lodge' surrounded by out-houses and small cottages. The cottages are occupied by the hotel staff, of which there are twenty-seven - including a gamekeeper and five professional ghillies. The hamlet can be reached - weather permitting - by road from Pitlochry. There are no other roads. There is, of course, the railway line that runs across the moor on its way to Fort William but in winter trains are not that frequent or regular. Often, if it has been snowing for any period, this line is closed, leaving the hamlet surrounding the hotel itself completely isolated.

Apart from Loch Laidon, the moor is dotted with small lochs (lochans) and countless streams. It is famous for its sport - hunting, shooting and fishing. The western edge of the moor is marked by the A82 road that goes north to Fort William, via Glen Coe. To reach this road from the hotel is extremely difficult, especially in winter. Apart from its natural beauty, Rannoch Moor is a dangerous place and should not be attempted without proper equipment and detailed maps. Even then, unwary travellers have frequently lost their way for the weather here can change dramatically, from bright sunshine to thick fog, driving rain or blizzard within minutes.

People have died on Rannoch Moor. Some people have even died from natural causes.

* * *

Colonel Blunt, accompanied by the estate's Head Gamekeeper and three ghillies, have now reached the western edge of the forest known as Ceann Caol na Cruaiche, two miles north of the railway station. On their left is the conical mass of rock known as Meall Liath na Doire, rising some five-hundred-and-eighty feet above sea level. Twenty minutes later Colonel Blunt and the hunting party emerge from the forest. The sun has now appeared from behind dark clouds, casting its light onto the bare mountain, its snow-covered cap now turned to a dazzling saffron yellow.

The hunting party leave the track and head north, skirting the western edge of a large forest of Scots pine and fir trees. Here there are deer tracks in the snow and some droppings. The Head Gamekeeper is now confident that some three or four deer are on the move. These deer have clearly eaten all the grazing close to the edge of the forest and are now needing to feed further away - on open moor-land at Glac Dhubh or even onto the rugged slopes of the mountain itself.

This might be the chance the hunters have been waiting for.

'Look', said a ghillie, suddenly pointing with his gun towards an outcrop of rock to their left, 'there they are!'

Sure enough, clearly silhouetted against the snow, stand three deer and in their midst a handsome, fully-grown stag.

The party at once divide into two, with Colonel Blunt leading the way, accompanied by Head Gamekeeper Jamie McBane some thirty-feet behind him. The others quickly moved further north and spread out - to cut off possible retreat for the deer should they make a dash back towards the forest and safety. Slowly, both groups move in on their targets - until Blunt is some two-hundred-and-fifty metres from the stag itself. He takes up a kneeling position, scanning the small group of deer on the horizon with his binoculars. Jamie kneels on the grass some twenty meters behind him and slightly to the colonel's right. He is carrying two slim, high-velocity rifles - one of which belongs to the colonel.

The others are now out of sight, hidden from sight behind a small hill further east. This rocky outcrop is covered in gorse and heather.

It is as Blunt is beckoning silently with his arm for Jamie to join him that a shot rings out, the high-velocity bullet whistling past Colonel Blunt's right ear. Although it does not hit him, the percussive force of the bullet causes Blunt to fall to one side, landing heavily in wet heather. He is momentarily deafened and blood begins to trickle from his ear.

'What the hell...?'

He at once scrambles to his feet, turning to face the man behind him. He is about to remonstrate when, to his horror, he sees Jamie McBane again taking aim. The gun, only thirty feet away now, is pointing straight at him.

The great stag and its deer have long since vanished by the time Blunt fully realises what is happening.

'Jamie, what are you doing, for God's sake? You nearly hit me, man!'

'Aye, that I did. I suggest you run, you bastard. I may not miss you a second time!'

With that Jamie again raises his gun and points it straight at the terrified man, now kneeling in the snow and holding a hand to his wounded ear. The other ghillies have now appeared from around their rock and are hurrying towards Jamie and Blunt. They are waving their guns in the air and are making whooping noises, like some ghastly pagan chant. Blunt stares in utter amazement at this horrifying spectacle. He is momentarily lost for words.

'Go on then! Run! Run for your life, colonel!', shouts Jamie, deliberately aiming his gun at the colonel's bald head. Blunt's cap has fallen to the ground and there is now blood spattered on the snow at his feet.

Blunt, quivering with fear, staggers to his feet. Before he can remonstrate further Jamie fires a second shot that whistles past Blunt's head. Instinctively, the colonel at once turns and runs as fast as he can, away from his assailant. He is slipping and sliding on the icy rock. He is now squealing with terror, like a pig that is about to have its throat cut.

Almost immediately, a third shot rings out, grazing Blunt's right arm. The noise of the gunshot echoes off the mountain. It is drowned by more whoops of excitement from the ghillies. Blunt can feel an excruciating pain in his upper arm and a heavy trickle of blood running down his sleeve. Driven now by absolute terror, he scrambles from one rock to another, heading towards a large, granite outcrop to his left. The fourth bullet strikes him on the side of the head, removing his left ear. He immediately falls to the ground, blood pouring from the gaping hole.

Although now seriously wounded he again manages to stagger to his feet and face his opponents.

'For God's sake, man, what are you doing? Are you fucking mad? Stop this, stop this madness!'

The McBanes ignore his cries for mercy and respond only with more wild whoops of excitement and triumph as all four move in for the kill.

Blunt, now absolutely terrified, scrambles to his feet and takes off again across the moor, splashing through large puddles of icy water, leaping from rock to rock and crashing through outcrops or stark, yellow gorse. Ahead of him the ground rises steeply towards a granite outcrop. Blunt's breathing is heavy, coming in sudden, terrified gasps. The blood in his head pounds and his wounds throb and pulsate. At each step the snow is covered in lurid drops of blood.

He finally reaches the granite outcrop. For a moment, as he scrambles up the mountain side, Blunt is silhouetted against an azure sky but the fourth and fatal bullet strikes him full in the back and catapults him off the rock and into a narrow, snow-filled ravine.

***

Oxford that afternoon is a far removed from the desolates wastes of Rannoch Moor as can be imagined.

For once the rain has vanished and Oxford, in all its glory, is this afternoon awash with sunlight. The sandstone walls of the ancient university buildings are now a rich, golden brown. The tiles on each slate-grey roof glisten, the sunlight bouncing off their wet surfaces. The streets are busy with shoppers. Students in their black academic gowns hurry about their business - heading for their next lecture or tutorial or, more likely, the nearest pub. It is a lively, bustling town. Too much traffic of course but a fine place to be that surprisingly warm, October afternoon.

Professor Elspeth Grant PhD is, therefore, in an excellent mood.

She is walking from her lecture theatre at the Department of Criminology, Manor Road towards All Souls College, situated at the centre of Oxford, just of Radcliffe Square. Elspeth Grant is a Fellow of All Souls. It is here - when teaching or studying in Oxford - that she resides.

All Souls is a graduate college. The entrance exam is said to be the hardest in academia, with only one or two appointments a year. It is also said that some of the finest brains in Britain are to be found here, often preserved in alcohol for the vast wine cellars of this distinguished academic establishment are famous. It is rumoured to have a financial endowment in the region of £220 million. It is therefore the richest college in Oxford and certainly its most exclusive. For Elspeth Grant, one of Britain's most distinguished Criminologists, its is simply her Oxford 'digs' and favourite watering hole.

Elspeth was on Catte Street, close to the Sheldonian Theatre and not far from the ornate gates of All Souls when she was approached by a young woman.

'Excuse me, Dr. Grant. Forgive me for contacting you in this way but I need to talk to you. Its very urgent.'

The woman is about thirty, slim and rather beautiful. She has raven-black hair cut in a severe bob and pale skin. Elspeth is impressed.

'Very well. Shall we find a pub? I could murder a sherry. When in Rome...'

Elspeth led the way beneath Oxford's very own 'Bridge of Sighs' adjacent to Hertford College, then ducked down a narrow, dog-leg alleyway. Moments later they emerged from this passageway redolent of cat piss into an area surrounded by old Victorian buildings and the high, ancient stone walls of New College. Before them squatted an old pub - The Turf Tavern, Bath Place. There was a walled garden to one side and another 'beer-garden' at the back. The pub itself had bare stone walls, low ceilings and a much lived-in feel. The Turf is one of Oxford's most celebrated pubs, famous for its wide range of real ales. And its sherry, served straight from the barrel.

Elspeth chose a table in one corner of the smaller of the three rooms. The barman hovered behind the bar, just a few feet away. Elspeth smiled at him (he was young and good looking) and ordered a schooner of Tio Pepe, Fino served straight from the barrel.

'What would you like, my dear?', she asked, turning to her unexpected yet extremely beautiful guest.

'Red wine, please, Dr Grant.'

'I don't recommend it. Not here. Try a sherry. The Bodegas Fernando de Castilla Antique is to die for.'

'Very well, thank you.'

Elspeth ordered the drink, waited until it had been served then raised her glass to the young woman sitting across the table.

'Cheers! Please call me Elspeth. And what is it that is so urgent that you need to follow me all the way from Manor Road to Catte Street before accosting me? Not that I am complaining, of course. Its not that often that a charming French woman comes up to me in the street in such a blatant manner. By the way, what did you say your name was?'

Wednesday, 17th October

Rannoch Moor is bathed in thin, wintry light. The wind has dropped somewhat but the clouds still threaten snow.

Some five miles from where the headless body of Mitchell had briefly lain that previous week can be found the single railway track that crosses Rannoch Moor, ending at Fort William, deep in heart of the Western Highlands.

The night-sleeper from London that in winter twice a week crosses these desolate moors is now powering its way towards the little station at Rannoch - carrying with it men and women, pleasure bent. Indeed, its carriages contain a veritable cross section of well-off, middle-class society - husbands and wives, friends and lovers, old and young. Stuffed in the racks above their heads are guns, fishing rods, nets and all the other paraphernalia of the British sporting-class determined, for a few days at least, to kill as much wild life as their hosts will allow them or luck determines.

Meanwhile, forty miles to the east, high above Loch Rannoch's grey waters, a silver seaplane banks steeply above the village of Kinloch Rannoch, aligning its sleek fuselage with the narrow road that follows the lake westwards. It is a Hughes HK-1 Hercules from the 1930's, lovingly restored by its present owner and pilot, Giles Beaumont . As it turns and adjusts its position for its final descent, its wings glint in the sunlight.

Inside, northern industrialist Sir Miles Ballard and his blonde mistress Cecelia Arnold, sip their champagne and peer down at the car far beneath them.

'Well, bugger me,' declared Sir Miles, 'I do believe that's Teddy Bosenquet down there. Cheeky young scoundrel. Trying to beat me, eh? Not bloody likely! We'll be there long before him. More Champagne, my dear?'

Cecelia, feeling slightly airsick, slumped lower in her seat. Moreover, she is still a little the worse for wear after a torrid night with Sir Miles at her flat in London's Mayfair. She groans inwardly.

'No thank you, darling. Are we nearly there?'

On the northern edge of the loch a 1932 Bugatti 'Royale' speeds along the narrow, winding road - the choppy waters of the loch to one side and dark forest on the other. The Bugatti is also heading for Rannoch Moor but is no match for a seaplane that soon leaves it far behind.

Cecelia does not share her lover's enthusiasm for classic aircraft, beautiful as they undoubtedly are. It was Ballard's idea to travel from London to Scotland by seaplane. Since cost was no object, Sir Miles had chartered one of the best seaplanes still flying. He had even spent some time at the controls. Boys will be boys, thought Cecelia. But then, if you are as rich as Miles Ballard ....

Minutes later, the sea-plane begins its descent and lands effortlessly on choppy water at the western end of the loch. It then taxis in a whirl of spray to the landing stage that serves Rannoch Lodge. Sir Miles and Cecelia disembark and climb into the minibus waiting there for them. Twenty minutes later they reach the Rannoch Moor Hotel - an imposing, mock-Gothic building close to a tiny railway station, largely unchanged since the 1930's.

They have finally arrived at the Rannoch Moor Hotel and Hunting Lodge - one of Scotland's most celebrated watering holes.

They are met at reception by the Manager, Ronald McBane.

'Sir Miles, it is so good to have you back here again. Madame. Stewart here will show you to your rooms.'

'Thank you Ronald. It's good to be back.'

Forty minutes later Teddy Bosenquet and his young fiancée, The Honourable Lady Olympia Garland, turn their Bugatti into the forecourt of the Rannoch Moor Hotel, screeching to a halt in a shower of gravel. They quickly check in at the reception desk and, with unseemly haste, take to their bed where Teddy pleasures his bride-to-be with all the energy and enthusiasm of the fit, young cad that he is - the most recent in a long line of cads that extends back to his great, great grandfather, Lord Arnold Bosenquet of Jodhpur.

That afternoon, other couples elsewhere in this sprawling Victorian hotel, unpack and restore the ravages of their journey with a dry sherry or two and a nibble of home-made shortbread from the tray their hosts have thoughtfully left on each bedside table. Some guests have also come by car but most by train - some from as far as London. Many are tired after their long journey. All are looking forward to their first meal in a hotel celebrated for its fabulous cuisine and lavish hospitality. Five Star. Sumptuous. Ruinously expensive but for gourmets and sporting types, the best that Scotland can offer.

Gleneagles might disagree with that claim but for those who regularly come here, this hotel with its wonderful food and unique sporting activities is an experience not to be forgotten.

* * *

Back in Oxford, Elspeth slips out of bed and totters from the bedroom into the sitting room, opens the mini-bar, takes ice, a slice of lemon and a bottle of tonic water and pours herself a refreshing drink.

It is ten o'clock on the morning of Wednesday, 17th October. She has a hangover and is hovering metaphysically somewhere between death and ecstatic spiritual elation.

The evening had not gone at all as she had expected. After far to many sherries in the Turf Tavern, she and the young French woman had staggered to the gates of All Souls where Elspeth had tried to smuggle her new companion into her rooms. She had been politely but firmly repulsed by the Porter. Undeterred by such effrontery, Elspeth had then hailed a passing cab on Hollywell Street and travelled the short distance to The Randolph Hotel, Beaumont Street where she took a room for the night.

Since Elspeth's former companion - a beautiful young man from Somalia affectionately known as 'Mother' - had vanished from her life, Elspeth Grant had lived the life of a celibate don. All that ended that fateful night when the young woman - who turned out to be Parisian - first kissed her, then undressed her and then took her to bed. Elspeth, who had not slept with a woman since she was a girl at Rodean School, Brighton, was a willing companion and spent the larger part of that night on a roller-coaster journey of violent passion mixed with moments of exquisite tenderness.

Her new lover's name is Gabriélle.

It was true - she *had* been following Elspeth that day after Elspeth's lecture in the Department of Criminology on Manor Road. She had even attended that lecture, sitting discretely at the back. Indeed, she had been following Elspeth for two days, stalking her every move. It was only on the third day, on Catte Street, that she had picked up enough courage to approach Elspeth and accost her.

Elspeth put her empty glass on the table and moved back to the door of their bedroom.

Gabriélle, naked, lay fast asleep on the bed. The sheet had ridden up, exposing one delectable thigh. Elspeth gazed at it lovingly, then quietly moved to the bed and adjusted the sheet to cover her new lover. She then bent and gently kissed her on the cheek. Gabriélle stirred but did not wake up. Elspeth then tiptoed out of the room, closing the door quietly behind her.

She moved to the telephone and dialled.

'John, is that you? Its Elspeth. I'm in Oxford. You have a problem.'

* * *

It is now seven o'clock on the evening of Wednesday, 17th October. The new guests that arrived earlier that day by rail or car at the Rannoch Moor Hotel are being summoned to supper by Stewart McBane, a lad of seventeen yet already a piper of some distinction.

Stewart is standing half-way up the grand, central staircase and playing his bagpipes. He is dressed in full Highland dress and looks very smart. He is playing what is called a *pibroch* or - more precisely - *Pìobaireachd*. This word, as the wee brochure readily available at the reception desk explains, is itself derived from the Gaelic for 'piper'. In Gaelic *pìobaireachd* literally refers to any pipe music, not merely the Ceòl Mór (big music) normally associated with the Great Highland bagpipes.

Thus it was that the guests that evening emerged from their respective rooms on the first floor and assembled informally together on the landing, listening appreciatively to Stewart's plaintive music. After a minute or two (there is only so much bagpipe music that one can endure, particularly if supper beckons) they all descend the grand staircase. On reaching the hall they fan out, some heading for the bar for an *aperitif* perhaps, others going straight on into the dinning room to begin their long-awaited, evening meal

No one knows from where exactly the McBane family first came to these parts, for they are not natives of Rannoch Moor. They are, however, numerous. Indeed, the hotel is now run entirely by members of the family - from Ronald McBane the Manager to young Stewart, now standing proudly on the landing. Even the Station Master and the local Postie are McBanes - as is the only policeman in the area. He is based at Bridge of Gaur, the nearest hamlet to this remote hotel and hunting lodge.

All, however, are dedicated to making their guests' stay at Rannoch as memorable as possible.

As to the building itself, it is said that Ronald McBane's great, great grandfather built the first proper hotel (he called it a 'hunting lodge') on this site in 1780. It had once been a modest, late 17th[th] Century inn until then but when the McBane family acquired the estate in 1778 they enlarged it year by year. Finally, in 1898, Charles McBane (Ronald's grandfather) hired Edward Calvert to double the hotel in size and redecorate it throughout. Today it stands as one of the more absurd examples of late Gothic Revival in Scotland but is still very impressive, never-the-less.

Dinner that evening - served in the vast, baronial hall that is the hotel's architectural gem - consisted of Scotch broth, turbot, boiled salmon, mutton collops, pigeon pie, boiled chicken, boiled ham and French beans followed by mushrooms, peas and lobster and rounded off with a 'fairy feast' of preserved strawberries, cherries and sweetmeats served with generous scoops of almond cream. Not only was the food and wine wonderful but the service unostentatious and highly efficient. McBane's staff are clearly well trained and attentive to their guests' every need. The hotel's reputation, well known throughout Scotland and increasingly beyond, is therefore much deserved.

Later that night, as the guests gradually retire to bed or linger in the bar over just one more fine whiskey, two men with guns slung across their shoulders, slip out of the back door of the hotel and set off west down the lane and past the railway station.

The weather has abated and a full moon now bathes the surrounding moor-land and countless small lakes in its light. Although the promise of snow still hangs in the air like an evil threat, the otherwise desolate landscape that stretches out on all sides from the hotel is truly beautiful.

The track the two men have taken leads due west from the railway station, towards a small loch (Dubh Lochan) at the head of Loch Laidon. The track here is well marked and largely free of snow.

It is here, less than five hundred meters from the hotel, that George Lowry and his younger brother Terence have decided to take the air for a while before retiring to bed. They have taken this short walk most evenings since their arrival a week ago. There are no clouds for once and the vast sky above them is full of stars. With the moon now full, the wild and rocky landscape - stretching off into the darkness - is very beautiful and tranquil.

George is surprised, therefore, when a shotgun, at point-blank range, suddenly blows Terence off the path and into an adjacent bog.

'Oh my God!. Terry! What's happened? Terry!'

George looks around him wildly. At first he can see no one and is about to go to his brother's body, now lying face down and spread-eagled in murky brown water, when another shot rings out and two figures emerge from behind a large rock. A third bullet strikes the ground close to his feet, causing splinters of rock to graze his legs. His feet buckle under him and he falls to his knees.

Terrified by this sudden and unexpected attack, George immediately stands up and takes off down the stony path, running as fast as he can away from the hotel. After twenty or so meters he stumbles but immediately regains his feet and staggers on down the track, his heart pounding. He glances over his shoulder and can now clearly see two men running after him and getting closer and closer. They are waving their guns in the air and shouting at him, loudly mocking his futile efforts to escape. The whole scene is lit by the moon, glancing off the waters of the adjacent loch and bathing everything in its sickly pallor.

The last thing George Lowry hears, before the second gun goes off and kills him instantly, are grotesque whoops of joy.

2
Thursday, 18th October

That evening, DCI John White clears his desk at Police HQ in Inverness and gets into his car for the start of what is officially called 'a well-earned vacation' - even if it is only for an extended weekend. It would prove to be anything but that but why remains to be seen. As far as his colleagues at police HQ in Aberdeen are concerned, however, DCI White's forthcoming weekend trip to Rannoch Moor is pure pleasure and wholly unconnected with police work.

The unexpected phone call from Elspeth Grant had changed his plans somewhat. They had not spoken much since the James Ledbetter trial, two years previously although they had written to each other in recent weeks on a matter of mutual interest. Now all that has changed.

That Ledbetter case - the discovery and capture of Scotland's most dangerous serial-killer - had brought DI White (as he was at that time) and police profiler Elspeth Grant together for the first time in 2012. It had made them both famous, although Elspeth's reputation as Britain's best profiler had preceded her trip to Portree and the Isle of Skye that year.

Now, here she is again, suddenly popping up out of the blue in person and with what is rather alarming news.

'Typical!' thought John. 'Just like Elspeth to stir the pigeons. Bless her!'

While DCI White's job in Inverness and the surrounding region was never as onerous as it had been when he was stationed in Carlisle some years previously, the distances he has to travel and the boring nature of much of his work now is quite as exhausting.

He has been stationed in Inverness for five years and has, as far as he can judge, done well. His promotion to Detective Chief Inspector had followed as a result of his part in the James

Ledbetter case. White had been widely praised for that investigation, although profiler Dr. Elspeth Grant had taken a great deal of the credit - deservedly so, in John's estimation. There was no animosity between them although after the Ledbetter case John was sad to have rather lost touch with the charmingly eccentric Elspeth. On the last occasion they had met, following Ledbetter's conviction, she had dined with John and his wife Poppy at their cottage in Dunkeld.

On that celebrated occasion, Elspeth - all of fifty-three and a little stout - had done cartwheels on their lawn - just for fun!

Since then John White's work has been primarily managerial. He badly misses the hands-on investigative work of his days as a Detective Inspector and although he now has additional responsibility for recruitment and training at Police HQ, Inverness, he misses his celebrated 'Gang of Five' and the excitement of a complex murder investigation and all that that entails.

Ever since his initial posting to Inverness and his subsequent promotion, John and Poppy have mutually resisted moving north - not only because they love their cottage in Perthshire but because Poppy has friends and neighbours in Dunkeld and Birnham whom she particularly likes. Poppy also enjoys her job with the Perth and Kinross Council. She is Senior Manager in their Child and Family Support unit, based in Perth. When the subject of moving north first came up, she resisted it strenuously. In the end John agreed that she was right, particularly as their Perthshire cottage has risen in value far more quickly than property in Inverness. Their lovely home in Dunkeld is, therefore, worth hanging onto. Meanwhile, John rents a small flat in Inverness where he stays during the working week.

John got home to Dunkeld that Thursday evening at about eight o'clock. After supper he and Poppy selected their clothes for the weekend and broke out the fishing tackle, nets and folding stools from the garage.

Since their cottage backs on to the river Tay, both husband and wife have taken up fly-fishing in recent years. John finds it a relaxing way to unwind after a week's work (far better than golf, which most of his colleagues play). Poppy, who is an excellent cook, finds the addition of fresh trout to their diet very attractive. John's plans for a weekend's fishing on Rannoch Moor, although somewhat unexpected, immediately appealed to Poppy's innate sense of adventure and she set to packing that night with some excitement.

Friday, 19th October

The following morning they loaded the car and set off at about ten o'clock. The journey by road from Dunkeld to Rannoch Moor will take them nearly two hours, provided the weather stays good. There is ice on the minor roads out of Dunkeld but once on the A9 they should be OK. Snow has been forecast but not until that Friday afternoon.

With luck they could be at the Rannoch Moor Hotel by noon.

It is, therefore, with this happy thought in mind that they leave Dunkeld and head up the A9 for Pitlochry - before turning west along the B846 for the remote yet stunningly beautiful wastes of Loch Rannoch. Beyond the loch lay Rannoch Moor itself - fifty square miles of rugged moor-land, lochs, countless lochans, peat bogs, and streams.

Anyway, that's what it said in Poppy's guidebook!

* * *

The guests at the Rannoch Moor Hotel awoke that morning to a bright but extremely cold day. They had all slept well after their magnificent evening meal. Not only had the food and wine yet again proved everything as good as the glossy brochure had promised, but the hotel itself was beautifully appointed. The beds were comfortable, the rooms elegantly furnished and the place itself very warm and cosy.

Cecelia Arnold did not get up early that morning although her lover - Sir Miles Ballard - was up and dressed by eight o'clock, anxious to take advantage of an un- expected lull in the weather and try and get some hunting in before the snows returned. Hunting was his passion - apart, that is, from making vast amounts of money, which he also did with consummate skill. Instead of getting up at such an unearthly hour, Cecelia lay in bed, luxuriating in silk sheets. She always slept naked, not least because she loved the feel of fine linen on her slim, exceptionally svelte young body.

Cecelia had met Sir Miles Ballard at the Formula 1 Grand Prix in Monaco two years previously. At that time she was working for a French PR firm, meeting and greeting VIPS at the racetrack. Some of the girls provided services over and above that for which they had been contracted but Cecelia had resisted that temptation. That alone had endeared her to Miles Ballard, whose penchant for pretty girls was widely known in racing circles but who always enjoyed a 'chase'. Cecelia kept him at bay for at least three days but, on the F1 race-day itself, finally succumbed - a relationship consummated on a veritable lake of Champagne in Sir Miles' bedroom later that night at Monaco's celebrated Hermitage Hotel.

Since then they have been almost inseparable - despite the existence of Dorothea, Sir Miles' ever-vigilant wife back in Tonbridge Wells. Cecelia now occupies a very smart apartment in London's Mayfair, paid for by her wealthy lover so there was little danger of the two women ever meeting. When not with his wife at the family home in Kent, Sir Miles is lavishing his attention on Cecelia. Although sexually demanding, he is a generous lover and showers his young mistress with expensive gifts - most of which she promptly banks (for a rainy day, as she always explains to her girl friends - some of whom are in the same 'business'). She loves Sir Miles in her way but like most girls in such a relationship, keeps her eyes wide open for either a better situation or ideally someone she could really love with all the genuine passion she knew she was still capable of.

That morning, at Rannoch Moor, Cecelia dozed in bed until about nine o'clock then took a warm shower, dressed and wandered down for a breakfast of fresh fruit and yoghurt, followed by kedgeree - a traditional dish consisting of flaked smoked haddock, boiled rice, parsley, hard-boiled eggs, curry powder, butter, cream and sultanas - followed by American coffee, black as it comes.

It is a hard life, but someone has to do it - or so Cecelia explained to herself that Friday morning.

* * *

John and Poppy White made good progress, despite deteriorating weather conditions *en route*.

They passed through the town of Pitlochry then headed west, following the northern edge of Loch Rannoch. That morning the water of the loch was slate grey - dark and ominous. Sudden squalls of rain and sleet made driving difficult. If they were going to get in any fishing this week-end or a walk or two into the mountains that surround Rannoch Moor, then they would need better weather than this seemed to promise.

The James Ledbetter case had had a profound effect on both husband and wife. Although it had concluded with Ledbetter's trial and conviction two years previously, John White still had nightmares of the gruesome murders that had characterised that investigation. Although Poppy's part in the investigation had been relatively minor - helping out, for example, with the fake photograph of Elspeth Grant's 'murder' - she had born the brunt of her husband's mental suffering. The pressure on him had been enormous and it had been largely up to her to sustain his efforts and nurture his self-confidence - at times seriously diminished - during the investigation itself and the long months leading up to Jim Ledbetter's trial.

In a strange way it had brought them closer together but both bore the scars, even now.

* * *

John and Poppy White were not the only travellers that morning.

Elspeth, now fully recovered from the rigours of her night of passion with Gabriélle in Oxford, was at the wheel of her Mercedes and well on the way to Edinburgh.

She had enjoyed her night with the young, strikingly beautiful French woman but when she discovered, later that day, the real reason for Gabriélle's presence in Oxford and why she was in Britain at all she became not only disturbed but somewhat disappointed.

However, such feelings did not last long.

There was no doubting Gabriélle's passion. That was genuine but that was only part of her attraction towards the older women, it would appear. Gabriélle needed not only information but Elspeth's professional help. The sex was a bonus, not part of the younger woman's original plans and certainly not a 'bargaining' ploy but a delightful, wholly unexpected and unplanned 'diversion'. That at least is what Gabriélle claimed. True, the mutual attraction and the sex that followed had rather complicated matters between them but then, how does the Paul Simon song go? 'Who am I to blow against the wind'.

That, anyway, was how Elspeth now viewed the matter - after careful consideration and a certain amount of heart searching.? However, there were issues that needed resolving, not least Gabriélle's reasons for being in Britain and the exact nature of the help she was asking of Britain's most celebrated Criminologist. That posed a number of problems - some of which she had imparted to her former colleague and friend in Dunkeld, Detective Chief Inspector John White earlier that morning. He had not been best pleased!

Elspeth glanced in her car mirror.

Gabriélle was curled up on the back seat in a tartan blanket. Her face was pale and she appeared to be fast asleep.

'No stamina, these young things!' thought Elspeth. 'Why, when I was her age….'

She glanced in the mirror once more, to discover Gabriélle stirring, sitting up on one elbow and gazing wanly back at Elspeth.

'God, she's beautiful!' though Elspeth.

* * *

John and Poppy White arrived at the Rannoch Moor Hotel at about eleven-forty-five that Friday morning - excellent going, considering the worsening conditions. They unpacked the car with the help of one of the porters then checked in.

'Detective Chief Inspector White, Mrs White - welcome. I trust your journey from Dunkeld was not too bad?'

It was the hotel manager, Ronald McBane, who met them at the reception desk. He was a tall, slim man in his mid-forties with a pale complexion, piercing blue eyes and a professional smile. John White took an instant dislike to him but Poppy smiled and thanked him for his consideration.

'Here is your key. Stewart will show you to your room. I will send up your luggage in a moment or two. Enjoy your stay. Lunch is still being served and the main meal this evening is from seven.'

They followed Stewart (now acting as Porter) up to their room on the third floor. Their luggage, brought on a trolley by a second young man, arrived almost simultaneously. John tipped both boys, closed the door after them and seized his wife around her very slim waist, gently lifted her off her feet and carried her towards their large, four-poster bed.

'John, what are you doing? Put me down! Put me down, you wicked man!'

They reached the bed and collapsed onto it in hysterics, all thought of lunch vanishing in a flurry of mutual kisses and giggles.

* * *

With lunch came the first heavy fall of snow, covering the mountains around Rannoch Moor in a treacherous white veil and making the only road to Kinloch Rannoch - the nearest village, at the far end of the great loch - exceedingly dangerous. An hour or two later it cleared but, according to the BBC weather forecasters at Fort William, heavy snow was expected to return later that day. The temperature was also dropping rapidly with a wind chill-factor to give any self-respecting brass monkey serious pause for thought.

Undaunted by the prospect of more snow to come and keen to use what snow there was, Frank Robinson grabs a light lunch then dons his skis and sets off across the snow-covered moors for some much-needed exercise - Norwegian style.

Frank is an experienced skier. He first learned to ski as a young man in the Swiss Alps but his preferred sport these days is Nordic skiing - a type of skiing in which only the toe is attached to the skis, leaving the heel free to rise with each forward thrust. In Norway itself Frank has won a number prizes for cross-country skiing - when younger. Although now in his mid-forties, he is still as fit as a fiddle and anxious that morning to get in some serious practice before the weather deteriorates.

Frank left the hotel that afternoon and headed west, towards Dubh Lochan. Here the water is dark blue beneath grey skies, with shafts of wintry sunlight occasionally penetrating the clouds and bathing the landscape in great pools of golden light. Reaching the lake, Frank turns south, following the narrow path at the water's edge. He has only gone a few miles when he comes across a lone fisherman, hauling in a large pike. Frank stops, greets the man and stands watching as the fish writhes and twists in the net - until a sharp blow with a gaff despatches it.

'What do you think it weighs?' asked the gillie, holding the blood-stained net out in front of him towards Frank.

'Well,' said Frank, stepping out of his skis and leaning over the net to get a better look, 'probably about….'

We shall never know what Frank Robinson thought that particular fish actually weighed because a sudden, sharp blow to the back of Frank's head causes him to plunge forward into the loch. As he struggles to lift himself up out of the cold water, blood already pouring down one side of his face, his assailant's Wellington boot - applied roughly to his exposed throat - thrusts him once more under the icy water. Frank thrashes and fights back but lacks the strength to overcome the full weight of that man's body pushing down on his neck and half-choking him into the bargain. A second man then appears as if from nowhere, takes a long gaff and shoves it onto Frank's chest, forcing him even further under water.

There, for at least three minutes, the two ghillies hold Frank under water until all movement stops. They stare down at him coldly as he lies there on his back in the loch, his face a deathly white, his eyes popping and his head and mouth smeared with blood. Each ghillie then grabs a foot and drags him up onto the bank where the stretch him out on the snow - as motionless and as dead as that gaffed pike, still entangled in its net.

3

Teddy Bosenquet did not slept much that second night, largely due to the attentions of Lady Olympia Garland, his fiancée. Not that he was complaining, mind you, but there is only so much love-making a fellow can take!

That Friday morning they ordered breakfast in bed - consisting of porridge, fresh orange juice, toast, lashings of butter and delicious Frank Coopers 'Oxford' marmalade washed down with buckets of black coffee. Once their waiter had left, they sat up in bed like two naughty children, the large breakfast tray balanced across their laps, and tucked in with relish.

'Not bad, eh!' said Teddy, through a mouthful of thick buttered toast and marmalade.

'Not bad? Its bloody *brilliant.* I think I like Rannoch Moor - as long as one doesn't actually have venture out into it. What?'

'Quite. My view entirely', said Teddy with some conviction.

Olympia lent over and kissed him affectionately on the cheek. Then, with her long, pink tongue, she deftly removed a portion of marmalade stuck to the corner of his mouth.

She sat upright again, selected a slice of toast, buttered it then looked for the marmalade pot. It was on Teddy's side of the tray.

'Pass the marmalade, darling - if there is any left, that is!'

They first met two years ago at a polo match at the Beaufort Polo Club where Teddy practices and regularly competes. Olympia is also a fine horsewoman and had once nearly been selected for the Badminton Horse Trials. She might have made it but for an injury earlier that season that put her out of the running for eighteen months. She never quite recovered her winning form thereafter. Apart from a shared passion for horses, both she and Teddy are independently wealthy, having inherited vast sums from their respective parents. They are, in that sense, an ideal match although Teddy's love of veteran cars is something Olympia feels she might need to curb somewhat once they are married.

Their wedding is scheduled for June next year - in the lovely chapel at Trinity College, Cambridge where Teddy had been a student. The wedding reception thereafter will take place at the Royal Society's splendid Georgian country residence, Chicheley Hall, near Newport Pagnell. They are expecting two-hundred guests at Chicheley, including Olympia's second cousin, the Princess Royal. It is going to be that big!

After breakfast Olympia slipped out of bed and retreated to the bathroom where she had a long, luxurious shower.

She was a very pretty girl, with long flowing blonde hair (which she usually kept in a pony tail), freckles and green eyes. She was remarkably slight for a horsewoman but very strong and athletic. Despite her recent accident she kept in training, competing whenever the opportunity presented itself. She was, therefore, extremely fit. In looks her friends had always said that she resembled Mia Farrow. Since Olympia was too young to remember who Mia Farrow was she could only take the comparison on trust.

After her shower she dressed in her riding clothes and went off to find the stables at the back of the hotel, leaving Teddy snoring away in bed. She had booked a horse for the latter part of their week's stay on Rannoch Moor and was now anxious to check her mount out - even if the snow on the ground might prevent even a modest canter. Since their arrival on Wednesday conditions had not been good for riding anyway and she had occupied herself with short walks in the snow, reading and writing letters - or making love. Now it was time to explore the stables and perhaps plan some modest equestrian excursion, weather permitting.

The hotel's stables are housed around a small, cobbled courtyard at the back of the hotel, close to the kitchens. Like everything at the Rannoch Moor Hotel, they are well appointed, clean and professional. There is also a small, indoor training and exercise arena. If all else failed, thought Olympia, she could at least exercise her mount and even try a few jumps.

'Morning, Madame,' said the stable lad. 'What's you name please?'

'Garland. Olympia Garland. And you are....?'

'McBane, Miss Garland. David McBane. Your mount is called Sebastian. Fifteen hands. Friesian. Lovely horse, is Sebastian.'

McBane led Olympia across the courtyard to the horsebox where Sebastian was housed. He proved to be a fine animal with a strong body, full black mane and thick tail. Friesians are always black but can have a small white star on the forehead. Olympia had ridden one once before, in Spain.

For a moment or two horse and rider eyed each other, then Olympia put her face close to Sebastian's and stroked him gently with one hand just below his ears. He seemed to settle almost immediately, thereafter allowing her to run her hand down his long, arched neck and across his shoulders and flanks. Sebastian's sloping shoulders looked and felt powerful, as did his compact, muscular body with its strong hindquarters and low-set tail. He was a very handsome horse and appeared to have been well looked after and properly groomed.

'Yes, he will do very nicely,' thought Olympia. 'Very nicely indeed!'

* * *

Poppy and John slept for the larger part of that Friday afternoon. Poppy was the first to awake and was somewhat startled when she realised that it was now almost four o'clock. She got out of bed, slipped on a silk dressing-gown and padded across to the window in her bare feet.

It had been snowing for most of that afternoon but had now stopped - although the clouds still looked dark and ominous. There was, therefore, a thick covering of fresh snow on the ground. In the forecourt below, men with shovels were clearing pathways to and from the hotel's main entrance. There were a number of cars in the forecourt, some of them in the 'very expensive' category.

Poppy knew next to nothing about cars but she could at least recognise a Bentley when she saw one and there were three down there, each one now partly covered with snow.

She noticed too a young man sweeping snow off the large plastic cloth that covered his veteran racing car. They had seen it when they arrived earlier that morning. John had said that it was a Bugatti - whatever that was!

She turned back into the room and looked at her husband, still fast asleep. He was clearly exhausted and although their love-making that afternoon had tired them both somewhat it was months of hard work and tension that had caused DCI White to collapse into a deep sleep afterwards. While it was a lovely idea to celebrate their eighteenth wedding anniversary in this splendid hotel, it was equally clear to Poppy that John badly needed to rest, or at least time to recharge his batteries. If the weather held good then they might plan a walk tomorrow or even a little fishing expedition but nothing too strenuous. Tonight, they had their first gourmet meal to look forward to.

Poppy ran a bath, added copious amounts of a green liquid she found in an elegant glass bottle by the sink, and lay down - luxuriating in a veritable cloud of bubbles.

She loved John and was very happily married but often wondered how it had come to pass that she had married a policeman. True, it had been love at first sight and she had always been a sucker for a smart uniform but it could so easily have been someone else. There had been plenty of suitors, that's for sure. But there was something about John White that had caught her eye.

After only a couple of years as an ordinary constable he had been selected for officer training at the Metropolitan Police Training Centre at Hendon and it was there that they first met, at a local dance in the town.

Mind you, John White was not much of a dancer but he was charming and a perfect gentleman. You could not say that much for many of the other young men there that evening. Within weeks they were engaged and as soon as he completed officer training at Hendon, they got married. That was in 1994. He was twenty-four and she had just turned nineteen. Five years later and with the rank of Inspector, John left the Metropolitan police in London and moved north, first to Wolverhampton and then to Carlisle. His appointment as Detective Inspector at Inverness followed three years later, in 2006.

After her bath Poppy wandered back into the bedroom. John was sitting on the side of the bed, rubbing his eyes. Poppy sat down beside him and gave him a hug.

'Well, the conquering hero awakes. About bloody time! Do you know what time it is, my darling Chief Inspector Plod? Four-thirty!'

'Goodness. That late? Anyway, you are looking exceptionally pretty - again. I love that dishevelled, wet-hair look. Like you have just had a bath after an extended bout of lovemaking.'

'Well, if you are going to be as frisky all weekend as you were after lunch then you had better get used to this look! Talking of lunch, may I remind you that we did not take lunch - we were otherwise 'occupied'. What's more, I am now absolutely starving and I'm not sure I can wait until suppertime. Fancy a cup of tea and a plate of sticky cakes? Are you up for that, my darling, or are you going to snore your head off all weekend?'

* * *

Sir Miles Ballard got up early that Friday morning, leaving Cecelia fast asleep, and set off for the forest just north-west of the hotel.

He had that morning persuaded one of the hotel's four professional ghillies to take him on a scouting expedition up into the forest, due west of the railway station. This was his first outing since he and Cecelia had arrived on Wednesday. There had been too much snow to do anything else, other than play backgammon with Teddy and prop up the bar - or bed Cecelia. Still, it was good to get out on the hills once more, even if there was little chance that morning of spotting any deer in such conditions.

Both he and his ghillie carried guns but this was essentially a tracking exercise, to check the movement of wild deer in that part of Rannoch Moor.

'If the weather holds off, ye might have a better chance of a kill tomorrow. Snow makes the beasts take cover. They might emerge from the forest if hungry but I doot we'll see any today, sir.'

'Aye, I think you may be right. What's the forecast?'

'Nay good, sir. Besides, you are cutting it pretty fine. If you are after a hart, tomorrow is your last chance. The hunting season ends on the 20th October here in Scotland.'

'No pressure, then Duncan! Eh?'

'Aye, sir. Nay pressure!' said the ghillie, winking as he did so.

At the time they were skirting the southern edge of a long stretch of coniferous forest, close to the black waters of Loch Laidon. Here the loch extends away to the south-west before dividing in two near Tom Dubh-mor, the most remote and inhospitable part of Rannoch Moor. It was on this loch-side track that Sir Miles' ghillie had spotted some deer tracks and droppings. Unfortunately, these tracks had then disappeared back into the dense forest. The deer had emerged from the forest, only to return all too soon to the safety of its dark interior. There was little point in following them there.

It had been a cold, bright morning when they first set out, with only an occasional flurry of snow or sleet. Later, however, it began to snow properly and by mid afternoon was snowing quite heavily. Despite his sixty-five years and the beginning of a distinct paunch, Sir Miles Ballard was still a fit man. He loved the outdoors, was a fine shot and an experienced huntsman. Even looking for deer was an exhilarating experience for him. This was his third visit to Rannoch Moor. The first year he had bagged nothing. Last year he shot a hind. Thus far, therefore, a stag had eluded him. Perhaps this year he might get lucky? Anyway, the hunting here was usually pretty good and the food at his hotel unquestionably the best in the Highlands. Perfect combination.

He took out his flask, took a long swig of whiskey and passed it to his ghillie.

'Thank ye, sir. Shall we head back?'

'Aye, Duncan. Tomorrow is another day, or so they say.'

They left the edge of the forest and crossed the track, moving quickly down towards the dark loch. Here the long grass was a golden brown, dry and febrile in the bitterly cold wind that parched everything in its path. The railway station in front of them was just visible through the flurries of snow and sleet that stung their faces.

If they were going to find deer tomorrow they would need to be well above the tree-line, further to the north-west. Up there was open ground and good feeding for the deer. Once back at the hotel. Sir Miles fixed an early start for Saturday morning with his ghillie, shook hands, bade him farewell and headed for the restaurant.

Sir Miles was thus back in time for lunch. Cecelia, who had spent a lazy morning in their bedroom, joined her lover for a warming Scottish broth with home-made bread rolls still hot from the oven, followed by profiteroles covered in sticky chocolate. Afterwards, they had coffee on the covered veranda and watched as scurries of snow and sleet struck the glass. There would be even more snow later, that was for sure.

There was no sign of Teddy or Olympia so for the rest of the afternoon Sir Miles and Cecelia lay on their bed and read - until it was time to get dressed for supper. When not reading Sir Miles sat on the edge of their bed, talking into the telephone. He hardly ever stopped work, even on holiday. That might explain why he was recently listed forty-seventh in the *Sunday Times* 'rich list' and why his company was said to be worth billions.

Cecelia liked Teddy Bosenquet but did not get on particularly well with Olympia. Chalk and cheese, or maybe it was a matter of class. The two women met occasionally at social gatherings in London but deep down Olympia did not approve of the younger woman whom she privately regarded as little more than an expensive courtesan and whom Sir Miles patently over-indulged. Olympia did not intend to invite Cecelia to her wedding next year.

Sir Miles would just have to bring his wife instead. So there!

Teddy had once worked for Sir Miles but had left after only a year or so to set up his own business. Since then, Sir Miles had kept an avuncular eye on the young man's progress and had even invested some of his own money in Teddy's company - a private jet-charter organisation based at London's Canary Wharf. It was Teddy who had arranged for the seaplane that had brought Sir Miles and Cecelia to Loch Rannoch a few days ago.

By seven o'clock that evening they were both dressed and ready for supper. The moment they heard the bagpipes on the stairs they left their room and headed for the grand staircase.

'Hurry up!', said Sir Miles to Cecelia. 'I am so hungry I could eat a horse!'

4

'My God, what on earth is that racket?,' cried John, as he brushed his hair in the bathroom mirror.

'It's the call to supper, darling. Its called a bagpipe.'

Poppy was seated on the bed, making a final adjustment to her stockings. She seldom wore tights, preferring real stockings instead - much to her husband's perpetual delight.

'That's not what I call it!', said John loudly.

'Well, it means that we can eat.'

'You already did, if I recall. Two cup-cakes and a chocolate éclair.'

'Yes, but that was then and this is now. Are you ready?'

John emerged from the bathroom. He was dressed in a smart, charcoal-grey suit, white shirt and dark blue, silk tie.

'My, what a handsome man! Will you accompany me, kind sir, to the banqueting chamber where roast venison awaits us?'

'My pleasure, beautiful young person in expensive Jean Muir-type frock. Follow me and I shall lead you to gastronomic delights beyond your wildest dreams!'

'Oh goodie, kind sir!'

It was while they were walking along the corridor leading from their room to the grand staircase that they both noticed something strange.

One of the bedroom doors on their corridor was ajar. Inside they could just see two chambermaids hastily emptying clothes and other personal items from a large chest of drawers and a tall wardrobe into two large suitcases they had placed on the bed. What was strange was that the two women were throwing these items into the suitcase, with no attempt to fold them or place them carefully. Poppy and John stared for a moment then moved on. The women did not seen them for they had their backs to the door.

'I hope,' whispered Poppy as they moved away from the door, 'that's not how *you* pack when I'm not there to do it for you. Positively sloppy, I would say.'

'What do you mean? I always pack my own suitcase.'

'Not last night, you didn't.'

'Yes, well, you said you would do it. Anyway, when I *do* pack I am a lot tidier than that, I assure you. Odd though. Very odd. I dread to think what the owner of those suitcases will think when they get home and look inside.'

The noise of Stewart's bagpipe was so loud by now that they were unable to speak further. For a moment they paused on the landing with a few other guests, also heading for supper, then descended the grand staircase arm-in-arm, quietly humming 'Hello Dolly' in unison and trying hard not to giggle too loudly.

* * *

Teddy and Olympia are seated in one corner of the bar, holding hands. They have just ordered a vodka and tonic each. There are about twenty other people there, enjoying an *apéritif* before moving into the dining room.

The bar is quite small but with a high, vaulted ceiling. The walls are covered in highly-polished, wooden panels in a rich Chestnut veneer. Victorian Gothic, probably. Sir Charles Barry, maybe? Art is Olympia's passion. That and horses. The tables, however, are the kind you might see in a smart French café on the Boulevard Saint-Michel - with white marble tops. Even the waiters have long black aprons. This is more Paris than Perth, thought Olympia. She had been to finishing school in Paris and knew every café on the Boulevard Saint-Germaine *et environs.* Ah, happy days!

The barman arrived with their drinks and two copies of the menu - single sheet, cream paper with the day's choices printed in ink that was slightly embossed. Very smart and very expensive. No wonder this place is costing an arm and a leg, thought Olympia, as she ran her eye down each choice.

'Ollie, you look great. I love that cream dress. Is it new?'

'Oh Teddy, I wore it only last week! You have such a shocking memory. I wore it when we saw Caroline and Rory. Do you not remember?'

'Nope. Sorry. Hungry?'

'Rather. What do you fancy? Apart from me, that is!'

She held the menu card again up to her face and peered at it. She was a little short-sighted but always hated wearing her glasses in public.

'What on earth is 'Seppie in Umido con Patate e Piselli'? Doesn't sound very Scottish!'

'Cuttlefish, I think. With potatoes and peas. It 'sounds' delicious, if you ask me. Is that what you are going to have?'

'Not sure. I quite like the look of fish soup from Ancona. Do you think the Chef is Italian? Anyway, its all quite delicious. What about you?'

'Mussels, followed by veal.'

At that point a waiter arrived and took their order.

'I will call you when your table is ready. Would you like another drink? I can send the barman over.'

'Yes please. Same again, darling?'

'No thanks. May we see the wine list, please?

'Certainly, Madam.'

* * *

The architectural jewel in the crown of the Rannoch Moor Hotel is its mock-Gothic baronial hall. It too has a vaulted ceiling and panelled walls but on a massive scale. The room can probably cater for one-hundred covers when full. The high ceiling is cream plaster dotted with ornate, embossed 'shields' listing countless Scottish clan leaders and their heraldic coats of arms in lurid colours, edged with gold. Tall windows - now draped with rich, dark-red curtains - fill one wall, running the entire length of the hall.

John and Poppy White were half-way through their meal when Teddy and Olympia entered the dining room. They paused briefly at Sir Miles' table, exchanged a few words. Their waiter then led them across the room and seated them at their normal table, next to the Whites.

Both couples exchanged glances and polite smiles but otherwise said absolutely nothing. Very British!

'So Poppy,' said John, leaning forward slightly to speak to his wife, 'how was your grilled pike?'

'Amazing! The real question, though, is what shall I have *next*? I rather fancy wild strawberries with zest of lemon. What say you?'

'Wild strawberries in late October? Wow!'
'You are right. Probably flown in from Morocco, especially for us!'

'Maybe, but when I was parking the car at the back of the hotel I saw they had a large hot-house. They probably grow their own. I know it was working because there was a bloody great chimney next to it, belching out black smoke. Mind you, I'm not sure how eco-friendly that is - just so you can eat strawberries in October, my darling.'

'Well, if they have gone to all that trouble just for *me* I suppose I had better have some. Or shall I have profiteroles? You decide for me, John. We are simply spoilt for choice here. Oh go on then, strawberries it is. Waiter!'

* * *

It should be noted that Teddy and Olympia did not join Sir Miles and Cecelia at his table that evening, although they were invited. They had dined together twice since arriving on Wednesday. Enough was enough, thought Olympia. She had, therefore, politely declined Sir Miles' offer. Cecelia was secretly relieved when that happened, although she could never admit as much to Sir Miles who was clearly very fond of the young couple. Too fond, though Cecelia, especially of the Garland woman.

'So...', asked Teddy, once they had ordered their meal, '...how is your horse?'

'He's splendid. He's called Sebastian. Bit of a handful, I suspect. I am going to ride him tomorrow. If its too bad outside I will exercise him in the small, indoor riding area they have. Do you want to watch?'

'Not really, darling. I think I will leave you to it. I fancy a walk, perhaps. Could do with the exercise.'

'Last night, if I recall, you were complaining of too much 'exercise'?'

'Yes, well, you know what I mean. More wine?'

* * *

In the lobby after their meal Poppy spoke briefly to the hotel Manager, Ronald McBane. He told them that although another heavy fall of snow was certainly expected later tonight it should be bright and sunny on Saturday morning.

'I hope so, that is,' he added. 'We have guests leaving tomorrow on the train from Fort William and others coming up from London and Glasgow on the Caledonian Sleeper. Sometimes, if the single track is covered by snow drifts, the trains are unable to get through. It has already happened twice this year and its still only October! Very bad for business. Would you like a morning alarm-call? Papers?'

It was as they were walking towards the lift that Poppy took John's arm and whispered in his ear.

'Did you notice those two suitcases behind the reception desk, next to the Porter's cubby hole? They were the ones we saw being 'packed' earlier this evening. If the trains are not due until tomorrow, why are they packed now?'

'No idea, my darling. Does it matter?'

'Yes, it does matter. There is something distinctly odd about those cases.'

'Look Poppy, I'm the detective in this family. Enough! We are on holiday - if only for a few days. Its none of our business whose cases they are. Anyway, I'm sure there is a perfectly good explanation.'

They had now crossed the lobby and were heading for the lift situated in a corridor leading off the main reception area.

'You know what,' whispered Poppy. 'This place reminds me of the hotel in *The Shining*. You know, that creepy film by Stanley Kubrick. The one where Jack Nicholson goes crazy. Well, the corridors here may not be as big or as long but they are awfully similar!'

They had now reached the lift. Poppy lent forward to press the button but then thought better of it.

'The last time I saw a lift like this,' she whispered, 'it was in *The Shining*. When the lift doors opened the corridor was inundated in blood!'

John glanced at his wife. He had a wicked grin on his face. He pressed the button to summon the lift.

'Well', he said, 'let's see if this one does the same!'

5
Saturday, 20th October

For once the weather forecast was right. Saturday morning proved bright and sunny. There had been a heavy fall of snow that night but, by the time the hotel's guests emerged for breakfast, the snow in the forecourt had been cleared. It promised, in short, to be a beautiful day.

The mountains to the south and west are now snow-capped but bathed in a brilliant, buttercup-yellow light. The forest, where Sir Miles and his ghillie had gone tracking on Friday, is now heavy with snow. The tiny lochs and tarns, scattered in all directions across the rocky landscape of Rannoch Moor, glint like shards of metal foil. While the snow is deep in places, paths leading from the hotel have already been cleared or covered in clinkers, still hot from the hotel's vast boilers. The short, macadam road leading south from the hotel entrance to the tiny railway station, is virtually clear of snow.

The McBanes must have been up early to clear that road.

The news from First ScotRail was that both trains due that morning - one from Euston and one travelling south from Forth William - were on schedule. The sleeper train direct from Euston Station, London would be the first to arrive. It was expected at about nine-thirty that morning - a slight delay, due to adverse weather conditions just north of Crianlarich. The Manager and staff at the hotel on Rannoch Moor had breathed a collective sigh of relief at the news that the London train was more-or-less on time. They were expecting at least another forty guests travelling on that train.

Meanwhile, back inside the hotel that morning, Sir Miles emerges naked from his morning bath like a Turkish potentate, drawing contentedly on a fat, Cuban cigar. Cecelia, dressed only in a silk bathrobe by Schiaparelli, stands before him, her arms outstretched. She is holding a large bath towel. She looks very pale, almost fragile standing there but Sir Miles sees none of this.

He takes the towel, wraps it round his large stomach, slaps Cecelia resoundingly on her bottom and strides off back into the bedroom.

She closes the bathroom door behind her and stares at herself in the mirror. The mirror is covered in steam so she has to wipe its surface with her hand before she can see herself properly.

She stared at her pale reflection in the mirror then sighed.

It is not that Miles treats her unkindly. Indeed, he is generous to a fault - what with the flat in Mayfair and money to buy clothes or jewellery whenever she asks. A rich man's mistress has its compensations but it was clear to her that Miles was entirely blind to her real qualities - her intelligence, her compassion and her wit. She knew deep down that she was capable of more, much more - that's why at times she felt trapped and unfulfilled. She knew within herself that she was capable of achieving something in her life that did not rely on another's patronage. But what, exactly?

She turned away from the mirror and ran herself a bath.

'Bye, Cissy.'

It is Sir Miles. He is now dressed and leaving their suite of rooms, heading for breakfast before meeting up with his ghillie as arranged.

'I'll be back later this afternoon. Be good. If not, be careful!'

Cecelia said nothing. She was still lost in her own thoughts. She lent over the bath, testing the water with one hand and adjusting its flow with the other.

She had money now. She had her secret 'rainy-day' fund but to what end? Where could she go if she left Sir Miles and struck out on her own? Did she even have the courage to do that, after two years of living in absolute luxury? She may have money now and jewellery she could sell but how long would that last? One year? Six months? And what then? Too many questions! She needed answers. She needed a plan but above all she needed someone to love her, to really look after her. Someone who cared about her above all else. Someone who would love her for herself and not as some kind of living Barbie doll whom rich men dressed and undressed whenever they felt the need.

Cecelia turned off the taps, dropped her silk gown onto the floor and lowered herself into the bath.

She lay there for twenty minutes, occasionally adding more hot water as the bath cooled. Her head spun with thoughts but this time she was not thinking of Sir Miles. She was thinking of Erik.

* * *

Behind the hotel, in the middle of a wood, is a small camping-site belonging to the hotel. It is usually only open in the summer.

It consists of a clearing reached by a narrow track that starts at the service road behind the stables. Its most notable feature is a tree walk - an aerial pathway that circles the clearing. It is about twenty feet above ground, with suspended walkways made of slats of wood on wires and with double ropes above acting as hand-holds. On some of the larger trees small platforms have been built where one can pause for a breather or allow the more adventurous to pass onto the next suspended section. Initial access to this aerial walkway is by a rope ladder attached to a large beech tree.

In the summer, when there are numerous children staying at the hotel, it is much used. It is also used from time to time by groups of young people on 'adventure' weekends or by boy-scouts or girl-guides on similar outings.

Today it is completely empty - except for a small, Skyledge 2.1 'artic' tent pitched to one side of the clearing.

The tent belongs to Erik Bergman from Volda, Norway

Erik is on a camping holiday and for the last three weeks has trekked his way across Scotland, sleeping only in his tent. He arrived, somewhat unexpectedly, on Rannoch Moor two days ago and persuaded Ronald McBane to allow him to pitch his tent for a few nights in the otherwise closed camp-site. McBane agreed, charging him only a token 'rent'. In return, Eric offered to chop wood or generally help out if required. McBane had thought that unnecessary but thanked the young man for his suggestion.

That Saturday morning Erik is sitting outside his little tent, brewing himself a can of tea for breakfast on a small primus stove. The trees all around him are heavy with snow and the temperature is only just above freezing but he appears not to feel the cold. He is humming to himself and stirring his can of thick, black tea with a broken twig.

He is a tall, handsome young man with a blond beard and long, blond hair that he keeps in a pony tale.

Although he had been asked politely not to frequent the hotel, Erik is allowed in the small public bar - a bar to which guests have access but which is also used by day visitors just passing through and other non-residents. Here Eric would buy a beer or two and a cheese sandwich perhaps. He is rather shy and his English not that good so he tends to keep himself to himself. He is, however, polite and very clean - which is more than can be said for many of the hill-walkers that sometimes used that bar during the summer months. The bar staff appear to like him. They call him by his first name. At night the public bar is closed, the only bar remaining open being the saloon bar within the hotel proper. This is used exclusively by residents. Erik, as a non-resident, is not allowed in this bar.

At night Erik would therefore sit in his little tent and read or write. He is an aspiring novelist. Stieg Larsson is his hero.

It was in this little public bar that Cecelia had first caught sight of Erik - two days ago. It is there that, when not reading her book in the lobby, she now hangs out whenever she can do so without attracting attention to herself of rousing her lover's suspicions.

She had actually sat near Erik on Friday but she had been too shy to say anything to him. He had glanced at her and smiled, but that was only as he was leaving. She had watched him through the pub window move off down the lane past the station and strike out for the moor with his rucksack on his back. He also carried Norwegian skis and ski poles so she assumed that his explorations of the moor were extensive. He seemed very self-possessed and independent. She liked that. He was his own man. That she found attractive. He was also terribly good looking, a bit like Brad Pitt. Brad Pitt as Achilles, that is.

Cecelia got out of her bath and, still dripping wet, walked naked into the bedroom, dragging a large bath towel behind her.

She had not seen Erik since Friday lunchtime but perhaps, with Miles up in the hills for some hours, today might be her lucky day.

* * *

Poppy and John White were up and dressed early that morning. They had a less-than-indulgent breakfast - although the temptation to try a little of everything on offer was almost overwhelming. In the end they settled for porridge, freshly squeezed juice from blood-oranges, hot-buttered toast with lemon butter and Arabica coffee, made in Trieste by Illy.

Their plan was to go for a short walk, then have a light lunch. If the weather held they would try and get some fishing in before supper.

Garbh Ghaoir, a brisk hour's walk from the Rannoch Moor Hotel, was their first choice but much would depend on visibility and how deep the snow was on that part of the moor. Garbh Ghaoir is a long, thin waterway that connects the Loch Eigheach reservoir to the head of Loch Laidon and although not that far from the hotel does include some spectacular views down the loch and towards the Black Corries far to the west.

They left the hotel at about eight-thirty that morning and headed south, following the road past the railway station. They then crossed over the railway line using the narrow foot-bridge and struck out due west, with the forest on their right. It was a crisp morning and although the sun shone brightly it was still very cold. They were well dressed for Highland weather, both being seasoned walkers but soon Poppy's nose had turned a very delicate pink and John's had begun to run.

He sniffed all the way to the banks of Dubh Lochan.

Here the track they had followed thus far divided into two, one heading off into the forest and the other following the northern bank of the great loch that now stretched off into the distance in front of them. They opted for the shorter route, turned due south and headed towards Garb Ghaoir.

The landscape here was truly dramatic, with rust-red heather poking through the snow in places. The sun, shining fitfully, glinted off the standing water of the lochans all around them. Poppy stopped and took a number of photographs on her digital camera.

'How did you sleep last night?'

'Very well, thank you, Poppy. Mind you, I woke up in the middle of the night. Jack Nicholson was trying to batter down our door. I'm surprised it did not wake you up too, it was loud enough!'

'Stop it, John. I have my own nightmares without needing to share yours!'

They paused for a slurp of coffee from their thermos and nibbled on a biscuit or two. Poppy showed her husband her photographs.

'Very good', said John. 'Amazing landscape but it will certainly look far better when its finished!'

'Ha, ha! Very funny', said Poppy. She put the thermos back in her rucksack and the camera in her pocket.

'Here, take this'.

She handed her husband a wad of paper tissues.

'If you sniff all the way *back* to the hotel I might have to kill you. Nothing personal, my darling Inspector Plod'.

'Thanks.'

John took the tissues and blew his nose loudly on one of them.

'By the way, please do not call me Inspector Plod.'

'What then?'

'Supercop would do. Yes. Detective Chief Inspector John 'Supercop'. I think I could just about cope with that!'

They continued south, looking for the railway line that would lead them back to their hotel. After two miles they could just make out the single-track railway line ahead of them. This was the Great Western line that started at Crianlarich and snaked its way across the bogs of Rannoch Moor and on to Fort William, some thirty-five miles further to the north. Even then, as they peered through their binoculars, a train was moving, somewhat slowly, towards them

'Let's head back,' said John. 'I doubt this weather is going to hold much longer. Look at those clouds to the east. Snow is on its way, for sure. No fishing today, I'm afraid, Poppy.'

They turned and headed back towards their hotel, four miles to the northeast. Here the ground was wet and very boggy. Tough terrain but possible with the right boots and sufficient determination.

Since the area was also dotted with lochans (tiny lochs, some only yards across) it meant frequent diversions, skirting these somewhat treacherous, water-filled depressions - ancient legacy of the great ice sheets that once covered vast areas of pre-historic Scotland.

They could now hear the diesel train to their right, drawing closer. In the old days it would have been a steam train, with its white cloud of smoke streaming back behind its powerful engine and sparks flying as its wheels stuck each link of the uneven track. It was a remarkable example of engineering that there was even a single track across these desolate wastes.

When the West Highland Line was first built across Rannoch Moor, its Victorian engineers had to float the rails and wooden sleepers on a mattress of tree roots, brushwood and thousands of tons of earth and ashes. Rannoch station opened to passengers on 7th August, 1894.

Or so John had read in his guidebook.

'Steam trains across Rannoch Moor! What a wonderful sight that would have been', thought John.

6

The railway station at Rannoch Moor - with its single island platform - is what one might call a collector's item. It has not changed much since the 1930's but the original turntable of 1898 for reversing trains has gone, as has one of the shunting yards. The little signal box, although now automated, looks much as it did originally. More recently, they have added a gift shop and a small café where you can buy tea and cakes and soft drinks.

It was here that the delayed Caledonian Night Sleeper from Euston, London stopped and disgorged some forty or so new visitors to the Rannoch Moor Hotel, before moving on to complete its long journey at Fort William. It is nine-thirty in the morning of Saturday, 20th October. The new guests were all met on the platform by porters from the hotel, pushing rather old fashioned wheelbarrows on which to carry luggage, fishing rods and nets and all the other paraphernalia of the British sportsman or woman. It was a noisy, bustling scene.

One or two of the residents had gone along to inspect the new arrivals. Amongst them was Cecelia. She badly needed a little fresh air. Perhaps outside she might spot Erik. She had no idea where he lived, since he was clearly not a resident. Perhaps he was staying in one of the cottages near the station? Perhaps today they might finally meet.

The weather had just about held off but the temperature had dropped alarmingly during the morning. While the sun still shone (somewhat weakly, admittedly) it was clear that the weather was about to change - probably for the worse. More snow was expected soon. While the snow itself might not end up particularly deep, strong prevailing winds across the moor often caused drifting that blocked both the one road onto the moor and this single-track railway line. Indeed, it was not uncommon for the tiny community of Rannoch to be cut off for days. There was no mobile phone links in that part of Scotland and even landlines were subject to storms - high winds and heavy snow-falls sometimes causing telegraph poles to crash to the ground.

Cecelia gave a shudder, wrapped her fur coat closer about her slim body and headed back for the warmth and comfort of the hotel lounge.

The lobby was full of noise and confusion as the new guests fought with each other to sign in, collect their keys and luggage and then head upstairs to their respective rooms for a refreshing shower, perhaps, after the long journey from London. Many made a beeline for the dining room where breakfast was still being served. This extended breakfast service was only available on those days - twice a week, Wednesday and Saturday - when the hotel accepted new guests.

Many other guests never got further than the bar which appeared to be open for alcohol at all hours of the day.

* * *

Meanwhile, on the northern edge of the long, narrow coniferous forest and close to Creag Dhubh-mhor, Sir Miles and his ghillie Duncan are edging their way towards an outcrop of rock some two-hundred meters to their left.

There are in fact two ghillies with him that morning. Duncan has been joined by a young man in his twenties. He is called Neil. Sir Miles assumed that they were related since most of the staff at the hotel seemed to be part of one enormous family. Piercing blue eyes was the most commonly shared family characteristic - that and a certain dour temperament.

Although Duncan had been Sir Miles' ghillie on the two occasions they had hunted together in previous years, it would be fair to say that they had hardly exchanged any proper conversation throughout that time. After several attempts to strike up some kind of rapport, Sir Miles had given up. Duncan spoke only of deer and their chances of seeing any. Nothing else - unless asked a direct question. Ronald McBane, back at reception, might have an easy, convivial way with his guests but it was not a quality the rest of his relatives had obviously acquired. Still, thought Sir Miles, we are out and about and for the moment the weather is holding up.

Perhaps there might be a kill after all.

'Look, yonder', hissed Duncan suddenly.

He had fallen to one knee and was pointing with one arm ahead and slightly to their right. Sir Miles stared in the direction he was pointing.

There, silhouetted against a dull grey horizon was a hind, grazing. She was about thirty yards in open ground from the forest.

'She's too young for us, Sir Miles but there will be others nearby. Follow me. We need to be further right of her.'

Sir Miles moved off right, following his ghillie. Neil stayed where he was, knelt down on one knee and attended to his rifle.

* * *

Breakfast at the Rannoch Moor Hotel is always served between seven and ten, by which time most of the guests are out and about. The only exception is Wednesday and Saturday when the trains arrive from London. Then breakfast is served until 10.30.

When Paula Leamington eventually arrived at ten-forty-five that Saturday morning, the waiters were already clearing away the great silver tureens and dishes that held the remains of that morning's Finnan-haddie with poached eggs, Ayrshire bacon and mushrooms, cold venison pasty, potted grouse, scones, heather honey, toast and Audrey Baxter's blood-orange marmalade.

Undeterred by sour looks from the waiters anxious to prepare for lunch, Paula takes her seat near the great, baronial fireplace and orders black coffee and toast, to be followed by three boiled eggs.

'I'm afraid we are closed, Madam. We stop serving breakfast at ten-thirty. Seven to ten-thirty on Wednesdays and Saturdays. I'm very sorry.'

'Stuff and nonsense! Black coffee and toast and three boiled eggs. Four minutes each and not a second longer.'

It was as if she had not heard the waiter. She stared hard at him until he had no choice but to nod and retreat rapidly to the kitchen to attend to her order.

Paula Leamington was used to getting her way.

Paula Leamington is not one of the hunting set but a gourmet who had heard of the hotel's reputation and had decided to treat herself to a long weekend of unashamed gluttony. She is short, fat and about fifty years old. She has raven black hair and is 'something in the city' - or so she claims. In the male dominated world of finance, powerful female executives are still a rarity. It partly explains her gruff, often aggressive manner but behind this somewhat manly exterior there lurks a woman who is actually quite lonely - although she would never admit it, least of all to herself. Either way, she *always* gets what she wants - even if it means bullying her long-suffering staff back at her office at London's Chancery Lane.

Her eggs arrived ten minutes later. She is surprised, however, when one of the waiters - one Edmund McBane - suddenly holds her arms behind her chair in a vice-like grip.

'What? What are you doing?' she screams in alarm. 'Let go of me, you little bastard! Let go at once!'

It is at this point that a pretty but diminutive waitress - Edmund's sister, Emily - steps forward and stuffs the three eggs, still in their shells, into Paula's large mouth. Emily then hold's Paula's nose between finger and thumb while with the other hand she shoves the eggs deeper down Paula's throat.

Naturally, Paula struggles manfully, her eyes popping and her face quickly turning a remarkable shade of blue but the two McBanes are much too strong for her and after four minutes - and not a second longer - Paula Leamington is well and truly dead.

* * *

Poppy White is not the only woman in the hotel that week who is curious about the behaviour of the two McBane chamber-maids.

Cecelia Arnold, when not attending to her lover's sexual needs, has taken to loitering near the lobby - partly out of boredom, partly out of curiosity as to the comings and goings of her fellow guests and partly also, she must admit, in the hope of catching a glimpse of the elusive yet hugely attractive young man she now knows is called Erik Bergman.

On these occasions she sits, for example, in the small lounge preserved for smokers. This is just off the lobby but with a good view of the main entrance to the hotel.

Here she pretends to read a book or magazine while surreptitiously peering over the top and watching whatever is going on. It was, she imagined, like being a private detective.

She is there now because of something strange that she had observed taking place in Paula Leamington's room earlier that morning.

She had passed Paula once or twice on the stairs and had frequently seen her elsewhere in the hotel, especially the dining room; it would appear that Paula was exceptionally fond of her food. Although they had hardly exchanged a word on any of these occasions, Cecelia had soon discovered that Paula occupied a room by herself on the opposite side of the corridor from where she and Sir Miles had their suite. This particular morning, when she returned to her room to fetch a book at about eleven, she naturally passed Paula's room. The door was wide open and the trolley containing fresh sheets and cleaning materials was parked outside. There was no sign of Paula herself but it was clear that two chambermaids were doing something with Paula's clothes and possessions.

Cecelia hesitated for a moment but then unlocked her own bedroom door and entered. She then closed the door behind her - but not entirely, leaving a narrow gap through which she could peer in to Paula's room without herself being seen. From here, for the next minute or so, she secretly watched what the two women were doing.

Every now and then, one of the maids - the one partly hidden from Cecelia's view behind Paula's door - would fling a pile of clothes onto the bed. The other chambermaid, sitting on the edge of the bed, would rifle through them, select one or two for examination, putting aside any article of clothing or object that she apparently approved of. She would then fling the rest into the suitcase. At one point the woman selected a silver hairbrush, brazenly slipping it into the pocket of her white tunic.

It was absolutely clear to Cecelia that they were stealing Paula's clothes and personal possessions. Not at all what you would expect in a respectable hotel. But where was Paula?

It was just as Cecelia was about to leave her room, cross the corridor and remonstrate with the maids - or at least find what was going on - that a third chambermaid, carrying neatly folded towels in her arms, appeared further up the corridor. Cecelia immediately changed her mind about intervening and retreated back into the safety of her bedroom, quietly closing her door behind her.

Minutes later, having thought more about what she had just seen, she opened her door and stepped back into the corridor. She was holding a paperback novel in one hand. Paula's door was now shut so she hurried past and took the lift down to the main reception desk.

'I wonder if you can help me', she said to the receptionist - a young woman called Marie, thought to be the hotel Manager's eldest daughter. 'I am looking for Miss Paula Leamington. She lent me this book the other day and I would like to return it to her. She's not in her room. Do you know where I can find her?'

Marie was about to speak when the Manager, Ronald McBane emerged from the inner office and approached the desk.

'Thank you Marie, allow me. I'm afraid Miss Leamington left after breakfast this morning.'

'Oh, I see. Did she leave a forwarding address?'

'No. It would seem that she had to return unexpectedly to London on business. She caught the sprinter train to Crianlarich, at about ten-thirty this morning.'

'I see. Thank you. Thank you very much.'

Unconvinced by this explanation, Cecelia took up her familiar position in the small lounge off the lobby and pretended to stick her nose in a magazine. Sure enough, thirty minutes later, a young man appeared in the lobby with Paula Leamington's suitcase, dumping it unceremoniously in the porter's lodge next to the reception desk.

If Paula really had left for London why had she not taken her luggage with her? Single lady, travelling alone and without her luggage. Very odd!

If, as Cecelia suspected, Paula Leamington had *not* checked out that morning and the McBanes were simply lying, then what could have happened to her? Why, if she had not left, would the McBanes lie?

More importantly, where on earth was Paula now?

* * *

Poppy and John White arrived back at the hotel in time for an early lunch. They had thoroughly enjoyed their short walk but were glad to get back into the warm. They were heading for their room to change out of their walking clothes when Poppy suddenly stopped and grabbed her husband's arm. They were now near the entrance to the saloon bar, leading off from the main lobby.

'Look, John! Through there, at that table near the bar. Could it be….?'

'Oh my God, its Elspeth!'

'What's she doing here? And who is she with?'

Sure enough, Dr. Elspeth Grant, the celebrated Criminologist was seated near the bar. Sat with her was a beautiful young woman with raven-dark hair. They were blatantly holding hands across the white marble table and gazing into each others' eyes. Neither seemed to be talking.

'Did you know she would be here this week-end, John?'

'Of course not. I have not seen her for two years, not since the Ledbetter trial. I cannot imagine what she is doing her. She's hardly the hunting and shooting type, as you well know.'

'Well, we cannot ignore her. Let's go and say hello.'

'Are you sure that's such a good idea? She seems to be, er, otherwise occupied.'

'All the more reason to find out why she is here and who that gorgeous young woman with her is. Come on, John!'

Poppy let go of her husband's arm, crossed the lobby and entered the bar. She went straight up to Elspeth, whose back was slightly towards her, and threw her arms around her shoulders, kissing her on one cheek.

'Of all the gin joints, in all the towns, in all the world, she walks into mine! What brings you here, Elspeth? And who is this *lovely* young woman you appear to be fondling so outrageously?'

7
Sunday, 21ˢᵗ October

Douglas Tait - and his friend, Robert Wellington - had arrived at Rannoch Moor on Wednesday, on the local train from Fort William.

They were both keen rock climbers and had, individually, conquered most of the Munros while still students. They had first met at university in Aberdeen, where for four years they had studied geology. Douglas now works for an American oil company operating in the North Sea while Robert is contracted as a surveyor with the Norwegian Petroleum Directorate, operating out of Trondheim. Now both in their early thirties, Douglas and Robert have also acquired in recent years considerable experience from winter ascents in the Swiss Alps and free-climbing expeditions in the Italian Dolomites.

Rock climbing in Scotland held no fears for them. Today's ascents would be a 'walk in the park'.

Unfortunately, their respective wives did not share their enthusiasm for the outdoor life. They preferred - whenever the 'boys' went off somewhere, climbing or walking - to meet up in London or Edinburgh or even occasionally Paris. They would check into an expensive hotel and then shop all day, ending at a smart restaurant for a meal together or to meet up with other girl friends.

This schedule was repeated each day that they were away. They called these girlie outings their 'credit-card recreationals'. This had been going on for some years now. The two women were good friends. With similar tastes and interests, they had always found each other's company enjoyable. Since their husbands were both exceedingly well paid, everyone seemed happy with this particular holiday arrangement.

Douglas and Robert had sought detailed directions from the hotel receptionist on Saturday night and had booked with Room Service an early breakfast, to be delivered to their respective rooms at six the following morning. After breakfast they left the hotel and set out for Buachaille, about fifteen miles due west from Rannoch. It was now seven o'clock and still dark but dawn was just starting to break, turning the wastes of Rannoch Moor into something quite miraculous. Although wild and desolate, Rannoch Moor can be breathtakingly beautiful at times. This October morning was no exception.

The trek across country was going to be tough but both men were seasoned walkers and used to difficult terrain. They crossed the railway line and followed the main track through the forest, until it petered out in open moor land, pitted with lochans and crossed by countless streams.

Their route thereafter was not difficult - as long as they kept the long loch on their left-hand side and stayed on high ground. There were also electricity pylons to follow, although occasionally they took short cuts, staying well north of the complex mix of lochs and lochans at the western end of Rannoch Moor.

When the loch split into two sections, they turned west-north-west until they struck Alt Lochaim Ghaineamhaich - a long, narrow loch leading to loch Ghaineamhaich itself. Here they turned due west, aiming for Dubh Lochan. Ahead of them loomed the mountains leading to Glen Coe, including the range of steep rock faces known as Buachaille - or Stob Dearg, to give this peak its proper name. It was here that they intended to tackle Rannoch Wall, a south-east facing rock-face dauntingly steep, rising to seven-five meters.

Throughout their long trek they do not waste energy by talking but settled into a steady pace, striding across the moor with remarkable speed.

However, what Douglas and Robert do not know is that throughout this cross-country trek they are being followed by two men on a quad-bike. The quad-bike is pulling a small cart, normally used for carrying animal feed to remote parts of the moor. Today, however, the cart is empty. The men are keeping their distance, every now and then stopping to observe the two climbers through their binoculars.

From two miles away the sound of their vehicle is inaudible, partly because of the prevailing wind but mainly because they do not wish to be seen or heard and are careful to maintain their distance.

They are, in effect, stalking the two climbers.

By eleven that Saturday morning, Robert Wellington and Douglas Tait finally arrived at the base of the triangular-shaped mountain called The Buachaille and the south-east facing section known as Rannoch Wall. One hour later, after a scramble up the rugged terrain of Crowberry Gully, they arrive at the foot of their chosen rock face - the aptly named 'Bridge Too Far'.

'Wow! That looks fantastic', says Robert. 'Fancy a coffee?'

'Cool. What kit should we take?'

'Chalk bag. Maybe a couple of wire nuts. Belay tape and quickdraw carabiners. Here, take a few of my Nitrons. That should do. Keep it simple.'

'OK. Simple it is!'

They poured themselves a cup of coffee from a thermos and munched on a banana or two. It had been a long walk across inhospitable ground, but they feel good and are ready to climb. After refreshments, they switch from their walking boots to climbing shoes and shed a layer of two of clothing. The sun is now well up, quickly warming the rock face. They will be warm enough, even without the exertion of the climb itself. The rock face soars above their heads, incredibly steep but without snow clinging to its surface. That is a good sign.

'I'll go first.' says Robert. 'Give me about fifteen feet clearance then follow. It looks dry enough. I'll stick with 'Bridge Too Far', you follow 'Game of Dice', slightly to my right. Safer that way, perhaps.

If I fall off I don't want to bring you with me, eh?! By the way, watch out for the hanging grove, about fifty meters up. Some loose rock round about there. OK?'

'OK. Enjoy!'

'You bet. I have been looking forward to this all week.'

With that Robert began climbing, first following a vertical crack in the rock towards a shallow grove with a second crack-line above. Without ropes or the usual climbing tackle, Robert free-climbs the first twenty-five meters with ease, quickly finding his rhythm. Douglas watches admiringly, then begins his own ascent, starting slightly to Robert's right but within talking distance.

Some three hundred yards below them and in a narrow gully, the two men who have been following them all the way from Rannoch, are now crouched low, hidden from view behind a rock fall. They have left their quad-bike hundreds of yards away, further down the gully. They are both armed with high-velocity rifles with telescopic sights.

It took Robert twenty minutes of strenuous climbing to reach the grassy bay, just beneath the headwall. Here he rested, occasionally glancing back down at Douglas, some thirty feet below him and to his right. Douglas appeared to be making good progress.

'How are you doing?'

Douglas paused for a moment, clinging to the rock face with two hands but leaning out slightly and enjoying the view - a magnificent white, lunar landscape stretching in all directions, including the flat wastes of Rannoch itself.

'Fine, I think. Great view, eh?'

'Even better from the top. Meet you there!'

Both climbers resumed climbing. The rock face here, slightly in shadow, was peppered with snow and some ice so they both proceeded with caution.

In the gully, some two-hundred-and-fifty meters below them, the two men who had followed them this far - one much younger than the other - were loading their rifles and adjusting their telescopic sights.

'Now son,' said the older man, whispering, 'you shoot first. Go for the lower of the two. We dinna want ye bringing one doun on t'other.'

'Aye', said the young man, barely in his teens. 'What should I aim fer? Neck or head?'

'Neither. He's moving his head tay much, looking for hand-holds. Play safe. Aim for middle. Between his shoulder blades.'

'Very well, fader. Wish me luck! How far, do yer reckon. Two hundred?'

'Adjust for two-fifty. There's nay wind, not that it would make much difference at this range. Nay rush, either. They have twenty minutes before they are anywhere near the top. Time enough, son!'

The boy adjusts his sights once more and takes aim.

The high velocity bullet struck Robert exactly between the shoulders, slamming his body flat against the rock face. That single bullet generated such an explosive force on impact that Robert's lungs and heart simply disintegrated. He was dead, even before he fell backwards off his narrow ledge and plummeted to the ground, some fifty meters below.

It is not clear at what point Douglas fully realised what had just happened. The gun shot was clearly audible but at first he did not associate it somehow with the sudden fall of his companion. He looked down and saw his friend's body spread-eagled on the rocks far below.

Robert's blood was already staining the snow.

Suddenly, a second shot rang out, then a third. Shrapnel and chips of rock flew past Douglas' head, some striking him on the right cheek and nearly blinding him. The impact of the high velocity bullet so close to his ears instantly deafened him, sending a searing pain into his skull. Blood immediately began to trickle from his ears. He was also now bleeding profusely from shrapnel wounds on his right ear and cheek. He could feel the warm blood trickling down his neck. Then a fourth shot struck the rock to his left, at head height. More shrapnel, more cuts to his head and face.

He began to climb upwards as fast as he could, panic rising like a torrent in his throat, his heart pounding fit to burst.

Far below the boy was jumping up and down with delight as his father deliberately, maliciously placed each shot close to the tiny figure, now scrambling up the precipitous face.

'Kill him, da! Kill the bastard!'

The older man grinned at his son, nodded, then adjusted his sights once more and fired. The bullet struck Douglas on the back of the head, the shock disintegrating his skull with devastating power.

Son and father even had time to watch the young man's precipitous descent through their binoculars until Douglas landed with a sickening crash close to his dead companion.

Three hours later the quad-bike reached Rannoch Moor Hotel. Father and son had taken the A82 as far east as they could but had then cut back across the moor itself. Their cart now contained two bodies in black, plastic body-bags.

It had, by all accounts, been another satisfying day's hunting for Alistair and his son, seventeen-year-old Stewart McBane.

No one saw them arrive at the back of the hotel, unload the two bodies and dump them in an outhouse just behind the stable block.

No one, that is, except Erik Bergman.

8

When Douglas Tait and Robert Wellington left the hotel early that fatal Sunday morning, they were not the only ones up and about.

Like any large hotel, even one in a remote part of Scotland, there were staff going about their business all through the night. Indeed, the skeleton night-staff, including two night porters and two cleaning ladies, finished their shift at six o'clock that morning, just as the early-morning shift, including kitchen staff, arrived to start theirs.

Erik was woken up by the murmur of voices in the cobbled courtyard at the back of the hotel and by some engine, a tractor perhaps, starting up. Although his tent was pitched in the small wood at the back of the hotel and unseen by the night staff returning to their cottages near the railway station, he could hear everything in the stillness of that early morning.

He turned over in his sleeping bag, pulled the hood over his head, and tried to grab another hour's sleep. It was still dark - a raw, October morning with fresh snow on the ground.

Inside the Manager's office just behind the main reception desk, Assistant Manager Marie McBane was completing her shift. She finished at seven o'clock and was responsible for supervising the departure of one shift and the start of the next, together with ensuring that preparations for the guests' breakfast service were well in hand.

She was also responsible for the office paperwork.

For the larger part of Saturday night and into the early hours of Sunday morning she had been effectively 'cooking' the books.

On the desk, spread out in front of her, she had that particular morning the wallets, credit cards and personal effects - letters, photographs and address books - of George and Terence Lowry. According to the information now on her computer screen, both brothers had checked out of the hotel on the morning of

Thursday, 18th October. Indeed, she had before her a copy of their separate bills, signed by both men individually, together with a print-out of their credit card payments covering their (shortened) stay at The Rannoch Moor Hotel.

Although George and Terrence had 'left unexpectedly' they had only been charged for the three nights they had been there and not for the entire week they had originally booked.

Marie made digital copies of both the bills and the credit-card payment slips and attached them to an email assuring Mr James Lowry of Merridale Road, Wolverhampton that both his sons had definitely left the hotel on that date. She added that as far as she knew they had been planning to return to Wolverhampton and had left no other forwarding address. She had assumed at the time they checked out that they were leaving early because of the bad weather. She hoped it had not entirely spoilt their holiday and that they would turn up soon.

Marie despatched the email, gathered the objects on her desk together and placed them in separate plastic envelopes, clearly labelled with their respective names. These she then put in the safe - not the regular safe but one that was behind a 'secret' panel; a clever, hidden device that her grandfather, who had rebuilt the hotel in 1898, had thoughtfully concealed in the office wall.

* * *

Apart from Douglas Tait and Robert Wellington, the other guest up early that Sunday morning was Lady Olympia Garland.

Indeed, she was the first guest to take breakfast, sometime around seven-thirty. She was dressed in her riding gear. After a light breakfast, she headed for the riding stables behind the hotel. As she left the dining room she passed John and Poppy White. They too had opted for an early breakfast that Sunday morning and as soon as it was light were intending to take their second walk across the moor. They smiled at Olympia at the entrance to the dining room but otherwise said nothing to the serious young woman in tweed jacket, jodhpurs and riding boots.

The Manager of the stables is called Emelia McBane, Ronald's eldest sister. She is a short, somewhat stocky woman in her mid-forties. She has the wide hips and plain look of an experienced horse-woman, with her long hair in a tight knot and no makeup.

'Good morning, Lady Olympia. Sebastian is ready for you. Enjoy your exercise. If you need anything I shall be in my office.'

'Thank you, Emelia. Cold morning, what?'

'Indeed, your Ladyship.'

The indoor riding arena was small - little more than a converted barn - but it was better than nothing. There was too much snow on the ground to risk taking her mount outside that morning. When Olympia entered the barn she found the stable boy standing waiting patiently in the ring and holding Sebastian by his reins.

'Hello David.'

'Good morning, your Ladyship.'

'He's looking good. I fancy a few jumps this morning. Nothing high. Can you set some up, please?'

'Yes . Of course.'

While David builds a few jumps in the arena, Olympia mounts Sebastian and gently walks him round a few times. She then takes him for a short canter before pointing him at the first, and lowest obstacle - a single bar, no more that twelve inches off the ground. He hesitates for a moment but encouraged by a swift dig of Olympia's heels in his sides, immediately clears the jump with ease.

For a good hour Olympia worked hard with Sebastian, occasionally raising the jumps a little but never by much.

Sebastian took all in his stride, growing in confidence each time she put him to the jumps.

It had begun to snow slightly so Olympia gave up all hope of taking Sebastian out that day.

By ten-thirty she had had enough. Two teenage girls, guests at the hotel and both pony mad, had come to watch. Or was it young David that they had come to stare at? Anyway, they leant on the guard rail and studied Olympia as she gave her mount a few more canters round the ring before calling it a day.

It was clear even to these two novices that they were watching a very experienced rider. What they could not know was that at their age, Olympia had been taught by Captain Mark Philips himself, at his equestrian academy at Gleneagles. It had been expensive but what better training could one get except from a former Olympic gold medallist.

Olympia was herself fully aware of her social advantages. It was one thing to be the only daughter of rich parents with close links to the royal family but Olympia's mother had been one of Queen Elizabeth's Ladies in Waiting in the 1980's and a second cousin to the Princess Royal herself. That helped somewhat in life's upward struggle. Now that she was about to marry Teddy Bosenquet she had an exciting future to look forward to - even if, sadly, her own international show-jumping career was now over.

Olympia dismounted, handed Sebastian back to David, smiled at the two teenagers and returned to her bedroom for a long, hot bath.

Teddy, whom she had left snoring in bed, was nowhere to be seen.

Olympia undressed, stepped into her bath and lay there, luxuriating in warm, soapy water for at least an hour.

* * *

Sir Miles came off the moor that Sunday afternoon in a foul mood. Not only had he failed to bag a deer but had fallen out with his ghillie - big time.

There had been, for five exhilarating moments, a chance to bag his first stag. It was a handsome beast, seen briefly silhouetted against the sky on an outcrop of rock, posed as if from some Victorian paining. He was taking aim when Duncan, his ghillie, pushed his gun aside. The bullet flew off to the right, crashing into rocks some thirty yards away.

Within seconds, the stag and the three hind close by him had vanished into the morning mists.

When Sir Miles expostulated, the ghillie told him that it was illegal to take a stag now since the hunting season for harts ended on the 20th October. This same ghillie had, on previous occasions, turned a blind eye to these rules - once even with Sir Miles, from whom he had accepted a large 'commission' for his troubles. Sir Miles therefore found the man's behaviour on this occasion inexplicable - and told him so in no uncertain terms. Since Sir Miles was of the opinion that money could buy anything and that every man had his price, the 'moral' stance now adopted by Duncan McBane was not only peculiar but uncharacteristic of someone who was, by reputation, little more than a poacher.

Miles Ballard had a temper on him and it was as much as the younger ghillie with them could do to stop the two men from coming to blows, there and then.

The upshot was that Sir Miles turned on his heels and angrily stomped off down the hill, back towards the hotel.

The two ghillies watched his departure impassively.

'Good riddance, ye old bastard!' said Duncan under his breath. 'Mind you, I'll have you one day, you miserable sod. Just you wait and see!'

He spat into the snow, broke his rifle, pocketed his cartridges and set off across the moor, following Sir Miles' footsteps in the snow. The younger man loped after him, chuckling to himself in a strange, idiotic manner.

* * *

Cecelia did not manage to 'bump' into Erik that morning although it was not for lack of trying. He was nowhere to be seen.

She assumed that he had gone off on one of his long, solitary journeys across the moors on his strange little skis. Cecelia was not sporty in any way and found the activity of many of the hotel's guests - particularly the men - somewhat manic. Even Sir Miles, gallivanting about on the moors with a gun almost as long as himself, seemed absurd to her.

What was *not* absurd were her feelings of unease about this hotel and its somewhat weird staff. Apart from a certain physical resemblance - not least a preponderance of piercing blue eyes - they all had a look about them that she could not quite 'place'. Something about the skin, perhaps. Pallid, bloodless. Whatever it was, her woman's instincts had been aroused. The odd behaviour of the two chamber-maids she had spotted rooting through Paula Leamington's belongings was disturbing in itself. The more she thought about that, the more troubled she became.

She longed to tell someone but who? Miles would not listen to her. In fact he would probably laugh at her and tell her that, anyway, it was none of her bloody business. No, she had to tell someone soon or she would burst. The question was, who, for heaven's sake? Erik seemed one obvious choice but who was he and, more importantly, where was he? He was the most elusive young man she had ever come across.

Where was he now that she needed him?

* * *

Elspeth Grant and her new companion, Gabriélle Fourés, spent the larger part of Sunday afternoon in bed. Talking.

They were an odd couple.

Elspeth was in her late fifties, short, stout and not particularly beautiful. She was a brilliant, highly qualified Criminologist and fellow of All Souls ('Arseholes', she called it) at Oxford University where she sometimes taught, at the Department of Criminology. She was also a Consultant Psychologist, or 'Profiler', for the British police. It was she whose remarkable deductions had led to the discovery and prosecution of Consultant Pathologist Dr. James Ledbetter as a multiple murderer, Scotland's most notorious serial-killer - as the tabloid press chose to describe him. This and other related police gossip had occupied the larger part of their conversation the previous evening over supper with the Whites. The food as usual was fantastic and together they put away three bottles of expensive wine. It was a most enjoyable evening and something of a welcome reunion between friends and fellow professionals after too long a gap.

Poppy and Gabriélle had hit it off from the moment they met although Poppy noted, that even when pressed, Gabriélle was reluctant to reveal much about herself or say why she was in Britain. Poppy got the impression, from some of the things Gabriélle said that evening, that she was some kind of journalist. Poppy thought it best not to press too hard - at least not until they both knew each other better. Slowly, slowly, catchee monkey.

Much as Poppy liked Gabriélle, she had therefore some misgivings about Elspeth's new lover; misgivings that she found hard to define exactly. Some woman's instinct, however, told Poppy that Gabriélle Fourés was not quite what she claimed to be.

It had been Detective Inspector John White (as was) who had been the Investigating Officer on the Ledbetter case. He and Elspeth had worked well together, become friends but - as often happens with professional relationships - had lost touch with each other in the intervening years. True, they had throughout that period corresponded regularly on police matters of mutual interest but they had not been in each other's company - formally or otherwise - since the Ledbetter trial was done and dusted. Now they were together again.

Gabriélle Fourés did not, for reasons of her own, quite share Elspeth's enthusiasm for this 'reunion'.

Gabriélle was a classic Parisian beauty - well groomed, sultry, sophisticated, highly articulate, well-educated (despite predatory nuns), naturally sexy - and a chain-smoker (even in public). Since Elspeth also smoked like a chimney, it was not surprising to find them that Sunday afternoon both sitting up in bed, puffing away while each balanced an ashtray on their knees. They were smoking Gitanes Brunes - the dark, aromatic version of this classic French cigarette. Gabriélle had hers especially imported from the Netherlands each month, as Brunes were almost unobtainable in France. The fact that the smoke-alarm in their bedroom had not gone off was entirely due to Elspeth's legendary dexterity with a screwdriver and a pair of pliers.

'Just my luck to find us sharing this hotel with a bloody *flic*! Did you know he was going to be here, Elspeth?'

'Of course not, my darling. Anyway, I thought you had rather taken to his wife. Poppy is very bright and an absolute poppet.'

'Tout à fait! The wife, she is gorgeous but senior policemen always give me the creeps. In France they are always so fucking arrogant. Why, I would not put it past him to arrest me for trespassing on his patch.'

'I hardly think John White is going to arrest you, Gabriélle - unless its for smoking these disgusting cigarettes in bed!'

Elspeth stubbed out her half-smoked Gitanes with a look of distaste on her face, picked at the shreds of tobacco still sticking to her upper lip, rolled out of bed and tottered to the bathroom. She was wearing only a large pair of silk knickers.

'Anyway, he may be able to help you in your 'research', my darling.'

This was said from inside the bathroom. Elspeth then flushed the toilet and reappeared at the bathroom door, pausing there in what she hoped was a rather sexy pose.

'Très belle, ma chérie, but please stop posing over there like some old tart from Rue Saint-Denis and come here and show me how much you really love me. Then, maybe, I will tell you *exactly* why I am here in this weird, fucking hotel at the frozen end of the known universe!'

9

Since Erik lived in a wood with an aerial walkway, he had taken to climbing the great chestnut tree each evening and spending some time aloft. This was partly exercise, partly to relieve the boredom of camping in a remote part of Rannoch Moor with limited access to the hotel itself, and partly so that - on a clear night, such as there was on Sunday evening - he could gaze at the stars.

It was in this elevated position that evening, at about six o'clock, that he first heard the distinctive noise of a quad-bike crossing the cobbled yard of the stables behind the hotel. This yard had been cleared of snow earlier that day and some clinkers and ash spread to cover the thin layer of ice that remained.

Out of curiosity and for no other reason, Erik quickly scampered along his aerial walkway towards that part of the wood nearest to the stables. He knew this walkway like the back of his hand now and was able to reach the far end within a minute or two. From that position he was able to peer down at two men hauling long black bags from off the back of their trailer and dragging them, one by one, towards an outhouse adjacent to the vast boiler that even then was belching smoke into the night sky. A strong shaft of light from the open door of this building illuminated the scene with dramatic intensity.

There was something about the shape of those plastic bags that worried Erik, so much so that he immediately descended from his tree by a rope there for that purpose. Landing softly on the snow-covered ground he crept towards the lighted window of the outhouse and cautiously peeped in. The floor of this large room was covered in white tiles, as were the walls. It looked like a milking parlour or dairy facility for there were pipes and taps and other apparatus for washing attached to the walls. In one corner there were tall, aluminium vats and on a metal shelf at one end of the room, aluminium buckets and bowls

It was while Erik was taking all this in that the men entered from the yard, each dragging one of the plastic bags behind him.

They then closed the door and began unzipping the bags. They contained the bodies of two young men, one of whom had no head. As Erik watched with increasing horror, they stripped the bodies, searched pockets and removed all personal belongings from the two corpses. Some of these - including wallets, keys and money, they pocketed. The clothes, together with two rucksacks and some climbing equipment, they stuffed into a sack which they then carefully placed by the door.

The two bodies - one without a head - naked and covered in blood, now lay spread-eagled on the white, tiled floor.

The elder of the two men then took a hose pipe from the wall, turned a tap and began to hose down both bodies. Erik watched, trying hard not to vomit, as the bloody water swirled across the floor before disappearing into a drain in the centre of the room.

Meanwhile, the younger of the two ghillies took the bag, opened the door and stepped into the yard. Erik had seen enough of the bodies to last a lifetime so he immediately left the window and hastened to the corner of the building, peering round cautiously. Diagonally across from where he knelt in the snow was the entrance to the boiler house. The door was open and light flooded into the yard. From his hidden position, Erik watched the young man fling open the iron door to the furnace, and hurl the sack into the flames. He then shut the furnace door, turned and re-entered the yard, closing the door behind him.

It was at this point that that Erik disappeared into the shadows and retreated into the safety of the dark wood and back to his tent to think over what he had just witnessed.

As he zipped up the entrance to his tent he noticed that his hands were shaking and his heart pounding.

* * *

Supper that Sunday evening was served as usual - at exactly seven-thirty. The guests, who had spent their day in a variety of activities (some more sporty than others, perhaps) shared one thing in common - they all had a ravenous appetite and were looking forward to yet another sumptuous evening meal at the Rannoch Moor Hotel, celebrated for its unique cuisine.

Young Stewart, scrubbed up and polished after his murderous adventures on the moor that afternoon, was now standing as usual on the great stairway, piping the guests into supper. They dutifully paused on the landing to appreciate the lad's undeniable musical skills, then filed downstairs and into the dining room. There were some forty-three guests in the hotel that evening - excluding, naturally, the seven who had gone missing since Thursday, 11th October.

Poppy and John were amongst those making their way down the stairs that evening. Poppy was dressed in a low-cut silk dress with a distinct Japanese motif. She wore her dark hair up, with a flower above one ear. She looked stunning - this was, after all, her eighteenth wedding anniversary. She had to look her best for that and was pleased to see that John fully appreciated her efforts. As they went down the stairs, arm in arm, she could see that he was as proud as Punch to have such a beautiful woman on his arm.

Poppy was also wearing a new Chrysoberyl (cat's eye) gemstone set in gold next to her wedding ring. This was John's present to her to celebrate their eighteenth wedding anniversary. It had appeared, as if by magic, from behind her ear. This was no mean feat as they were both naked in the shower at the time! Since John was something of an amateur magician and frequently entertained young relatives by discovering a sweet or even an egg hidden about their person, Poppy might have expected some such trick that evening - but not in the shower together. Who said Romance was dead?

Their chance meeting with Elspeth Grant in the bar had surprised John and Poppy but within minutes of falling into conversation with Elspeth and her new partner it was as if they had never been apart.

Supper that evening had brought back many fond memories of

time spent at Dunkeld, including their final get-together to celebrate Ledbetter's trial and convictions. On that memorable occasion, fifty-three-year-old Elspeth had executed cartwheels on their lawn - just for fun. At that time Elspeth's companion was a handsome young man from Somalia who turned out to be a brilliant cosmologist. He had taken up a new research post at CERN not long afterwards and so Elspeth's relationship with 'Mother' had subsequently ended sadly. But now she had a brand-new lover - the delectable Gabriélle Fourés.

Although tonight was meant to be their celebratory meal for two, both Poppy and John were happy to share a table with Elspeth and Gabriélle. If truth be told, Poppy was secretly relieved. Much as she enjoyed her husband's company, she was naturally gregarious and certainly liked Elspeth. It would be fun to share their special evening together and to find out more about Elspeth's startlingly beautiful new girlfriend.

'We met in Carcassonne, in the south of France. I was on holiday, quietly minding my own business, sipping my wine in the square outside Chez Felix when this gorgeous brunette sat down beside me, ordered herself a large beer, calmly lit a cigarette and then proceeded to seduce me!'

'Not true, Elspeth. Not true at all. I never drink beer!'

Indeed, none of it was true. Elspeth and Gabriélle had met in Oxford (as John well knew) but Elspeth's love of the dramatic gesture was one of her more harmless eccentricities - so John said nothing.

Their waiter arrived and took their order. It was eight o'clock and the great Baroque dinning room was full. Candles had been lit on each table and the overhead, electric lights dimmed. A wood fire roared in the vast baronial hearth at one end of the hall. The wine-waiter poured them each another glass of fine red wine (Elspeth's choice) and then withdrew.

'What do you do, Gabriélle? Elspeth seemed to imply earlier that you worked for French television.'

'I did, once. I was a TV director at Planète+, making documentaries. Now I am a freelance writer, film director and producer.'

The waiter arrived with their first course, closely followed by what can only be described as a gourmet banquet.

Their meal that evening consisted of cock-a-leekie broth or Cullen Skink (Finnan-haddie, onion, mashed potatoes, butter and milk), followed by haddock in brown sauce, followed by Meg Dods' haggis, kailkenny and neep purry (stewed turnips) followed in turn by Whim-Wham (cream, white wine, lemon, Naples biscuit, red currant jelly, candied citron and orange peel,) or Atholl Brose (oatmeal, water, heather honey-whisky and cream) and rounded off with Orkney cheese and homemade, oatmeal biscuits.

After their meal they withdrew to the enclosed veranda for coffee and brandy. The curtains were open this evening. Coloured lanterns had been hung in the trees close to the window, creating a charming effect. It was snowing gently. It almost felt like Christmas although it was still only October.

'I am still not clear how you both came to be here in Rannoch Moor of all places. Was it your idea, Elspeth?'

Elspeth withdrew her nose from an enormous brandy glass, grinned at John and indicated with a tip of her head towards Gabriélle, now sat on the sofa next to her.

'It was my idea, John,' said Gabriélle. 'I was in Edinburgh with Elspeth for a week or so and came across an article about this hotel in *Scottish Life*. We both love good food so on impulse I booked us in for a few nights. After the meal we have just had, I think I made a good choice, did I not my darling?'

At this point Gabriélle patted Elspeth affectionately on her knee. Elspeth grinned like a Cheshire cat who has just been given yet another enormous bowl of cream. She did not look at John, though. John was well aware that Gabriélle's choice of Rannoch

Moor was far from random. Elspeth herself had told him as much. For the moment, however, he would go along with the story Gabriélle was weaving so effectively - like some fabled storyteller from Baghdad.

Although the temptation to talk once more about the Ledbetter case was considerable, both Elspeth and John held back during the meal. Both were more interested in what the other had been doing *since* then. This therefore occupied the larger part of their conversation for the rest of the evening - once they had all adjourned to the bar for a whiskey or two. The saloon bar at the Rannoch Moor Hotel boasted a choice of twenty-seven single malt whiskeys, excluding inferior foreign products from Ireland, America, Canada or even Japan. Elspeth chose Edradour and John opted for his favourite, Talisker from the Isle of Skye. Poppy and Gabriélle stuck to red wine.

'Are you working on any specific project at the moment, Gabriélle?', asked Poppy.

They were now sat together in the lounge drinking hot chocolate, having left Elspeth and John talking 'shop' in the bar.

'Not really. I have a number of projects on the go at the moment. The problem is always funding. That seems to occupy a large part of my time. That is the disadvantage of being self-employed. I love the freedom but raising money, even for the initial research, is very difficult.'

'Is it any easier here in Scotland?'

'Maybe. I have some European Documentary Film contacts in Scotland. In fact, I came to Edinburgh this time not just to be with Elspeth but to meet a friend and colleague. Noé Mendelle is part of EDF in Edinburgh and a member of the Scottish Documentary Institute. She is helping me find money for a film I want to shoot here in Scotland later this year, hopefully.'

'What's is you documentary about?'

'Don't ask, Poppy!'

It was Elspeth. She and John had left the bar and now joined them on the enclosed veranda. Elspeth was tottering slightly, clinging to John's arm. She had clearly enjoyed her meal - not least the two bottles of fine claret they had drunk between them and the whiskeys that had followed.

'Gabriélle is a very naughty girl! Very naughty and very secretive. She never tells me anything, do you darling!?'

* * *

Erik had spent much of his day worrying about what to do, having seen what he had seen. Should he report it to the police immediately or at least tell the hotel manager?

Mile after mile that afternoon he had crossed the moor on his Norwegian skis, frantically racking his brains. When it began to snow heavily mid-afternoon he retraced his steps. By the time he finally got back to his tent that evening he was cold and exhausted and not a little frightened. He had resolved nothing in his head, although he had rehearsed a number of the more obvious options facing him - or so he thought.

He made himself a hot drink of soup, which he drank, then crawled into his sleeping bag and pulled the hood over his head.

His first instincts told him to get off Rannoch Moor and move on. Easier said than done! It had been snowing since mid-afternoon and did not look like stopping soon. Even with his Norwegian skis, crossing the moor in these conditions and at night would prove extremely difficult.

If he stuck to the road going east it might just be possible to get to Kinloch Rannoch but that would take him back the way he had come. He did not want that, not after the long time it had taken him on foot to get to Rannoch Moor in the first place. No, he'd rather move further west, towards Glen Coe perhaps and then, as per his original plans, on towards the Isle of Skye.

Alternatively, if he struck out north, he could follow the railway line all the way to Fort William. If he left immediately, he could - with luck - make the youth hostel at Corrour by dawn but it would be a long, hazardous trip in these conditions. The railway line was raised above the bog and that encouraged snow drifts, at least on that side where the prevailing winds struck the embankment. No. Stay put. Keep your head down low and say nothing. Not the most courageous choice perhaps but for once - or so he hoped - common sense prevailed.

Erik spent an uncomfortable night in his tent. He was unable to shake the violent image of those two dead men out of his head. He assumed that they had been murdered and that they were guests. But why? What was going on in this strange hotel? Moreover, was he safe or could he be the next victim?

When he eventually dozed off, through sheer exhaustion, he slept fitfully - a sleep full of nightmarish dreams, fear and anxiety.

10
Monday, 22nd October

The next morning Erik woke early, cleared the fresh snow from the entrance to his tent, lit his primus stove and began a new day with a strong cup of black coffee and a steaming-hot bowl of Scotts porridge oats. The trees all around him are now heavy with snow, the sky above his clearing dark, with the promise of more snow to come perhaps.

It is now Monday, 22nd October and although Erik does not know it yet, the Rannoch Moor Hotel and the tiny hamlet that forms part of its vast estate is now entirely cut off from the rest of the world.

It had snowed heavily all night and the hotel itself and its cottages where the staff live are blanketed in snow. Strong winds have caused massive snow drifts along the length of the main road as far as Kinloch Rannoch in the east. Both the B846 and B847 are therefore closed. To the west, the A82 is still in use but the local authorities are struggling to keep it open. The single-track railway line that crosses Rannoch Moor from Crianlarich to Fort William is completely buried. It is, according to the local Station Master, unlikely that there will be any trains from either direction for several days.

That may partly explain the glum looks on the face of Ronald McBane as he coped with a host of questions from anxious guests crowded in the lobby.

'No Madame, we will not starve! We have plenty of food. I assure you sir, the boilers will not run out of oil and you will not freeze to death. Yes Madame, there are no trains, nor cars come to that. The roads are entirely blocked - for the immediate future, that is. Yes, we are doing our best to clear the roads but they are still far too dangerous in places, even for tractors. No, we will not run out of electricity. Even if the power lines do go down, we have our own generators. Yes Madame, breakfast will be served as usual and no, my mobile phone does not work either!'

The Rannoch Hotel, consisting entirely of either staff or clientele, is a small community and news that it was now cut off had spread like wild-fire to every one of its fifty or so guests.

They each greeted this news with a measure of concern - ranging from annoyance to sheer panic. This was surprising, considering the range of experience these largely wealthy, middle-class people shared. Perhaps it had something to do with busy schedules or forthcoming appointments. There were, after all, a number of hugely prosperous business men amongst the guest for whom severance from work appeared to induce a kind of terror.

When it was discovered that the telephone lines were also damaged and that there was no means of communication with the outside world whatsoever, then they appeared to enter some kind of catatonic state unique to workaholic entrepreneurs. Mobile phones had never worked this far from the nearest town and satellite coverage did not seem to cover Rannoch Moor. In short, there were neither landlines nor mobile phone links with the outside world. For some of the guest thus trapped, this was somehow far worse than the physical isolation caused by snow blocking the roads in all directions.

Erik was one of the last to discover the extent of the hamlet's isolation when he tried to use the public telephone near the bar. He shouldered his way through a group of perplexed guests, milling around somewhat listlessly outside the bar. It was as if they were waiting for the phone to suddenly ring of its own accord and put them out of their misery.

Erik entered the booth, pulled the sliding glass door shut and picked up the receiver. He was putting a few coins in the slot when someone tapped on the glass. It was a short, middle-aged man in a kilt.

'Nay bother, son. It disna work. Line down somewhere.'

'What do you mean?', asked Erik, opening the door. 'What's down?'

'The telephone line. There's no way of calling anyone. We are cut off. Bloody scandalous, if you ask me.'

Erik didn't ask him but shouldered his way back through the crowd and stood in the doorway to the hotel. He remained there for a while, staring forlornly out into the forecourt where a few porters were struggling to clear some kind of path. It was not immediately evident where this path was leading to for there was, in effect, nowhere to go! The snow was everywhere. Even getting from his tent to the hotel entrance had been difficult and no one yet had tried to clear the cobbled yard by the stables. The wood where he had pitched his tent had sheltered him from the worst but now, in the full light of day, he could see the extent of last night's blizzard.

Well, thought Erik, that puts pay to any plans I might have had of telling the police. I should have called them last night instead of dithering. Now what can I do? There is no point in telling the Manager. He is almost certain to be part of whatever horrible events are taking place in this ghastly hotel. Was he, Erik, the only one who had seen two dead men being treated as if they were little more than carrion? How come one of those terrible corpses had no head? What kind of place is this, for God's sake?

This, he concluded, was turning into some kind of horror movie - and he was a reluctant member of the cast, trapped in a cinematic nightmare!

* * *

Dr Thomas Neep was a portly gentleman in his early seventies, from Carlisle. It was thought that he had been a GP all his working life but who, seven years ago, had finally retired.

The story he told fellow guests was that he was now enjoying retirement with course-fishing, good food and occasional visits to his three grandchildren in Newcastle - in that order. His wife had died eleven years ago so he had long since made himself self-sufficient. He had seen too many of his medical colleagues retire, take to drink and pop their surgical boots in less time than it takes to perform a vasectomy. Even doing up a cottage in some remote part of the Highlands could not slow down that process or prevent retired doctors from sliding down the slippery slope of alcohol dependency and gout. That was his view, anyway. He was not going to make *that* mistake!

No, stay fit, stay active - that was the way to enjoy life.

Last year, or so he claimed, his treat to himself had been a trip to Disney World in Orlando, Florida with his daughter and her three children. That had been hard work. His treat to himself *this* year was a week's course-fishing on Rannoch Moor - all by himself. Mind you, the bloody weather had put paid to any fishing this week but the excellent food and exceptional service at the Rannoch Moor Hotel had more than compensated for that.

Soon it would be lunchtime. He could hardly wait.

* * *

Cecelia left Sir Miles in bed, reading yesterday's newspaper. He was in a foul mood. The deer hunting was proving disastrous, with little prospect now of getting anything. As for being cut off, that in itself was not so bad but to be without either his mobile or a landline was really getting him down.

'Where are you off to now?' he asked, somewhat testily.

Cecelia picked up her mink coat and wrapped it around her shoulders. She was wearing slacks, a roll-neck sweater and furry moon boots. On her head she wore a brightly-coloured woollen bobble hat with flaps that covered her ears.

'You look like a Technicolor gnome!'

'I'm going to get some fresh air. I hope that you are in a better mood when I get back, otherwise you may be eating by yourself this lunchtime.'

'Yes, yes! Don't get lost, Captain Oates.'

Cecelia had no idea what he was talking about so she said nothing but left the bedroom, slamming the door behind her.

When she reached the lobby there was a small crowd of people hanging around, as if looking for something to do. The staff were doing their best to give a feeling of normality to the day but the idea that the hotel was cut off clearly still troubled some of the guests.

Coffee and morning tea was now being served in the lounge and although tempted to join the guests already there, Cecelia stuck to her plans, left the building and stepped out into the forecourt.

It was very slippery underfoot but one of the hotel porters was shovelling hot cinders from a wheelbarrow onto the narrow path they had cleared earlier.

'Watch yer step, Miss!'

He flung a shovel-full of cinders onto the ground close to her feet. She watched the ash sizzle as it hit the snow and ice. She gingerly stepped over the smear of fresh ash and moved on - before he threw another shovel-full.

The railway station was completely deserted. The little gift shop was closed, as was the waiting room that had been converted into tea rooms for day-visitors and hill-walkers. Cecelia stood on the platform and looked in both directions - across a white waste, smooth and flat and now largely featureless. She could just make out the railway track itself in places, curving away to the south but soon that too disappeared. It was a desolate sight but also curiously beautiful. The mountains, partly covered in cloud, loomed on the distant horizon - ominous blue shapes on a lunar landscape. The sun was trying to emerge through the morning mist, giving the entire panorama a somewhat eerie, spectral hue.

'It reminds me of home!'

Cecelia, startled by this unexpected voice, spun round to discover Erik standing just behind her. He had his binoculars to his face and was searching the barren landscape to the north.

'Home?'

He lowered his glasses and smiled at her.

'Yes. I am from Norway. Where I come from it is often like this.'
He raised his glasses once more and pointed them up the line - towards Fort William, thirty-five miles to the north. Here the railway track disappeared only yards from the platform where they stood.

Cecelia followed the direction of his gaze. She was trembling slightly, although she did her best to hide it. So, here she was at last. With Erik. He looked even better close to. Brad Pitt in snow-boots and anorak!

'What are you looking for?'

'A way out of this place, that's what I'm looking for!'

'Why. Do you not like it here?'

He lowered his binoculars, turned and looked at her. He glanced around to see if they were alone and then took something from his jacket pocket. He held it out to her to hold in her gloved hand. She took it . Because she was slightly short-sighted and without her reading glasses, she held it close to her face. It smelled strongly of damp charcoal.

'Do you know what that is?'

'Is it bone. Charred bone?'

'Yes. It's a lunate carpal. Wrist bone, or at least a burnt fragment of one. I found it on the path this morning, in front of the hotel.'

'You mean it's a human bone?'

'Yes. From a body that has been freshly cremated. It was in among the ashes they were throwing on the path near the entrance to the hotel.'

'Oh my God!'

'It was still warm when I picked it up. That is exactly why I want to get out of this dreadful place'.

11

Chief Inspector John White and his wife Arabella (known as 'Poppy' to friends and family) spent the larger part of Monday morning playing Scrabble in the lounge and drinking far too much coffee. Since there was no sign of Elspeth and Gabriélle, they were obliged to amuse themselves.

Enforced idleness was not something Poppy took to well but John thoroughly enjoyed their morning together. Time to relax. Time to talk about their plans for the cottage back in Dunkeld and the garden - Poppy's pride and joy. Time too to discuss Christmas arrangements and holiday plans for next summer. Last year it had been Turkey. Greece this year, perhaps? Corfu? Now that he was a Chief Inspector they could afford somewhere even more exotic. India? Maldives? But not, definitely not, the Isle of Skye!

'MBAQANGA? What on earth is that when its home, Poppy?'

'Mbaquanga is a type of African music.'

'Yeah. Pull the other one! You are clearly cheating again, I can tell.'

'I am not cheating. I never cheat at Scrabble. Life is too short. Anyway, if you add that word to my score I think you will find that I have won. Again! More coffee, darling?'

They summoned a waiter who refreshed their coffee cups. It had started to snow again outside, but not heavily. Through the large windows of the lounge they could see children building a snowman on the lawn.

'Have you thought any more about what we saw those chambermaids doing the other day - you know, the ones that looked as if they were stealing clothes?'

'Not really. But I did notice that that particular suitcase was in the Porter's lodge yesterday and that today it has gone. Since no one left the hotel yesterday or this morning because of the weather I am wondering where it might have gone to. I could not see any other storage space in the lobby.'

'Should we not raise the matter with the Manager?'

'Possibly. The trouble is, we have no real evidence that they were stealing someone else's property. I suggest we wait and see. Let's keep our eyes open, in case something similar happens again. I'll tell Elspeth and Gabriélle. They too can look out for anything suspicious. Elspeth will love that!'

'But that does not explain what happened to the owner of that suitcase.'

'Yes. His name is Frank. Frank Robinson.'

'How on earth do you know that, John?'

'Well, I had hoped - just out of curiosity - to check the hotel register at the reception desk for that room but everything here is computerised. Anyway, when I was next in the reception area later that morning I noticed that the door of Porter's lodge was open. I sat down on a chair in the lobby and pretended to clean my binoculars with my handkerchief. From where I sat I could just make out through my binoculars the label on the suitcase at the back of their cubby hole. Frank Robinson.'

'Very clever, darling. All we need to do now is find out where Frank Robinson has vanished to! That should be a 'walk in the park' for the devious, cunning and thoroughly ingenious Inspector Gadget here!'

'Mbaquanga. I should think he's in Mbaquanga by now. Yes, that's where we will find the mysteriously missing Frank Robinson. What do you think, Little Miss Cleverclogs?'

* * *

Sir Miles did not enjoy his bath. He knew he was in a foul mood and that he had treated Cecelia rather brusquely that morning but seeing his lover talking to some good-looking young man did not help matters. He had been standing at the bedroom window in his dressing gown when he saw Cecelia and Erik walking back together from the station. He did not at that stage know who the young man was but he made a mental note to damn well find out.

No, he was in a foul mood and that was that. Maybe a whiskey or to with Teddy in the bar before lunch might cheer him up. They had arranged to meet there at eleven-thirty.

Teddy was already in the saloon bar when Sir Miles arrived half-an-hour later. They shook hands and ordered another whiskey. Teddy was drinking Glenmorangie. Sir Miles ordered the same.

'When do you have to be back, Miles?'

'Wednesday, Thursday. Not that fussed but not having a bloody phone is bugging me. I don't like being unable to talk to my people.'

'Cannot say it worries me! My lot are probably glad to see the back of me for a few days. Not being able to talk to Canary Warf is like having a real holiday. Mind you, we might need to order you a helicopter if this weather continues.'

'Cant be more expensive that that seaplane you found me, surely?'

'Maybe not but what a great experience, eh? Landing on Loch Rannoch in a Hughes HK-1 Hercules does not happen every day, now does it?'

'True. Great fun. Where's Olympia? Riding that bloody horse of hers again?'

'Yes, I guess so. Still, it keeps her busy.'

'I wish Cecelia had something to keep her busy - other than spending my money, that is. Right little moody bitch she was this morning.'

'Women! Love 'em, hate 'em. Can't do without 'em!'

'I'll drink to that. Slange!'

* * *

But Olympia was not riding that morning. Sebastian had shed a shoe that needed to be sorted before he could be exercised again. The nearest blacksmith was based at Kinloch Rannoch, miles away and still cut off by snow drifts. He would not to be able to fix it for some days yet - assuming the roads could be cleared, that is.

However, Emelia McBane, the Stables Manager, was confident one of the ghillies could. She would see that it was done later that day.

Meanwhile, Olympia had discovered the hotel's library. It was a beautifully panelled room just off the corridor leading to the main lift. It faced due east. It was small but entirely furnished with its original Victorian arm-chairs and tables. It must have been someone's study once. The walls were lined with book-shelves. Of course there was the usual mix of cheap thrillers, run-of-the-mill detective stories (Ian Rankin mostly, this being Scotland) and thick paperbacks about World War II but on the long wall there were shelves from floor to ceiling full of very old, properly bound books.

Olympia had borrowed the key for these shelves from Ronald McBane and had been given a pair of cotton gloves with which to examine these precious books. That was what she was doing when Gabriélle entered.

'Oh, sorry to bother you. I did not think anyone other than me had found this room. What are you looking at?'

'No problem. Come in.'

Gabriélle entered, closed the green baize door behind her,

crossed the room and stood beside Olympia, looking down over her shoulder. Gabriélle was surprised to see that the young woman was dressed in riding boots and jodhpurs.

'Look', said Olympia excitedly, 'It's the original designs for this very room. Isn't that fantastic!'

Spread out on the table before her is a large book of bound, architectural drawings. There, sure enough, are the plans and elevations of the room itself in which she is actually sitting. Little has changed. Indeed, it must be one of the least altered rooms in the hotel. Exactly as its architect had envisaged.

'Who is the architect?' asked Gabriélle.

'Edward Calvert. These plans are dated 1897. According to the hotel brochure, this building was built in 1898 on top of a much older farm house that goes back to the end of the 18th Century.'

'I'm Gabriélle, by the way.'

'Hello Gabriélle. I'm Olympia. Olympia Garland. I've seen you around. You here with your mother?'

'Well, not exactly. More like an aunt. So who was Edward Calvert?'

At this point Olympia pulled another book closer to her across the table. It was a copy of *Who's Who,* dated 1920.

'It says here that Edward Calvert was a Scottish architect, born in 1847. He died in 1914. He specialised in what is called 'baronial tenements' - whatever they are. He also built mock-Gothic villas for the wealthy. There are, it says, 'examples of his domestic architecture in Colinton Road, Merchiston'. Not sure where that is but I assume that it's in Edinburgh.'

'Fascinating. May I sit down?'

'Sure. Look, this house has been owned by the McBanes since 1778. Ronald McBane's great, great grandfather bought the farm house that year and turned it into an inn or, as they rather grandly called it at the time, a 'Hunting Lodge'. The original farm house itself is early 17th Century.'

'Have you found out who owned this house at the time of its Victorian conversion?'

'Yes. His name was Charles McBane. He must be the current Manager's grandfather. There's not much more about the McBanes before that but according to this book there is a tradition that the family originated from Fife, on the east coast, north of Edinburgh.'

'Fife?'

'Yes. Why? Are you interested in the McBanes?'

'Very. The more I can find out about them the better. Will you help me?'

'Sure. But I think refreshments are needed first. Shall I order a pot of tea for two and maybe some biscuits?'

'Perfect. Thank you, Olympia.'

* * *

Erik spent several hours that Monday afternoon taking photographs. He started at the station and worked his way up the railway line in both directions, as far as the snow drifts would allow him.

His camera had a powerful lens and he was able, whilst pretending to take shots of the snowy landscape, to cover most parts of the hotel itself. Later, when it began to snow again, he retraced his tracks and ended up back at the wood behind the hotel where his tent was pitched. They had cleared the cobbled yard in front of the stables but the rest of the out-buildings and passageways between them were covered in a layer of fresh snow. The wood itself was covered in a deep blanket of snow.

Even the little patch he had cleared earlier that morning in front of his tent was covered once more.

Making sure that no one was around, he climbed the rope ladder on the large chestnut tree and got onto the aerial walkway. From here, by making his way to the edge of the wood nearest to the back of the hotel, he was able to photograph from his elevated position most of the out-buildings - including the white-tiled room where he had seen them washing the bodies and the room with the furnace. The actual boiler-room that heated the hotel was further to the left, with a large oil tank behind it. Next to that was the greenhouse, heated by the furnace and beyond that storage buildings of one kind or another. Later tonight, when the kitchen staff have left the building after the evening meal, he will take a closer look at these out-buildings.

He had not told Cecelia about the two bodies he had seen.

He had, though, told her enough about his general concerns; concerns that it would appear she shared. She told him about the chamber maids and Paula Leamington's suitcase. It was not a lot to go on, she admitted, but some instinct, she added, convinced her that there were evil things going on in this hotel. Erik, knowing what he knew, concurred. So far as they knew there were at least three people missing - the two rock climbers and Paula Leamington.

Who else, they wondered, had either died or disappeared in mysterious circumstances?

They agreed to say nothing to anyone as yet but to keep their eyes and ears open for anything else suspicious and swap notes next time they met - on Tuesday morning at ten o'clock, by the railway station.

Erik was glad he now had someone to share his fears with - particularly someone as pretty as Cecelia Arnold.

The feeling, moreover, appeared to be mutual.

12

Cecelia was late joining Teddy, Sir Miles and Olympia for lunch. Throughout their meal she hardly said anything. Sir Miles, sensing that she was still angry with him, tried to be nice to her but his smiles and jokes and compliments fell on stony ground. Olympia was full of her discoveries about the McBanes and her new friend, some French woman called Gabriélle Fourés. When she started telling them about their discoveries in the library Cecelia perked up.

'Did you say you had seen plans of the hotel, Olympia?'

'Yes. Very detailed plans. Why?'

'Well', said Cecelia, 'I am interested in history, particularly old buildings. Does this one have cellars and secret passages?'

'Probably. Smuggling of one sort or another was common in these parts at the time of the original farmhouse on this site. I should imagine there are quite extensive cellars here. I know for a fact that they have a massive wine cellar and when you think of it, the kitchens must be below ground for the food always comes up by lift from somewhere beneath the main dining room.'

'Dumb waiter', said Teddy.

'I beg your pardon, darling. Whose a dumb waiter?'

'That's what they call it. Dumb waiter. That lift thing.'

'Right. Anyway, the McBanes have been here yonks. Very old family.'

'Very *odd* family, if you ask me.'

'Odd? It what way, Miles?'

'Well, look at them. Blue eyes, pale skin. Some of them, including one or two of the ghillies, are exceedingly odd. Not quite there, I suspect.'

It was at this point that their blue-eyed, pale-skinned waiter came to take their order so little more was said on the subject.

The dining room that lunchtime was full. Since there was little to do outside, except volunteer perhaps to clear the roads leading out of the hamlet, most folk had opted to take luncheon instead.

Normally, during an ordinary day when people are out and about on the moors, lunch is a light affair with mostly self-service dishes. Today, however, the Chef has pulled out all the stops and provided something special - to take people's minds off the fact that they are effectively trapped.

The meal that Monday consisted of:

Pea and broad bean ravioli, Iberian ham and *jus gras*; Ballottine of *foi gras*, peach carpaccio and almond milk; Home-smoked Scottish lobster, warm lime and herb butter; strawberries, pistachio sponge, vanilla ice-cream with coffee and chocolates to end with.

Afterwards, once they had retreated to the bar for a whiskey or two, Sir Miles expressed his full satisfaction with the meal.

'Bloody good food here. We might be stuck in the middle of nowhere but they certainly know how to dish up great grub. Did you enjoy your meal, darling?'

Cecelia smiled at him and held his hand across the table.

'It was delicious. Thank you.'

It was one of her winning smiles - sufficient at least for Sir Miles to believe that he was once more in her good books.

After knocking back his whiskey Sir Miles stood up.

'I think I'm going to have a lie down. Read the paper, perhaps.

See you two later. You coming, Cissy?'

* * *

Elspeth had spent her morning grooming. She had a long soak in the bath, washed her hair, sat in front of the mirror with her hair dryer and makeup and thoroughly enjoyed herself for an hour or two.

She was not normally this concerned about her appearance but ever since she and Gabriélle had got together she made every effort to make herself attractive to her young, beautiful lover.

They were indeed an odd couple but Elspeth did not care a fig if that's what people thought.

Gabriélle was the best looking woman in the hotel and she was with Elspeth and no one else. That made Elspeth feel good, and proud and even sexy. Despite their differences in age, their love-making had been, from the start, both passionate and inventive. There was mutual satisfaction and a great deal of fun. She made Gabriélle laugh and Gabriélle made her feel wanted. It was a good combination.

They had arranged to meet Poppy and John for lunch, followed by a short walk, weather permitting.

Over lunch in the saloon bar (delicious open-sandwiches and home-brewed beer) Gabriélle talked about the origins of the hotel and the information Olympia Garland had given her regarding the McBanes.

'What's your interest in the McBane family?', asked John. 'Professional?'

'No. Just curiosity. I studied Sociology at the Sorbonne when I was young. People always interest me. Perhaps that's why I became a journalist.'

'So who is this Olympia Garland, when she's at home?' asked

Elspeth.

'Just a guest, bored with this bad weather. I found her in the library. She is more interested in the architecture of this place than its owners.'

'Is she pretty?' asked Elspeth.
'
'Elspeth! Stop it. You know I only have eyes for you!'

'So, who's up for a short walk?', asked Poppy. 'Its not snowing and I think they have cleared a path or two. I need some fresh air.'

They got up and left the bar, gathered their coats from their rooms and stepped outside into the cold air.

They walked as far as they could (mostly up and down in front of the hotel), ending up on the small lawn facing the lounge. This was where some children had built a snowman. Poppy had her camera with her so all four of them spent a happy half-an-hour or so taking photographs of each other. The competition was who could make the silliest pose next to the snowman. Poppy won that one. Then the challenge was who could make the silliest face. John won that one with ease. The glamour pose prize naturally went to Gabriélle. To his surprise (and ill-disguised delight) John was voted runner-up in this category.

By this time a small crowd had gathered at the window of the lounge, watching the fun. The climax came when Elspeth executed two perfect cartwheels. This prompted looks of astonishment from her friends and a round of applause from those watching from the warmth of the lounge.

* * *

Thomas Neep was amongst those guests applauding Elspeth's antics that afternoon. He had had a thoroughly enjoyable lunch and was sipping a coffee when he was drawn, like the others, to the lounge window. Their antics on the lawn brought back happy memories for him - sunny days on the beach at Weymouth with his late wife when they were younger and building snowmen with his young daughters in their garden in Guildford.

He returned to his seat, finished his coffee and resumed reading his book. It was called *But who killed Caroline?* He had never heard of its author but it was dark, very dark. Severed limbs and serial killings on the Isle of Skye. Wonderful nonsense but a damn good read.

Anyway, that's what Thomas Neep thought. Book sales of 250,000 proved that he was not the only one who thought this particular crime thriller was 'a good read'!

* * *

Erik sat outside his tent that evening and cooked himself a plate of baked beans, sausages and mushrooms on his primus stove, followed by a scalding mug of black coffee.

He knew, even as he squatted there in front of his little tent, that the guests in the hotel would be sitting down to a five-course meal, with wines that cost at least £30 a bottle. He knew also that they would then move to the saloon bar (the one to which he was not admitted) and consume large amounts of expensive whiskey and brandy. He knew all this but he did not envy them one jot. Indeed, he felt some sympathy for them for he sensed, as had Cecelia, that they were part of some horrible scheme of things; some dreadful calamity that was unfolding around them and about which they themselves knew absolutely nothing.

He washed his frying pan, plate, knife and fork in the snow, packed his primus stove away carefully in its metal box and stowed everything in his tent in its designated place. He then checked his camera. He had recharged it from an electric point in the public bar that afternoon, thanks to an accommodating barman - even if he had piercing blue eyes! He put on his darkest clothes, including a dark blue cagoule and a grey woollen hat, zipped his tent flap shut, and stole off into the night.

* * *

Poppy slipped into bed beside her husband and snuggled up to him. They had enjoyed their evening meal and all four of them had spent some time over coffee afterwards, giggling at the photographs taken that afternoon.

'Elspeth is amazing. Do you remember the last time she did cartwheels for us? In Dunkeld, just after Jim got sent down.'

'Yes. Then there was that time when 'Mother' dared her do it in Princess Street. I think that made the local papers!'

'What do you think she is doing here, John? I do not believe Gabriélle's story about a 'spur-of-the-moment decision' to come to this remote hotel. I'm not even convinced that she is a journalist. There's something fishy going on. Do you think Elspeth's involved?'

'Maybe. You never know with her. She can be very devious. Its Gabriélle I do not trust, though. I do not doubt her affection for Elspeth but she has another agenda, I am sure. She is here, I suspect, to discover something or pursue some kind of research but what it is I can only guess. I asked Elspeth but she genuinely seems to have no idea what she is up to. Let's hope though that its legal! Elspeth and I have reasons to be worried beyond that. Something to do with an on-going police investigation that we do not want compromising. With Gabriélle here, snooping around, there is a danger that that police investigation could be damaged.'

'What investigation, John? Tell me! What's *really* going on here and what exactly do you think Gabriélle is up to? Is Elspeth being used? Tell me, John. I need to know and I also need to know what exactly we are doing here if its not to celebrate our wedding anniversary!'

* * *

It was now eleven-thirty. Erik had watched most of the kitchen staff quit the hotel and head back to their cottages near the station. The Head Chef had also left, as had most of the waiters. Erik had watched all this from the security of the aerial walkway that provided a good view of the back of the hotel.

He knew that there were still staff in the hotel - night porters, cleaners perhaps and at least one manager - but they would stay there until the morning. There was no reason for any of them to visit the outhouses and it was there that Erik wanted most to explore and, if possible, take photographs.

He checked once more that the cobbled courtyard was clear and then sprinted across it to the far end, by the large greenhouse. He peered through the windows. Inside it was a veritable jungle of flowers in full bloom, potted plants including ferns and palm trees, and a whole section of fruit and vegetables, rack upon rack. When he placed the flat of his hand against the glass it felt warm. That meant that the furnace was on.

That was where he wanted to be. That was what he needed to examine closely. He was sure that that it was in that furnace that the human wrist bone he still had in his pocket had been partially cremated.

* * *

It was now midnight. Cecelia slipped out of bed and put on her dressing gown. Her lover was snoring away as usual, dead to the world.

She quietly opened the bedroom door and disappeared into the corridor, then tip- toed down the stairs in her slippers. The lobby was empty although she could see a light on in the inner office. The place was silent except for the distant noise of Hoovers, which meant that the cleaners were at work somewhere at the far end of the ground floor, probably in the dining room.

She found the door to the library, glanced back down the corridor to see that it was empty and that she was unobserved, opened the heavy wooden door and entered.

Olympia had told her that afternoon where the book she had been reading could be located. Fortunately, Olympia had forgotten to relock the cabinet so that Cecelia was able to take the book from its shelf and place it on the table. It was the bound edition of Edward Calvert's architectural drawings of the 1898 reconstruction of the Rannoch Moor Hotel but it was not its reconstruction that interested her but the hotel's 18th Century origins.

On page seventy-three she found what she was looking for - an outline plan of the hotel's ancient foundations.

As she had guessed, the Victorian hotel was built on top of much older foundations, including a complex of cellars and underground chambers that seemed to run in all directions. There were no secret passages as far as she could tell but the size and scale of this hidden part of the hotel was really quite astonishing.

Cecelia took from her dressing-gown pocket a pencil and paper and began making a rough plan of the cellars.

It was at that point that the library door opened and Assistant Manager Marie McBane appeared in the doorway.

'Miss Arnold? May I ask what you are doing here at this hour?'

* * *

Erik had now found his way to the furnace, adjacent to the greenhouse. It was a small room with roughly plastered walls and with a large brick furnace built into the end wall. Erik had noticed earlier that the brick chimney that rose into the night sky above this building was still smoking so it was safe to assume that the furnace was definitely on. Indeed, he could actually feel the heat from the iron door. The room itself also felt warm, particularly after the intense cold outside.

Erik first took a photograph of the room, with the furnace at one end. He did not dare use his flash so he had earlier set the camera for a long exposure. There was some light from the courtyard spilling in through the room's only window so he managed to get at least once decent exposure of the room itself.

With his gloved-hand Erik then opened the furnace door, quite expecting to see the half-cremated bones of some unfortunate guest.

What he in fact found was a pile of ashes, still glowing hot. The stove might be on but it had all but consumed its contents. He felt somewhat disappointed but on closer examination he found some metal objects amongst the embers. They were too large to have fallen through the grate into the tray below. These metal objects he managed to gather together and extract from the furnace, using his ski gloves to pick them out of the still hot ashes.

Half-an-hour later he was back in the safety of his tent, having photographed both the furnace interior and the tiled room where he had seen them hosing down the two bodies. He had also discovered a small garage at the back of the greenhouse, containing a quad-bike and trailer.

If he and Cecelia were ever going to escape from the Rannoch Moor Hotel that quad-bike might be their only hope - particularly as the ignition key was still in the ignition keyhole.

13
Tuesday, 23rd October

Sir Miles woke up early and dressed. He had arranged the evening before to do some gun practice in a field behind the hotel.

It had been Jamie McBane's idea since the snow was still too deep to hunt. Besides, the deer would not venture out into deep snow. They preferred the security of the forest. The fact that Jamie would be paid handsomely for his services, even when not hunting, may have induced the Head Gamekeeper to suggest this compromise. Since money was never a problem with Miles Ballard, he had jumped at the man's suggestion.

They met after breakfast behind the greenhouse. Here a large field lay adjacent to open moor-land. This area, facing east away from the hotel, was designed primarily for gun practice for grouse shooting. In summer they also set up several traps here for 'clay pigeon' practice. Today though, Jamie had erected a large wooden target about five hundred meters away on a small outcrop of rock.

Sir Miles was happy to be out in the fresh air once more. He had slept exceedingly well. Sex always refreshed him and Cecelia had been particularly accommodating both that afternoon and later that night, after dinner. Now, fresh as a daisy, he spent a very happy hour or two peppering Jamie's wooden target with high velocity bullets; bullets quite capable of blowing a man's head off from three hundred meters against a granite rock face.

* * *

Erik met Cecelia at the railway station at ten o'clock that morning, as arranged. He found her in the gift shop, looking at postcards. The shop had been opened that morning, despite the lack of day visitors. It was something else for the trapped residents to do, spending money in the process. The café, however, remained closed.

Erik did not enter the shop but indicated with a slight movement of his head for Cecelia to join him outside. They met at one end of the station, hidden behind the main waiting-room. Here they would not be seen by anyone entering or leaving the shop, unless they chose to visit the signal box behind them. Fortunately, the Station Master was nowhere to be seen either - not surprising, since there were likely to be no trains for a few days.

'Well, how did you get on?'

'Very well. Look what I found in the furnace.'

Erik took from his jacket pocket a small plastic bag and handed it to Cecelia. She took it somewhat hesitatingly.

'Not more bones, I hope, Erik?'

'No. Metal, this time. Can you tell what they are?'

Cecelia looked into the bag and took out a handful of metal pieces. They were badly discoloured, as if they had been subject to intense heat.

'It looks like some kind of metal lock or catch. These bits are the supports for a handle. My guess is that they are from a suitcase or something similar. Am I right?'

'Spot on. Someone has been burning suitcases in that furnace. At least its an improvement on bodies but still very suspicious. It may explain Paula Leamington's missing property.'

'So, what do we do now? Tell the police? We must do something, before they pick on someone else.'

'I agree but that is not as easy as it sounds. These bits of metal prove nothing and we would be hard put to 'place' that wrist bone at the hotel's furnace. No, we need more evidence before we can go public. Besides, if they find out what we have been doing we could be at risk ourselves.'

'I think we should try and get into the basement. If something is going on it is the most likely place.'

'Possibly, but creeping around out-houses at night is one thing but breaking into the hotel basement is quite another. Very high risk. I'm not quite sure I'm up to that!'

'Well, last night I did some research of my own. I found in the library a book with plans of the basement. Look, here's my sketch. Pretty basic, I know, but I was caught in the act.'

'Caught? What do you mean?'

'Well it was midnight and Marie McBane, the Assistant Manager, found me in the library in my dressing-gown. She was very cross - not because I was there but because I was not wearing cotton gloves when handling her precious books.'

'Wow! So you got away with it. Was she not at all suspicious?'

'On the contrary. I told her I could not sleep and had come to the library to borrow a paperback when I saw this book about the hotel and got interested.'

'Did she buy your story?'

'Not only did she buy it but she sat down with me and showed me a couple of other books about the history of the building. I told her I was primarily interested in Gothic decoration, to stop her thinking I was only curious about the basement or cellars. She fell for it and we spent quite an enjoyable hour looking at furniture designs and wallpaper patterns, circa 1898.'

'Did anyone else see you visit that library? What about your husband?'

'Miles is not my husband. Anyway, he was still fast asleep when I got back to our room. He knows nothing about any of this.'

'Good. Let's keep it that way. So, we now have plans for the cellars but how on earth do we get down there without being seen? It will have to be at night. The back door to the hotel is self-locking - I checked it last night. No entry that way. The real problem, though, is that there is always someone on duty and the only way down to the basement is past the Manager's office. Any ideas?'

* * *

It might be important at this stage to say that Dr. Thomas Neep is not quite what he appears to be. His public persona is certainly that of a respectable gentleman, a former GP and pillar of the community but in reality he is something else. He is here at the Rannoch Moor Hotel incognito, or so it would seem. Neep is not his real name, nor indeed is he a Thomas. He is a doctor all right, but not of medicine.

He is, in fact a Michelin Red Guide food Inspector.

He has been a Michelin Inspector for about ten years now, following a career as Senior Research Chemist with the Institute of Food Research in Norwich. Before that he had a distinguished career as a hygienist in the food industry and later a Consultant on food hygiene to a chain of hotels and restaurants. He combined his scientific, professional knowledge of food with a true gourmet's understanding and appreciation of it, having written a food column for the *Guardian* for about eleven years under an assumed name. In 1998 he acquired a *sommelier's* certification, for his knowledge of fine wines was as exhaustive as his appreciation of high quisine. When he retired from IFR in 2000 he was invited to attend an interview in France. He was appointed a European Inspector, one of about fifty, soon thereafter.

Indeed, it was 'Thomas Neep' who had been partly instrumental in awarding the much-deserved two Michelin stars to the Andrew Fairlie Restaurant in Gleneagles, Perthshire. Since then, he had travelled Britain evaluating and secretly inspecting countless restaurants.

This was his first visit to the Rannoch Moor Hotel and thus far he was enjoying the experience enormously.

He had originally planned to stay only two nights but this enforced extension of his (official) visit was something of a Godsend. If it meant a few more wonderful meals from the kitchen of Head Chef Moray McBane then so be it. Last night, for example, his waiter had presented him with a large, white plate at the centre of which was *foie gras*, a short pillar of puréed duck-liver on a piece of crisp toast with a lacy web of caramelized sugar on top. The sides of this miniature 'tower' were studded with cherries and sprinkled with pistachios. A transparent sauce, made of white port *gelée* surrounded the entire creation like a moat.

Outstanding!

'Dr Neep' could barely contain his excitement at the prospect of tonight's menu although his experience and training had taught him to be anything but demonstrative in public. It was essential that he stay anonymous and that his presence (as a Michelin Inspector) in Rannoch remain a closely-guarded secret, especially from the staff.

'So, what riches has Moray prepared for lunch, I wonder?'

* * *

Elspeth and John had lunch together in the saloon bar - little more than a prawn sandwich each and a glass or two of dry, white wine. Poppy and Gabriélle had decided to skip lunch - on the grounds that if they ate any more this week they might not be able to get out through the front door of the hotel when it was time to go home - if they could ever get off Rannoch Moor, that is. It was also an opportunity for John to tackle Elspeth about a number of matters of mutual concern, not least why she was here in the first place.

Since the bar quickly became crowded, they took their sandwiches and glasses of wine into the resident's lounge next door and chose a quiet corner where they could talk in private.

Elspeth was, as it turned out, surprisingly candid.

'We are here because Gabriélle is preparing a documentary on incest and the McBanes appear to be a prime example.'

'Incest? Is that all?'

'Yes. That's all. Look around you John. The entire place is run by the McBane tribe. I have counted at least forty adults, all of whom are closely related. Bright blue eyes and pale skin are just two of the more obvious characteristics of familial inbreeding.'

'Wow! I am absolutely gob-smacked. Elspeth Grant, you never cease to surprise me. How come Gabriélle chose the McBanes for her documentary?'

'Because she thinks they are unique. There are not that many examples of families who breed amongst themselves on this scale The Goler clan of Nova Scotia, for example, is perhaps the most notorious. When it came to trial in 1985, sixteen family members were convicted of sexual abuse and incest that had been going on for years. The McBanes may well be another such family although she only has anecdotal evidence as yet.'

'Does that mean you are here officially, Elspeth?'

'No. I am here only as 'cover' for Gabriélle. Its her documentary, although she is keeping me properly informed. In due course, when she has the material she needs for her programme, she will disclose all her evidence to the police. I have her assurances that she will give them everything.'

'Can you trust her, Elspeth?'

'Yes.'

'But you hardly know her! How long have you two been together? Months? Weeks?'

'She has been very frank with me - well, most of the time. She has not told me in detail *everything* she is doing but quite enough for me to trust her intentions.'

'Elspeth, you are in love with her! Are you sure that makes you a good judge of character? She picked you up, remember.'

'John, you are a dear man but you know very little about women. Yes, its true I am in love with this gorgeous young woman but I am also a freelance Criminologist. If I can help her expose these people then I am confident that I am behaving professionally. Anyway, you are wrong. I picked *her* up and it wasn't in Carcassonne - it was in Oxford, last week.'

'Last week? Really, Elspeth! Are you sure you know what you are doing? You know nothing about her or her background. She could be using you. Had that not occurred to you?'

'Of course. But then I might be using her! I know that your colleagues in Inverness have an ongoing, professional interest in the McBanes and that Gabriélle snooping around now could compromise that investigation but this way I can at least keep a much closer eye on her than you can. Besides, you are not even on duty here. According to Inverness you are officially 'off duty' and celebrating your wedding anniversary.'

'That's as maybe, but your initial phone call to me in Dunkeld set the alarm bells ringing back at Police HQ. In fact, they wet themselves with anxiety. Its pure coincidence that I chose Rannoch Moor to celebrate my wedding anniversary but my being here now is the best, short-term, damage-limitation strategy Inverness has. My 'unofficial' job is to keep an eye on Gabriélle, make sure that she does not screw things up for us and ensure that as and when the police make their move she does not get in the way. You too have a responsibility in that regard, whatever your particular involvement with this woman.'

'Point taken. That's exactly why I called you in Dunkeld and told you what I thought Gabriélle was up to and that she was planning to come to Rannoch Moor herself.'

'OK. I'm grateful for that. I am not sure Poppy is, though. She knows that we are here now for more than our wedding anniversary. She is not at all happy about that and there is only so much I can tell her at this stage.'

'She's a very smart woman, John. She already knows that Gabriélle is not what she seems. She also told me privately that she was concerned for my emotional well-being. That was very sweet of her and typically Poppy. If she knows that both you and I are keeping a professional eye on our charming French journalist then I am sure that she will come round. She might even enjoy the process. Tell her more. Let her in on the 'larger picture'. That way she can be part of the team. I want to nail the McBanes just as much as Inverness. Incest is only part of the picture, I am sure. We are dealing with a very weird bunch of individuals, a family that has serious issues. Incest is probably only part of the problem, as you well know.'

'Indeed. Has she started filming yet?'

'Yes, but very discretely. She has an array of special cameras, some with a lens little more than the size of a button. She's only getting what she calls 'actuality' at the moment. I have a feeling, though, that she is going to try and interview Ronald McBane sometime soon. General stuff about the hotel, that kind of thing.'

'Oh, my God! Its worse than I thought. Elspeth, I do *not* want her filming the McBanes. Secretly or otherwise. That could ruin everything if they became suspicious. There is far too much at stake here. Its not the adults but the numerous children here on this estate that we must take into consideration. We are dealing with child-abuse on a large scale, something that has been going on for years. These children will not only have to be rescued but given careful protection and support. If the McBanes find out what Gabriélle is up to then all our preparations will have been wasted. Elspeth, she has to be stopped, or at least seriously curtailed.'

'I take your point. Not easy, though. If the police start interfering with the legitimate work of an investigative journalist that could open up another can of worms for you.'

'Maybe, but why concentrate on incest? Incest amongst consenting adults is one thing but the widespread abuse of their own children is far more serious. Besides, what actual *evidence* does Gabriélle have? It all sounds a bit vague to me. When were blue eyes and pale skin a crime?'

'True, but look closely John and you will see a plethora of medical evidence. For example, have you noticed how difficult it is for Ronald McBane to rise from his chair when you approach his office and need to speak to him? Marie, his daughter, has exactly the same problem. Some of the other staff, especially the ghillies, have back issues and most walk like sailors. One of them even has rickets. All that is down to distal renal tubular acidosis.'

'What on earth is that?'

'Poor renal excretion, which leads to acidemia, which causes osteomalacia. In other words, weak proximal muscles. This is a typical symptom of inbreeding. The average adult size of this family is probably about five feet, six inches - way below national averages, even for Scotland. There are also a few examples of facial asymmetry. Look at our waiter, for example. His left eye is marginally higher than his right. These are all classic characteristics of inbreeding within a small community. You know better than I the extent of child-abuse going on here amongst the McBanes but inbreeding is all about incest - at that is what Gabriélle's documentary is about.'

'Elspeth, this is a police matter. It's not something to be used for commercial exploitation - no matter how well-meaning a documentary producer might be. If Gabriélle is freelance, then she's doing this for money. The investigation of child- abuse and the rest is best left to the police.'

'Maybe but its also Gabriélle's story. She has done all the hard work over the last six or seven months, or so she claims. I have no reason not to believe her. There are other examples of incest in Scotland that she is looking at so her documentary is not just about the McBanes of Rannoch Moor. We must let her do her stuff. The police will do theirs in due course. Meanwhile, I will do my best to stop her compromising any police investigations into child-abuse that you, or your colleagues in Inverness are pursuing. That, John, is a promise - no matter what I might personally feel for Miss Fourés.'

14

The restaurant was fairly busy that lunchtime. Since the weather prevented most of the guests from being out-and-about, Chef Moray had made a special effort to make lunch an even more enjoyable experience than usual.

'Thomas Neep' chose his usual seat near the window. Although it looked very cold outside, the restaurant itself was warm and cosy. He studied the menu with great care. It changed each day and although not a wide choice it was more than adequate for a light lunch.

He fancied Artic char for his first course but was undecided about his second. His waiter, a charming young man in his early twenties, waited patiently, pen in hand.

'Tell me, please, about the crab toast,' asked Thomas.

'It's Peekytoe crab, a chiffonade of tarragon as well as chives topped with white sesame seeds, toasted in the oven, finished with a miso mustard, and a pear salad on the side,' he said.

'Is it new?' Thomas asked.

'Yes sir. It was added to the menu about a week ago.'

'Thank you. I'll have that, please.'

The waiter took the order and left.

Well, thought 'Dr Neep', so far so good. It is always an excellent sign when a waiter knows the menu properly. It is also refreshing to see that the menu changes regularly - partly as a reflection of seasonal changes and the availability of fresh produce but also because the Chef is naturally creative.

'Yes. Pretty impressive!'

*　*　*

After his lunch with Elspeth Grant, Chief Inspector John White did not go and find his wife but left the hotel and headed for the railway station. He needed time to think and to reflect on what Elspeth had told him.

The station was deserted. He sat on a bench and lit his pipe.

The landscape was looking particularly bleak, with snow stretching as far as the eye could see. There was no wind but the sky was a dull grey, with the promise of even more snow to come. Sat there, by himself, on a deserted railway platform as if waiting for a non-existent train, John suddenly felt that he was in a painting by René Magritte.

He was deeply worried about what Elspeth had told him of Gabriélle's plans, not least her crazy notion of 'secretly' interviewing Ronald McBane, or any of the other McBanes for that matter.

He knew, however, that there was little he could do if push came to shove to stop Gabriélle making her documentary.

According to Elspeth, Gabriélle had promised to give the police her files once the documentary was released. This was not that unusual an arrangement between a professional journalist or TV Production company and the police. In Manchester, the police once had an arrangement with Granada TV whereby *World in Action* would broadcast its programme and simultaneously give the CID access to evidence or information of specific interest to them. That way, for example, a number of IRA operatives had been immediately arrested or traced following their initial exposure on British TV.

The problem was that Gabriélle's research ran parallel with the police's own secret, ongoing investigations on Rannoch Moor.

DCI White had, as yet, played no part in that investigation although he *was* aware of it - hence his concern when Elspeth first told him of Gabriélle's intention to visit Rannoch Moor.

Elspeth knew a little of that investigation, enough to see that her new lover's plans might cause problems for the police. At least she had had the presence of mind to warn John the moment she discovered what Gabriélle was up to. However, the police could not possibly wait until Gabriélle's documentary was aired, whenever that might be. That would be too late - not least because there were abused children who needed to be to rescued - just as soon as there was evidence against the McBanes sufficiently robust to stand up in court. Any police intervention - because of the possible scale of the abuse - would need to be carefully planned. The last thing Inverness wanted was a journalist snooping around on their patch.

What also concerned him was Elspeth's involvement in all this.

Elspeth was a freelance, independent criminologist and academic who acted as Consultant Psychologist (Profiler) for the police when required. Her day job, as it were, was that of teacher - lecturing on criminology at Oxford. She was perfectly free to assist Gabriélle or any other journalist for that matter but if, in the course of that work, she came across proven cases of child-abuse then she was duty bound to report it to the police at the earliest opportunity - not least in order to protect the child or children involved.

This she had not done so as yet. At least, not officially.

If she (or Gabriélle) had evidence of inbreeding amongst the McBanes then it followed that there could well be child-abuse. Indeed, the police were already absolutely convinced that that was the case but the issue now was what happens if, because of her (emotional) involvement with a journalist, Elspeth Grant deliberately (or even inadvertently) withheld information that might assist the police with their ongoing enquiries?

Regarding consensual incest between adults, that was a particularly tricky area. John was not sure where the law currently stood on that issue. If that was what was going on here within the McBane family, then it needed to be exposed. That clearly was Gabriélle's intention but she was also involved in the commercial exploitation of that situation. That raised all kind of ethical issues.

Moreover, where did that leave Elspeth Grant, for example? Where, for that matter, did it now leave him, Chief Inspector John White? He was happy to keep an interim eye on the situation for his colleagues in Inverness but at what stage ought he to actually intervene?

It could well come to that if, between them, they discovered criminal activity here at the hotel.

* * *

Head Chef Moray McBane was a remarkably shy man, despite the flamboyance of many of his finest dishes.

He never left his kitchen to meet his guests, nor did he take kindly for requests from favoured clients to meet him. He was remarkably tall, well over six feet. That made him the tallest of the McBane clan, of which he was titular head. He had a somewhat elongated face and wore a thick, 'walrus' moustache. He had something of the appearance of a figure by El Greco. He was the clan's father figure, the 'Patriarch' of a large family that went back many, many generations. He was their Clan Leader, in effect.

It is now three-thirty and the kitchens are deserted. Moray loves this time of the day. When his staff go home and rest for a couple of hours, he always remains behind, quietly preparing food for the evening meal. He always butchers his own meat but his particular favourite occupation is preparing fish. On the menu this evening there is grilled fillets of sea bass with clams and sea vegetables or sautéed squid. It is the sea bass that he is attending to that afternoon, applying his knife with the skill of a surgeon.

What is truly remarkable is that he is entirely self-taught. He has never worked in anyone's kitchen other than his own, nor has he ever been trained by another chef. Everything he knows about gourmet food he has either discovered himself by experimentation or garnered from books - many of them very old books. Indeed, in his personal library he has several cookery books that go back to the 18th Century - which partly explains the unique Scottish-ness of most of his best 'signature' dishes.

He lives alone in the largest cottage on the estate, close to the railway station. Since he is usually up in the morning long before anyone else and the last to leave the building after the evening meal has been served, few people ever see him in daylight. When at home in his cottage he either sleeps or spends hours reading his cookery books, endlessly devising new dishes. He lives and breathes cooking and is hardly known to leave the hamlet or travel, even to Pitlochry. No one can remember when he last took a holiday.

It is widely thought by those in the region that he is very rich. Since the hotel is itself hugely prosperous, that is not an unreasonable assumption. However, if he is rich then it does not show. Not only does he not have a car but his cottage is modestly furnished with few possessions of any value. He has neither a radio nor a television, although it is thought that he is fond of classical music so he may well have had a gramophone of some kind.

He is, by all accounts, an odd fish.

In the kitchen he is absolute God and yet no one can ever remember him shouting or swearing or throwing his weight around. Since his entire kitchen staff are his family, direct relatives every one of them, domination appears unnecessary. His staff are in awe of him but they do not fear him. When they do well, he praises them; when they made mistakes, he quietly corrects their errors and explains where they have gone wrong. He is meticulous in everything he does and is known to use a magnifying glass and a pair of tweezers sometimes when preparing fish. He is a model employer and an exceptionally gifted Master Chef whose reputation is growing steadily. The staff enjoy his fame and feel part of his success. They are, in short, intensely loyal to their celebrated Patriarch.

Moray is particularly pleased with the way lunch has gone. He made a special effort to entertain his guests with his menu this day, not least because he knew that many would rather be out hunting, or fishing or walking during the day than stuck indoors because of the weather.

To be honest, he enjoys those periods when the hotel is entirely cut off from the outside world. It is, for him at least, an opportunity to shine and rise to the challenges such isolation poses.

* * *

John told Poppy everything that Elspeth had told him.

'Do you believe her?', she asked.

They were dressing for supper. Poppy had spent a pleasant hour after lunch talking with Gabriélle and some other women they had met in the bar. She had then returned to her room and taken a nap. It was there that John had found her after his meeting with Elspeth and his meditation on the icy platform of Rannoch's historic (circa 1930) railway station.

'No entirely', said John.

He was struggling with his bow tie. Poppy came up to him and fixed it for him. She gave him a kiss on his cheek then returned to the dressing table where she continued brushing her hair.

'She seemed to know an awful lot about the medical condition (allegedly) of the McBane family. It did not strike me as idle observation. I know Elspeth is an acute observer and hugely intelligent and usually very well informed, but it all came a little too pat to be utterly convincing. I think she's up to her neck in Gabriélle's investigation. She is not here as 'cover' as she claims but as a direct participant. Knowing her love of the dramatic, she could well end up an on-screen contributor to Gabriélle's controversial and ill-time documentary!'

'What's wrong with that? She's freelance. She can do what she likes, surely?'

'Not entirely. It may be that she is being *paid* to assist Gabriélle. If that is the case then she could be in danger of compromising her position as an independent and entirely neutral police Profiler.'

'Is what she doing not research, albeit for a third party? That is what she does professionally, after all?'

'No. What I think she is doing is not research *per se* but making a TV documentary for money. Whatever crimes the McBanes have committed - and that still has to be proven - Gabriélle is exploiting them for commercial gain. I'm not condoning the McBanes or their alleged behaviour, especially if it involves child-abuse or child-exploitation, but Elspeth is in danger of possibly destroying her professional reputation.'

Poppy stood up and crossed to where John was still struggling with his tie and collar. She put her arms round his neck, sorted the errant collar and kissed him gently on the mouth.

'Perhaps, my darling, Elspeth is doing it for love. It has been known for someone to love another person so much that they would risk everything. I would! Would you, my darling Inspector Gadget?'

* * *

Since the landlines were still down and there was no satellite coverage in that area, Rannoch Moor was well and truly cut off from the outside world.

This did not worry Marie McBane.

Indeed, it was something of a blessing in disguise. Last week, before they were cut off completely, she had been trying to deal with additional requests for information from either relatives or business associates of both the Lowry brothers (again) and Paula Leamington whose absence from her office in London had caused a great deal of concern. 'Assurances' had been given in all three cases that these individuals had certainly paid their bills, checked out of the hotel and left the region. Marie was able to 'prove' this and had done so, forwarding all the relevant 'documentation' by email - before the internet disappeared.

No one had yet enquired about Douglas Tait or Robert Wellington, whose attempt to climb the south-east facing section of Buachaille (known as Rannoch Wall), had afforded Neil McBane and his son Stewart so much sport a few days ago. Tait and Wellington were booked in until Friday next so it was unlikely that anyone, least of all Douglas and Robert's respective wives - gallivanting about in Paris, or so it would seem - would miss them until then. Not being able to contact either of them by phone was clearly an advantage which Marie McBane relished.

Once the lines were back and anxious enquiries made, then Marie was ready with the relevant documentation - proving, beyond all shadow of a doubt that both men had left after an exceptionally enjoyable holiday on Rannoch Moor - despite the bad weather.

What they did thereafter, or where they might be if missing, was not something any of the Rannoch Moor Hotel staff need worry about - least of all the hotel's hard-working and thoroughly reliable Assistant Manager

So far, so good.

What *was* surprising was that, as yet, she had heard nothing about Charles Mitchell whose head - her elder brother Neil had also reliably informed her - had been blown to bits on Thursday, 11th October - some twelve days ago. True, the boys had found nothing of his personal documents, credit cards and the like about his person but there was enough information on the hotel computer from his booking to fabricate some kind of formal response to any outside enquiry. As yet, however, no one had shown the slightest interest in the late Charles Mitchell.

While she and her mischievous siblings always targeted lone guests, it is curious that no one appears yet to have missed Mitchell. Perhaps, mused Marie, he was never very popular.
Perhaps no one loves him sufficiently to care what has happened

to him. Just in case, though, Marie decided to forge the relevant documentation from what information she already had online in order to prove, if required and beyond any shadow of doubt, that Charles Mitchell had indeed 'checked out' the very same evening that his brains had ended up in a gorse bush three miles away.

15

Erik had not been idle. After his secret meeting with Cecelia that morning he had donned his Norwegian skis and, armed with his OS Explorer map, had set off - to plan their escape route.

Since no one knew when the roads out of Rannoch Moor might be clear of snow, Erik had resolved in his own mind to escape at the earliest opportunity with Cecelia (hopefully) on the quad-bike he had discovered in the garage at the back of the hotel. The road east was too thick with snow but he was sure that he could find a route across the moor itself, heading west. This had the advantage of making it difficult for anyone, even in a Range Rover, to follow them. It would also have the element of surprise for who in their right mind would think of setting off, in the dark, across a desolate moor covered in deep snow?

Erik was now convinced that murder had taken place and that Douglas Tait and Robert Wellington had died at the hands of the McBanes. Perhaps Paula Leamington had suffered a similar fate? Erik as yet had no idea why or, indeed, if there were other victims murdered by the McBanes, but the sooner he got off the moor and informed the police the better.

The moor that afternoon was stunningly beautiful, with broad stretches of snow giving its normal 'lunar' appearance even greater impact. Drifting was extensive but Erik soon discovered that if he kept to higher, more exposed ground, there was far less snow since what had fallen on higher ground had largely been blown away, exposing bare rock. This might be difficult terrain but a quad-bike with snow chains (he had spotted those already on the quad-bike in the garage) should be able to cope with it.

During the course of the afternoon Erik got lost several times and had to retrace his steps to avoid deep snow-drifts or partially concealed lochans. Some had frozen over and been covered with a treacherously deceptive layer of wind-blown snow. The ice was thin and at one point Erik found himself on cracking ice. He managed to slither off just in time. However, after three or four hours, he had marked on his map a possible escape route. It was somewhat circuitous and in places extremely hazardous but - all things being equal - it might just work! There was a moment though when, within sight of the main road leading to Fort William, Erik had been tempted to press on, abandon Cecelia and the others back at the hotel, and make good his own escape.

It was tempting but in the end he decided against such a selfish act. Cecelia had risked much in sharing her concerns with him. If any of the McBanes had seen them together then she would be targeted - once it was discovered that the quad-bike was missing and that he too had vanished. Then surely her life would be at risk. Besides, he sensed that her feelings for him were more than that of two scared people merely thrown together by circumstances.

Cecelia seemed to care little for her older partner, even if he was rich. She never spoke of Sir Miles Ballard with any obvious affection and once or twice had been quite disparaging of their relationship. That certainly was the impression she had given Erik in their few stolen moments together. Maybe, thought Erik, his feelings for this young, somewhat vulnerable girl were more than brotherly but then so what? If, as he suspected, she was attracted to him - even if shared anxieties added allure to that relationship - then so be it. Love can begin in many different ways, prompted by diverse emotions - including danger!

Who was he to 'blow against the wind'.

Now, therefore, it was only a matter of choosing when they might make their escape to freedom; escape from the clutches of a family that appeared to enjoy murdering its guests. In short, the sooner the better!

* * *

The evening meal that Tuesday night was something special. The reason for this was that normally it was the last evening meal for guests who arrived mid-week. Since those who booked in on a Wednesday would leave the following Wednesday, Head Chef Moray always tried to summon up something truly memorable on

Tuesday nights. However, due to bad weather and the fact that they were all snowed in, no guests would be leaving Rannoch Moor this particular Wednesday morning.

In well-run hotels habits die hard and Moray still wanted his guests to have one last, memorable meal - even if they were stuck and not going anywhere soon!

That evening then young Stewart McBane not only piped the guests down to dinner but led the way from the stairs and into the great baronial hall itself, accompanied by his younger brother, Rab on the Highland snare drum. They played their version of *The Black Bear.* When they finished, the guests - some forty or so - clapped the two boys then sat down.

The food on offer that evening was exceptional - even by The Rannoch Moor Hotel's own high standards. Moray McBane had surpassed himself - as 'Dr. Thomas Neep' was quick to observe.

The choice of starters was breathtaking. Crispy oysters with lemon and shallot vinegar or homemade black pudding, fried egg, bacon and lentil dressing or sautéed squid, fennel salad, orange and salami. The main course was either grilled fillets of sea bass with herb risotto, roasted cherry tomatoes and pesto or roast quail with herb butter or pork escalopes with Emmental cheese.

For desert the choice was between a gratin of home-grown Scottish raspberries, rhubarb and crème fraiche or roasted figs with spiced bread.

Poppy and John had arranged to meet Elspeth and her partner for coffee in the lounge after their meal. This would allow both parties to enjoy each other's company during their meal. Both John and Poppy opted for the sea bass for their main course. Their wine was a dry white Bordeaux - Le Sec de Rayne-Vigneau from 2010. They were guided in this choice by the hotel's *sommelier*, Rory McBane. At twenty-seven pounds a bottle it was one of the less expensive on offer.

'Darling, when do you need to be back at work?'

'Thursday, at the latest. I have a budget meeting in Inverness that morning. I am sure the roads will be open by then but the problem is we still have no means of telling them that I am stuck here if there are further delays. I checked with Reception - we are still cut off and so far none of the telephone lines have been fixed.'

'Perhaps they will send out a search party for you, John?'

'That could prove difficult , Gabriélle, since no one knows that I am here.'

This was not true of course. Inverness were very much aware that one of their senior officers was on Rannoch Moor. The problem was, that they too were unable to contact him either.

'If this weather continues we could be here for weeks', added Poppy. 'Mind you, I will have gained so much weight that I'm not sure I will be able to squeeze into our car. How are you doing, weight-wise, my darling?'

'Badly. Now, what do you fancy for deserts - raspberries or figs? Both have cream and about four thousand calories!'

'Tricky choice! I know! Let's order one of each - then I can have some of yours as well!'

* * *

Cecelia did not join Sir Miles and the others for dinner, claiming instead that she had a splitting headache. It was only partially true. She felt under the weather but it was entirely due to anxiety.

She lay on her bed that evening in a darkened room, trying very hard to think what to do. She had arranged to meet Erik at the station Wednesday morning, hoping that he had made some progress in his searches at the back of the hotel. They both needed concrete evidence of malpractice if they were to convince anyone of their suspicions. The two climbers and Paula Leamington were probably cremated by now, leaving no trace of their bodies at the hotel. The only evidence they had to go on was a charred wrist bone and some scraps of metal from a cremated suitcase or two. Not much, whatever way you looked at it.

Cecelia got off the bed and crossed to the window. She drew back the curtains and peered into the darkness.

It had begun to snow. Thick flakes fell slowly past her window, covering the cars in the forecourt once again. Under their protective sheets these cars looked like great burial mounds covered in white shrouds. There were lights still on at the deserted railway station but little chance of any trains stopping there anytime soon. Not only did that ghostly station make her feel very isolated but there was an air of despair and hopelessness about the whole place.

She gave a shudder, closed the curtains and retreated to her bed.

She had spent some time that afternoon in the Library, in the hope of finding out more about the mysterious basement. There was nothing on open shelves of interest and she thought it best at the time not to arouse suspicion by asking to see the same volume that Olympia Garland had discovered. What she *did* find, though, was a book with Douglas Tait's name written clearly on the flyleaf. This was pure chance for Cecelia had been looking for something to read for pleasure, if only to take her mind off her anxieties. He must have donated it to the library sometime during his stay.

That book gave her an idea.

Later that afternoon she asked Manager Ronald McBane - on duty at the Reception desk - if he had a forwarding address for Mr Tait. She said that she had borrowed a book from Mr Tait and would like to return it sometime. He said that he did and gave it to her - somewhere in Wolverhampton. Now at least she had a contact address for one of the missing men. No doubt McBane would claim - as he had done regarding Paula Leamington - that

Douglas Tait had checked out and left of his own accord but if he *were* missing then she now had the means of checking with his own family or friends.

It also meant that she had an authentic copy of Douglas Tait's signature. If, as she and Erik suspected, the McBanes were forging guests' signatures - either for financial gain or simply to prove that they had paid their bills and 'checked out' in the 'normal' way - then she had a signature to compare with those that appeared on the bogus credit-card slips or hotel bill receipts.

There was a lot of speculation on their part but if Erik was right and that there was a financial scam also at work, then that signature might prove significant. If guests were being systematically murdered for financial gain, then at least they now had some evidence. Not much but it was a start.

* * *

There had been a tacit agreement that evening that John and Poppy would not talk 'shop' with their friends and that all mention of Gabriélle's documentary project was forbidden.

By-and-large both parties stuck to this arrangement and over coffee and whiskey in the lounge, after a truly wonderful meal, they chatted amicably amongst themselves on a wide range of subjects - including wine, food, sex and where to buy sensible knickers. Marks and Spencer seemed to be the preferred choice, and that included John. As to the efficacy of skin lotions or anti-mosquito cream, Ponds won hands down.

'I have often wondered what we might do if deprived of all such creature comforts, as on the proverbial desert island, for example.'

This was Elspeth who, after three large whiskeys, had lapsed into philosophical mode - accompanied by a great deal of surreptitiously holding Gabriélle's hand under the table, not to say knee fondling.

'There is always your luxury choice. What would you chose, Elspeth? Apart from Gabriélle, that is.'

'Well, Poppy - good question. My luxury choice would be the Elgin Marbles, then I could fantasize about naked men and women any time I want.'

'I'm not sure the Greeks would approve, Elspeth. They still want them back.'

'That's OK. One day a handsome Greek sea-captain will surely arrive on my island, claim back the Elgin Marbles for his country and rescue me. Perfect! Gabriélle, what would your luxury be?'

'Since we are already marooned on a kind of island, my luxury would be the most powerful snow-plough on the planet - that way we can all get away from this fucking hotel and the really creepy people who run it. That's my luxury and I want it NOW!'

* * *

It was as they were getting ready for bed that Poppy asked the question that had been worrying husband and wife since parting company with Elspeth and Gabriélle on the landing .

'What was that little outburst all about, John? Gabriélle may be an investigative journalist but she didn't sound like one tonight.'

'I agree. But I think I know why. It was something Elspeth said earlier. Apparently Gabriélle got talking with one of the men clearing snow at the front of the hotel. Not only was he somewhat rude but he started making extremely suggestive remarks to her - so much so that she abruptly left him, with every intention of reporting him directly to the Manager. Half way to the lobby she changed her mind, not least because the man was clearly subnormal. Learning difficulties are one thing but his entire manner was very disturbing. I think it rather proved her point that the McBanes - or at least some of them - have serious issues but it also upset her as a woman. That may explain that outburst this evening.'

'Well, I'm half inclined to agree with her. There are a number of extremely odd people around here and only some of them are guests. It was a lovely idea to spend out wedding anniversary here, darling, and we have had some fantastic meals but I think I would like to go home now please. If, as you say, the police in Inverness are already investigating our hosts, then I suggest you leave them to it and get me out of here at the earliest opportunity.'

16
Wednesday, 24th October

Tuesday night it snowed heavily, undoing most of the work done beyond Pitlochry by the emergency services over the last two days. By Wednesday morning The Rannoch Moor Hotel therefore remained as cut off as ever.

Reactions amongst the guests were mixed. Those hoping to go home sometime that morning became angry and frustrated. Those who were not due to leave quite yet generally felt comfortable but began to fret at not being able to get out into the country and to pursue the hunting and fishing most of them had signed up for. The hotel had agreed to charge less for those guests who were now technically trapped - a reduction of forty percent which most people considered generous in the circumstances. Meals though - other than breakfast - would still need to be paid for at the usual extortionate rates. Most of the guests were wealthy and enjoyed their food so this was not regarded as unreasonable.

In addition to that, the McBanes did their best to make their guests comfortable, happy and engaged.

One corner of the lounge became a video area for the few children staying at the hotel. Although the DVDs on offer were somewhat old - *Raiders of the Lost Ark, Star Wars, Beverly Hills Cop* - it kept these lively teenagers out of mischief. One or two of the other children there were so young that even these 'oldies' had novelty value. While the telephone lines were still down there was TV and Local Radio and BBC Radio Scotland FM - thereby coping for most tastes. Indeed, local radio from Heartland FM became their primary link with the outside world, providing badly needed information about road and weather conditions.

There was, however, no internet links. These were tied to the landline that seems to have been cut or damaged somewhere between Rannoch Moor and Pitlochry. Mobiles had never worked on Rannoch Moor, which meant that at least three teenagers were now in meltdown mode, psychologically disturbed at being denied the ability to text their friends at will. All three spent hours in their bedrooms, sulking.

In the lounge itself card games, jigsaw puzzles, *Scrabble* and *Monopoly* acquired a new popularity. The favourite game was *Cluedo* over which grownups were occasionally seen to fight for possession. In the end Ronald McDonald had to arrange a 'booking system' to avoid tears and tantrums. Since it was no longer snowing that morning, Jamie McBane, Head Gamekeeper, cleared a patch of snow from the field at the back of the hotel and organised a clay-pigeon shoot with four traps. These were only used in the summer but he broke them out of storage and set them up.

It was there that Sir Miles and five other avid hunters staying at the hotel had a friendly shootout, the prize being a very large bottle of Lagavulin whiskey from Islay.

* * *

Cecelia met Erik at the railway station that morning, accompanied by the sound of gunshot only two hundred yards away. She personally found it unnerving but Erik was his usual calm self - or so it appeared to her. Moreover, he showed her how pleased he was to see her by unexpectedly kissing her on the cheek - once they were safely hidden behind the waiting-room.

'How are you coping, Cecelia?'

'OK but I want to leave this place, with or without Miles. He's as happy as a sand-boy. Listen to them! He's one of those letting off their guns. But me, I've had enough of this place. I know we have precious little proof of anything but every instinct in my body tells me that there is something terribly wrong with this hotel and the weird people who run it. I now feel absolutely trapped. What can we do, Erik? I'm really frightened!'

Erik took her in his arms and held her. She was trembling.

'I know there was more snow last night but there is a route across country that we can still use. All we need to do is steal their quad-bike and make a run for it.'

She stepped back and looked at him in astonishment.

'Where do they keep it?'

'It's in a garage behind the hotel. If we can wheel it out and away from the cottages we can then start it up and make a dash for it. They have two Land Rovers here on the estate. If they follow us we are vulnerable for the first three or four miles but then the track runs out and I doubt that they can follow us after that. If we head due west we can reach the A82. The nearest towns are Tyndrum and Crianlarich, some miles to the south. We can tell the police there everything we know. Its not much, I agree, but its not every day you find human remains scatted on the ground in front of a major hotel!'

'OK. When shall we do it?'

'We still need more evidence. They relit the furnace last night and its smoking. You can even see it from here. If I can get close to that furnace later tonight there may be something to photograph. Once we have that photographic evidence then I think we should go for it.'

'I agree. Does that mean tonight?'

'Yes, if you are up for it. But what about your partner?'

'Miles is not my partner. He's my rich lover whom I no longer love. If he really cared for me he would be trying to get us out of this place himself. Instead, he's fraternising with the enemy, even now.'

As if to endorse her observation there was a sudden volley of gunshot from the field behind the hotel.

'OK. Where shall we meet tonight?'

'Miles always has a drink with his cronies after dinner. I usually slip away then and go up to our room. Eleven is as good a time as any. The day staff usually disappear then, leaving only the night-shift. Once the others have gone to their cottages, the coast should be clear. I'll meet you just below the railway station, clear of the cottages. If we are heading west that's where you would need to cross the railway track anyway.'

'OK. Sounds good. Eleven o'clock, below the station?'

She nodded. There were tears in her eyes. He held her in his arms and then kissed her, this time on the mouth.

* * *

Gabriélle had spent an uncomfortable night, tossing and turning in her sleep. Nightmares of being raped by some moronic individual with a thick Scottish accent in a vast room, every wall of which was covered in mirrors, had haunted her all night and was still there when she woke. Her black hair was plastered to her forehead and her nightdress was wet with sweat. Elspeth was still snoring beside her.

She gave Elspeth a gentle kiss on her cheek and slid out of bed, heading for the shower.

Later that morning she Elspeth had a leisurely breakfast together. Elspeth chose fried kidneys, liver and home-cured bacon, followed by scones, cream and honey that tasted of heather blossom. Gabriélle chose fish as her main course. Very indulgent but both women felt like cheering themselves up.

Gabriélle's research had reached a critical stage. She badly needed to talk to the McBane children but it was difficult. Not only were they unruly and difficult to talk to anyway, but they kept themselves to themselves. The teenagers usually worked in or near the kitchens. It would seem that they were strictly forbidden to fraternise with the guests, especially the few teenagers amongst them so access was proving difficult. Gabriélle also felt now that she was being watched by the McBanes, especially the

Manager, Ronald. She may have been imagining this but it disturbed her, never-the-less.

Her encounter with the lad in the hotel forecourt and the lubricious nature of his comments had upset her far more than she had at first thought. However, if she complained to the management then it would draw attention to her even more. Elspeth's advice had been to ignore it as they were remarks of a disturbed young man lacking any of the social graces and clearly retarded. Easier said than done! Besides, some instinct told her that that young man and his obscene language was but the tip of an iceberg. There was something deeply disturbing about this hotel and its staff that went far beyond incest or even child-abuse. She had no idea what that might be but she would be glad when she and Elspeth could drive away, back to the comfort and safety of Elspeth's Edinburgh flat.

'So, my darling, what are our plans today?' It was Elspeth, chewing on her second cream-covered scone.

'I am going to try and tackle our chambermaid, the younger of the two. She's called Sonia I think. If I can get her into conversation I might be able to find out more about who is related to whom. She's no longer a teenager but she's the nearest I am going to get to the kids, I suspect. She usually does our room at about ten. I'll be there when she arrives.'

'OK. I'll work on young Stewart, the bagpipe player. He's on duty this morning at the Porter's desk. I saw him there when we came down this morning. From what I have seen of him around the place he has a lot of issues - far more than your average male teenager. Let's meet for coffee at, say, eleven and swap notes. Another scone, my darling? And do cheer up! This is still our holiday, remember, even if we are entirely surrounded by highly dangerous psychopaths!'

Gabriélle smiled and sipped her coffee. She reached for Elspeth's hand under the table and squeezed it gently.

* * *

Olympia was exercising her horse early that morning. She was becoming particularly frustrated by the weather. For months she had been looking forward to her stay at Rannoch and to exploring on horseback the surrounding moors. She had always known that October could be difficult but the snow this year was exceptional. While Sebastian had begun to enjoy his training and was now attempting much higher jumps, the indoor riding arena was far too small for what Olympia was attempting. Besides, both horse and rider were desperate to get out and about and enjoy the freedom that the great moor itself offered to the adventurous equestrienne.

The two teenage girls who had originally shown such an interest in Olympia's style and technique had stopped coming.

They both still rode occasionally in their own time but seemed more interested in young David than their mounts or in practicing equestrian skills. Perhaps they too were getting bored with the weather.

David, the stable lad, was one of the better looking of the McBane family. He was about fifteen, a year or so younger than his brother, Stewart. He was clearly flattered by the interest the two young girls took in him and was often seen hanging around in places that he was normally forbidden to be in - such as the station tea rooms or by the residents' parking area at the side of the hotel.

On one occasion, only a day or so ago, Olympia had seen David and one of these teenage girls - the blonde one called Tanya - actually disappear together behind the hothouse. That must have been on Monday. Clearly, not content with just looking, Tanya had found a more interesting way to pass her time - when not playing *Monopoly* with her parents or watching crappy videos.

Later that morning, after a vigorous work out, Olympia returned Sebastian to his stable and began to rub him down. She had started taking on these tasks, partly because she liked her mount but also because it helped pass the time. David did not seem to mind her taking over some of his duties. His thoughts were clearly elsewhere most of the time, anyway.

That morning though was different. Olympia had finished working on Sebastian when she heard a disturbance coming from near the Stable Manager's office, next to the tackle room. It was the cries of someone in pain, accompanied by angry shouts.

Olympia left Sebastian, closed his stable door behind her, and quietly approached the tackle room situated at the far end of the covered horse boxes. The door to the tackle room was partly open so that Olympia was able to see inside. What she saw horrified her for it was David who was crying out in pain as Emelia McBane laid about him with a horse whip. David was cowering in one corner as Emelia struck him again and again. There was blood on David's cheek. He lay curled up in a ball of pain, trying to shield his head from the blows raining down on him thick and fast

'Never go near that girl again, you young degenerate. Never, do you hear? It is strictly forbidden. Do you hear me, boy?'

Olympia was shocked at the violence of this encounter. Far too afraid to intervene, she tip-toed away. When she got to her bedroom back in the hotel she was still shaking.

* * *

Sonia McBane, the chamber-maid on the second floor of the hotel, was surprised to see Gabriélle still in her room.

'Do you want me to come back later, Miss?'

'No, no. I'm leaving in a moment. Please carry on.'

Gabriélle was brushing her hair at the dressing-table. From where she sat she could see, reflected in the mirror, Sonia changing the sheets on the bed.

'How old are you, Sonia?'

'Eighteen, Miss. My birthday was last week.'

'Congratulations. Have you a boyfriend, Sonia?'

Sonia looked distinctly uncomfortable, unaware perhaps that she was being observed by Gabriélle in the mirror.

'Not really, Miss. No time for boys. Far too busy, Miss.'

Gabriélle stood up and crossed over to where Sonia was bending over the bed. She took her jacket from the wardrobe and put it on, all the while watching Sonia at her work. Sonia seemed embarrassed by the other woman's proximity.

'I'm surprised that you do not have a boyfriend, Sonia. You are very pretty. Did you know that?'

'No, Miss. Thank you Miss.'

'Do you have any brothers or sisters?'

'Oh yes, Miss. Lots. Brothers and sisters. And aunts and uncles. We are all one big, happy family here, Miss.'

17

'Dr Thomas Neep' thoroughly enjoyed his breakfast. He had always enjoyed offal, especially when cooked to perfection - as it was that morning. He even had a second helping from one of the large, silver tureens that stood on the massive dresser against one wall of the dining room.

He was now fairly convinced that he would write an extremely favourable report for his masters back in Paris. One star, certainly. Perhaps even two, except that the location was somewhat remote. Still, that ought not to debar the Rannoch Moor Hotel from formal recognition of its exceptional gastronomic achievements it clearly deserved. At least, that is what he now thought.

He stood up, wiped his mouth on his napkin, and left the room. Back in his hotel bedroom he took out his laptop and began to write.

He, 'Thomas Neep', was about to make the Rannoch Moor Hotel restaurant one of the more distinguished establishments in the whole of Britain, let alone Scotland. His recommendations, if accepted - and why not, he was one of Michelin's more respected Inspectors - would bring fame and fortune to Moray McBane. Gleneagles may have its three stars but there is definitely a new contender now on the block and he - 'Thomas Neep', Michelin Inspector *extraordinaire* - would see to it that the entire world knew!

* * *

Poppy had decided that morning to have a massage. The Rannoch Hotel offered both massage and some basic cosmetic treatment - strictly by appointment. It was not cheap but then nothing in this hotel was particularly cheap. John had decided to make himself scarce so he toddled off to the resident's lounge for another cup of coffee, leaving his wife in the capable hands of Bridey McBane, the hotel's qualified masseuse.

Bridey was a twenty-something woman with bright red hair and piercing blue eyes. She was slim and attractive and, for a McBane, remarkable talkative.

Poppy, stripped down to her knickers, lay on her bed and surrendered to Bridey's skilful hands. The session lasted half-an-hour during which Poppy learned that Bridey was no longer engaged; that her father was Jamie McBane, Head Gamekeeper and that she was self-taught; that she had never been to Edinburgh but had been to Pitlochry several times but not recently; that she was very fond of Country and Western music, especially Don Gibson; that she did not want to marry her second cousin, which is what her father wanted; that she loved her job but sometimes wished she could travel abroad, like her eldest sister who lived in Castelnaudry, wherever that was; that there was a very dishy Swede living in the woods behind the hotel but she was not allowed to speak to him; that her brother Alec was a right little bastard, always moody and a thoroughly spoilt brat into the bargain and that she was now finished.

'That will be £30 please, Madam.'

Poppy remained lying on the bed after Bridey had left, utterly exhausted. The woman had not stopped talking once, throughout the entire session.

* * *

Teddy Bosenquet was not a happy bunny. He loved his Bugatti but thus far it had remained under its plastic cover. He had turned its finely-tuned engine over several times since they had arrived on Rannoch Moor but so far the car itself had not moved an inch from where he had first parked it.

Deeply frustrating.

Things were not going that well with Olympia, either. She was equally frustrated at not being able to get out onto the moors and had become moody and withdrawn. She no longer wanted to talk about their wedding arrangements, nor indeed their plans for a round-the-world honeymoon cruise they had been contemplating for some time.

Worse still, she had arrived back in their room later that morning in tears. Teddy was lying on the bed, reading, when she walked in. He looked up in surprise as she slammed the main door behind her. Concerned, he immediately got off the bed and moved towards her, as if to embrace her.

'Darling, what is the matter? What has upset you?'

Olympia brushed him aside and immediately headed for the bathroom, closing the door noisily behind her.

'Is it something I said? Tell me, please. I hate to see you so upset!'

Olympia remained in the bathroom and began to undress. Teddy could hear the bath taps running.

'Olympia, what is it? Talk to me, please.'

After a moment she opened the door. She had stopped crying but her makeup had run. Her familiar pony-tail was untied and her long, blonde hair was dishevelled, falling over her shoulders and down her slender back. She was in her underwear. She stepped forward and fell into his arms.

'Teddy, it was horrible! David was being beaten by Emelia. I saw it all. She was savage. Out of control. I was frightened.'

They sat together on the bed as Olympia told him the full story of her experience in the stables. At one point Teddy had to get up and turn the bathroom taps off. He was all for speaking to the Manager immediately but Olympia said no, best leave well alone. The McBanes were, she added, a very strange bunch. Weird. She wanted nothing more to do with them. No more riding and no more contact with Emelia McBane. Enough is enough!

'Darling Teddy', she added, throwing her arms around him and pressing her tear-stained face against his shoulder, 'I hate this place. I want to go home. Please Teddy, take me home.'

* * *

The residents' lounge was particularly crowded that morning so Elspeth and Gabriélle braved the cold and met instead in the tea-room, on the railway station. The McBanes had decided after all to open it up, partly to relieve pressure on facilities within the hotel itself. With a captive audience now, it was moreover yet another income stream. The McBanes were nothing but enterprising.

It was a cold, blustery morning but the little tea-room with its chintz curtains, gaily painted chairs and tables was surprisingly warm and cosy. It was also empty, apart from the girl behind the counter.

They ordered tea and biscuits and chose a table in the furthest corner of the room. Once the waitress had served them she busied herself in the tiny kitchenette behind the counter. At that distance both women felt confident that she could not hear them. They spoke quietly, just in case.

'Well, how did you get on, my darling?'

'Not particularly well. Sonia was not the most talkative eighteen-year-old I have ever met. Her body language, however, reeked guilt and shame. I know that is an extravagant claim on my part but she is a very repressed young woman. I managed to tape our conversation. I will show it to you later. You are a better judge than me and an expert on body language and speech patterns but for me this girl showed all the signs of having been regularly and persistently abused. What about our bagpipe player? Did you get anything out of that little degenerate?'

'Yes, as it happens. My late father - God bless him, especially his extensive wine cellar - once knew Alastair Milne, at that time BBC Director General. Milne was crazy about the Great Highland bagpipe and Pibroch music - the stuff young Stewart McBane plays every bloody night at suppertime. Well, I was able to regale our lad with tales of the Silver Chanter competition on the Isle of Skye and other such bagpipe ephemera. He was very impressed. Anyway, during the course of our little chat I discovered that he had five brothers and sisters, three step-brothers, two step-sisters and had been brought up largely by two aunts.'

'Wow! Impressive. And who was his mother and father?'

'Not surprisingly, he dodged that one. Ronald, who must have heard some of our conversation, emerged from his office at that point and promptly sent Stewart off on some task on the second floor.'

'You mean Stewart did not want to tell you his parents' names? He told you everything about his brothers and sisters but nothing about his mother of father? That's strange, is it not?'

'Its not that he didn't want to tell me. It's that he does not really know! He claims, somewhat unconvincingly, that Jamie McBane is his father but I'm not sure that's remotely true. More like his grandfather, perhaps. Either way, the lad is either confused or lying. His body language, his way of avoiding my eyes in conversation, his nervous ticks and gestures reveal deep confusion, anxiety and probably extensive guilt - not unlike Sonia. This young man often appears confident - as when summoning us all to supper, for example - but his whole persona belies that. He has all the characteristics of a fledgling psychopath.'

'Elspeth, how can you tell that from one brief conversation? That's impossible, even for you, surely?'

'Yes, I agree but its not merely based on our brief chat this morning. I have been watching him at every opportunity since we first encountered him on the stairs on the day we arrived. His behaviour appears odder the closer you observe him. Small things, like the way he manipulates his colleagues, especially the young women working here. He tries always to dominate, to humiliate and to exploit them. Last night he was one of the night porters. I heard him shouting at the girl who cleans the tables in the dining room. His manner towards her was little short of savage, for no reason at all. The girl had done nothing wrong. Moreover, she was clearly terrified of him. That's not remotely normal, particularly in a large family who generally appear quite close. Too close, perhaps but not openly hostile to each other. Young Stewart seems to be the exception.'

'But does that make him a psychopath?'

'Stewart may be seventeen but he behaves 'off camera' as it were like an angry, extremely bitter twelve-year-old. These children have a character disturbance. They devalue others and lack a sense of morality. Remember, psychopathy is not exclusively an adult manifestation. In fact, some of my colleagues who are child development experts believe that childhood psychopathy is increasing at an alarming rate. Not all these kids may become killers but they do learn how to manipulate, deceive and exploit others for their own gain.'

'But what causes such behaviour?'

'Difficult always to say exactly. It differs from child to child. In Stewart's case, I would say that he has failed to develop affectional bonds that allow him to empathize with another's pain or distress. In fact, he will delight in inflicting such feelings on others close to him, just to demonstrate his indifference. What they *do* develop, however, are traits of arrogance, dishonesty, narcissism, shamelessness, and callousness and that makes them potentially dangerous. As I say, we have in Stewart McBane the makings of a psychopath, and possibly a very dangerous one at that. Gabriélle, the sooner you finish this bloody investigation - and John and his mates can arrest the whole fucking family - the better!'

* * *

Detective Chief Inspector White spent a happy hour or two that morning in the residents' lounge reading old newspapers. In one of them - a local paper for Pitlochry, and nearly five weeks old - he came across an interesting article about Rannoch Moor station.

It told the history of the station (which John already knew about) but went on to describe the old signal box. Something in it caught John's eye, and acting on the spur of the moment, he asked at reception if the Station Master was to be found.

'You mean George, sir. He's in the public bar, even as we speak.'

It was Ronald McBane who told John this news.

'He's the one with the large moustache. George. George McBane, sir.'

John entered the bar. It was quite full - a few off-duty McBanes and one or two guests who preferred the beer on tap here rather than the expensive brew in the saloon bar. George McBane was sat in one corner, sipping a pint of bitter. He was even in his uniform although no trains were expected in the immediate future, or so it was thought.

'Mr McBane, I'm sorry to bother you but is there any chance I could have a look at your signal box? I'm a great train enthusiast and something I read in an article recently intrigued me. I hope you don't mind me asking.'

'Nay problem, Inspector. I'll sup up and meet you on the platform in ten minutes. Wrap up, mind you. Its cold out there!'

John was surprised that even the Station Master knew that he was a policeman. He supposed that word had spread rather quickly when he had first checked in. He had never sought to conceal his identity but he was slightly annoyed that it now appeared to be common knowledge.

Ten minutes later George let him into the signal box, situated rather unusually on the platform itself.

It was like stepping back into a railway time-capsule. The box was in beautiful condition, every one of its seventeen brass levers shining brightly.

'This is fantastic, George. May I call you George?'

'Of course, Inspector. What can I tell you about this signal box, apart from the fact that its unique on the Great Western Highland railway? Not many of these left, I'm afraid. I started in this very box, as a trainee signalman when I just fifteen. My dad and his dad before him were all railway men. They worked elsewhere of course but both ended up here towards the end of their careers. Just like me, I suppose.'

'What's this?' asked John.

He was pointing at a small brass contraption sitting on the signalman's desk.

'That, Inspector, is an emergency communications system. From the time of its opening in 1894, the West Highland Railway signals were operated by the electric token system but then, in 1967, the method of working between Crianlarich and Rannoch was changed to the Scottish Region's Token-less Block system. The semaphore signals here were therefore removed on 3rd November, 1985 in preparation for the introduction of RETB.'

'What's RETB, George?'

'Well sir, you must have heard of that if you are interested in railways. Its short for 'Radio Electronic Token Block'. It was introduced onto this line after the Banavie signalling centre opened on 14th June, 1987. Since all the signals were from then on controlled from Banavie railway station there was no need for this signal box here. That's when it closed, more's the pity.'

'But what is this little device, George?'

'Its for emergencies. In those early days the RETB was not particularly reliable. If something went wrong somewhere along this line we could use this to pass messages from one signal box to the next. The wire is buried beneath the actual railway track'

'But how does it work, exactly?'

'Morse code, sir. By tapping out your message using Morse code.'

'Does it still work?'

'Probably. Mind you, I have never tried in all the years I have been here. I keep it polished but as for using it, well no need, you see. No one at t'other end anymore. Besides, none of us here knows Morse code, least-a-ways me.'

18

Cecelia spent the morning in bed. Not with Sir Miles - he was with some of his cronies in the saloon bar. They had started drinking as soon as it had opened, not long after breakfast had stopped being served. He was drinking more and more, Cecelia noticed.

It was true that they were not getting on as well as they had previously. She sensed that he too was unhappy with their relationship. He had said nothing but after two years of intimacy she could 'read' him like a book. He was definitely not his usual, happy self and although he had tried to raise the subject of their troubled relationship a couple of times recently, he had on each occasion stopped short of a full-scale discussion. He was never good at expressing his feelings and would often cover his embarrassment over such intimate matters with his usual bluster and exaggerated *bonhomie.* It never worked. She could see through him every time but then neither did it improve matters.

Then there was Erik.

Cecelia had spent a troubled night thinking about Erik. He had kissed her in such a way the last time they met that she now felt that his interest in her went far beyond escape from this dreadful hotel and the horrors they both felt took place here. He might love her but did she love him? Perhaps not. It was difficult to tell, for her feelings for him were inextricably linked to her fears and anxieties. He offered escape - from whatever was going on in this hotel but also from her current lover and benefactor. That was a large part of his appeal. She had agreed to leave with him tonight, at eleven. That was a major, major step. Was she ready for such a severance from everything she had grown accustomed top - wealth, comfort, a measure of security and an impassioned, if not exactly loving, relationship?

She got out of bed and ran herself a hot bath. It would soon be lunchtime and no doubt Miles would come looking for her. He would have been drinking all morning. Drink made him amorous.

She stepped into the bath and slowly lowered herself into the warm, soapy water, allowing her body to relax as she stretched out.

By the time Sir Miles Ballard returned later that morning, she was dressed and perfumed and had dry-blown her hair. She looked stunningly beautiful. She kissed him, deftly avoided his groping hands, turned him around and gently pushed him back through the bedroom door and into the corridor.

'Not now. I'm famished. Let's have lunch. Later, if you are a really good boy, I shall be all yours, my darling.'

* * *

Lunch this day consisted of salmon *mi-cuit* with crab and avocado cream; ballottine of duck *foie gras* with rhubarb, almond and toasted brioche; hand-dived scallops with spiced yoghurt and sesame *tuille*; wild mushroom and artichoke gratin with peas and morels; summer truffle; home-smoked lobster with warm lime and herb butter; roast loin of venison with wild garlic, chorizo and parsley; St James strawberries with pistachio sponge and vanilla cream, followed by coffee and chocolates.

'Well, that was lovely!' said Elspeth, devouring the last chocolate. 'I think that is one of the best lunches I have ever had. The McBanes may be a bunch of psychopathic, incestuous degenerates but they sure know how to cook! What do you think, Poppy?'

'I think you exaggerate, Elspeth. Degenerate is far too harsh a word. Besides, my husband will tell you that they are all innocent until proven otherwise.'

'Speaking of which, Gabriélle, how are you getting on with your documentary? Almost finished?'

'Not exactly, John. As you say, it is one thing to suspect, quite another to prove our suspicions. Elspeth and I both think that the children on this estate have been abused and that some are already quite disturbed. I managed to....'

At this point their waiter came to their table with fresh coffee. He was a young man with a pleasant smile. He refreshed their cups, then withdrew.

'I managed to talk to two or three of the younger staff here in the hotel. When I showed Elspeth my footage she agreed that they all displayed signs of repression, guilt perhaps and a measure of learning difficulties. If the three or four we have met are anything to go by, then these young people are far from normal.'

'Time then', added John, 'for the authorities to intervene and make their own investigation.'

'Sure, but how the hell can we inform them? We are totally cut off in this God-forsaken place. No phones, no email. Nothing! Besides, I have a job to finish before either you or the local authorities get involved. I told you John, as soon as I have my programme I will pass everything over to the relevant people, including the police. Just let me finish, will you!'

At this point Gabriélle got up, threw her napkin onto the table and stormed out of the room.

'She's upset, John.' said Elspeth apologetically. 'Please do not take it personally. This place is starting to get us all down. She knows what she is doing. Trust her a few days longer. She will cooperate with you, I promise.'

Elspeth left the room and followed Gabriélle back to their bedroom, leaving Poppy and John staring at each other in amazement.

'Well', said Poppy, 'what did we do to deserve that?'

'I'm not sure but I am starting to know how they feel. The food here is wonderful, the service exceptional yet there is an atmosphere in this hotel that I too am starting to find very disturbing. Let's hope the road opens soon and we can get home to Dunkeld. Meanwhile, since we *are* trapped here, can I tempt you to more coffee in the lounge, my darling?'

* * *

The short, middle-aged man in a kilt whom Erik had briefly encountered by the telephone kiosk some days ago spent that afternoon lying on his bed, reading a novel.

His name was Gregor Mackintosh. He was staying at the Rannoch Moor Hotel on doctor's orders. He was still recovering from a serious lung infection and it was hoped that the fresh, clean air of the moors might well help his recuperation. He was also very fond of his food. Having lost his wife to breast cancer two years ago, Gregor was alone. However, because of the bad weather, he had now been here more than the week he had booked and was anxious to get back home to Glasgow. Although the hotel management had reduced his daily bill by 40% he could not really afford to stay much longer. Bloody weather!

Sometime that afternoon he must have fallen asleep for when he woke up his book had dropped to the floor and his glasses were missing.

He peered under the bed, picked up the book but could not at first find his glasses anywhere. He removed the pillows and felt down the back of the bed, between the mattress and padded headboard. He not only found his glasses but also a small cellophane bag containing a number of documents. A previous guest must have hidden them down there for safety and then forgotten them.

Gregor opened up the bag and examined its contents. It contained a passport and driving licence, set of car keys, together with some business cards and a few inessential discount cards - the kind of stuff you often put aside to lighten one's wallet when not travelling. Gregor had done much the same himself but his documents were in the safe in his room and not stuffed down the end of his bed!

He again examined the documents carefully. The photo in the

passport was that of a balding, somewhat overweight, clean-shaven man. His date of birth was given as 16th July, 1951 which meant that he was sixty-one. He was born in Watford, Hertfordshire which also meant that he was English.

The name on the passport was 'Charles Mitchell'.

*　*　*

After coffee in the residents' lounge, John and Poppy sat quietly in one corner of the room reading. Outside it was still very cold and gusts of wind were throwing sleet against the windows of the covered veranda. The snowman they had photographed a day or so ago was now little more than a broken pile of grubby snow. The paper lanterns that had once lit the garden beyond had been removed to protect them from the weather.

In short, it was - as the Scots say - a dreicht day!

It was while they were both engrossed in their books that they were approached by a short, middle-aged man in a kilt who introduced himself as Gregor Mackintosh.

'Chief Inspector, can I have a wee word with you? I know you are not on duty but I have stumbled on something that strikes me as very odd. I would like your advice, if possible.'

John was intrigued. He put down his book and invited the man to sit next to them. Poppy peered at Gregor over her reading glasses. He reminded her a little of the comic actor, Gregor Fisher although this Gregor was a lot better dressed. She had seen him in the hotel on a number of occasions, although they had never spoken to each other. She too was intrigued. Mind you, anything to relieve the boredom they were both beginning to feel was welcome at this stage of their enforced residency at the Rannoch Moor Hotel.

'How can I help you, Mr Mackintosh?'

Gregor showed John the documents and explained how he had

found them in his room on the second floor.

'Have you shown these to the hotel Manager? Surely he should be given them? Perhaps they can be forwarded to this guest.'

'Aye. I spoke to Ronald. I did'na tell him what I had found but spun some story about how I knew 'Charlie' Mitchell, that we had hoped perhaps to catch up with each other here on Rannoch Moor and wondered if he was expected at the hotel anytime soon? Ronald told me that, unfortunately, he had been and gone.'
'According to their records, he left on Wednesday, 12th October. I asked if he had left a forwarding address or had contacted the hotel at all. They said nay to both, which struck me as very odd. If I had lost my passport I would have contacted everywhere I had been, including this hotel. If Charles Mitchell has discovered his loss then he seems mighty indifferent to it.'

'Yes, that is odd, isn't it? What do you think, Poppy?'

'Yes, very strange. I'm curious, Mr Mackintosh, why you were so suspicious in the first place. Why did you feel you needed to spin a yarn rather than simply hand over these documents to Ronald McBane?'

'Because I do not trust that lot, Mrs White. And because I found this wee note tucked in the front of Mitchell's passport.'

He took from his pocket a slip of paper and handed it to John. John read it then passed it on to Poppy. It was a note, hand-written in biro on a piece of paper torn from a Filofax.

Poppy read it carefully then passed it back to her husband.

It read:

'If you are reading this then in all probability I am dead. Since I arrived here nine days ago, two men - both hunters, like me - have disappeared in mysterious circumstances. The management claim they left unexpectedly on urgent business but I know for a fact that that is not true. If, as I suspect, both have

been murdered then I may be next as they appear to target single men. I know this sounds crazy but something is going on here that the police should be told about.'

The note was dated Wednesday, 10th October and signed 'Charles Mitchell'.

* * *

Ronald McBane, Manager of the Rannoch Moor Hotel - while trying to keep his guests happy - was becoming increasingly frustrated in what was turning into something of a public-relations disaster.

This was not the first time the hotel had been cut off. Indeed, it happened quite regularly but usually only in December or January - never during the latter part of October. The weather this year had been exceptionally bad and had already played havoc with the hunting and shooting activities for which the hotel and its staff of professional ghillies were famous and upon which they depended for the larger part of their annual income. This was the longest they had been cut off since December, 2008. With the weather still deteriorating and more snow on the way, it was clearly not over yet.

Ronald McBane had been Manager since 2007, since he left Switzerland and took over from his uncle who had died of prostrate cancer that year. While he had been unable to complete his training in hotel management he had, on taking on the responsibility of running the Rannoch Moor Hotel at such short notice, learned fast. The whole operation was now a financial success, with bookings well into the New Year and beyond. Much of that success was due also to his uncle, Moray McBane, whose reputation as their Head Chef was now well established. The winning combination of exceptional gourmet food and fine sport was a formidable attraction for the wealthy patrons who regularly visited the hotel.

However, weather of the sort they were currently experiencing did little to enhance that reputation.

A number of guests, frustrated at being trapped, were becoming increasingly angry, demanding helicopter flights off the moor. Much as he would like to oblige them, there was at the moment no way he, or anyone else for that matter, could communicate with the outside world - until the only landline was repaired. None of his angry guests seemed to appreciate his helplessness. What could he do without the means to contact either the emergency services or even private helicopter companies?

Besides, with gale force winds and poor visibility, it was unlikely that any pilot would risk the trip. If the emergency services had helicopters then it was likely that they were being used for more urgent needs than helping a few disgruntled hotel patrons get back home. In such conditions it was normal for many remote farms in this part of Scotland to be cut off. If there were helicopters then they were surely being used to distribute animal feed or rescue stranded farmers and their families. Every one knew that the Rannoch Moor Hotel was largely self- sufficient so rescuing guests or residents would be low on anyone's agenda.

There was also the matter of the 40% reduction. With no new guests arriving, they still had to pay staff and provide all the regular services of a five-star hotel to those who were still trapped. They could probably recover financially later in the year but for the moment it was money lost.

Marie had been a great help during this present crisis.

She was entirely self-taught but handled the accounts like a professional, learning on the job as it were. She was also proving extremely adept at processing the documentation of those guests who had (how should he put it?) 'left early'. Her skills in this regard were exceptional. Without her, it was unlikely that the dangerous and at times irresponsible actions of his more 'excitable' relatives could be hidden from the outside world. It was a dangerous game that he and his extraordinary family were playing but so far so good. Let's hope, thought Ronald, that it remained just that - their little secret!

19

After their meeting in the lounge, Gregor Mackintosh had agreed to surrender Mitchell's note and the documents - as 'evidence'. John had given him a receipt scribbled on the back of an envelope and assured him that he would look into it as a matter of urgency. He told Gregor to say or do nothing for the moment. John had then asked Elspeth and Gabriélle to come to their bedroom to discuss this latest and somewhat alarming development.

Elspeth was the first to speak - once she had read Mitchell's note.

'Its not a lot to go on, John. In fact, its little more than speculation. We do not even know at this stage if Mitchell 'left unexpectedly' or whether or not he is alive and well somewhere. True, he clearly does not have his passport and, if Gregor is right, does not seem to have called the hotel in case they had found it. But again, there could be a simple explanation for that.'

'Such as?'

'Well, if Mitchell did not need his passport immediately he was not likely to miss it. Who here has not panicked when, getting ready to travel abroad, you suddenly realise with hours to go that you have misplaced your passport? We have all done that, I'm sure. I know I have!'

'Yes, but what of the note? If he was so worried that he *deliberately* hid those documents and that note in a place where no one else was likely to see it, he's not likely to forget it later. If nothing happened to him then it would be easy enough to retrieve his passport and destroy that cautionary note. If something did indeed happen, then his fears were entirely justified. Gabriélle, what's your take on this?'

'I think he was genuinely scared. It is not easy to write a note like that. True, his fears are not specific yet sometimes they are the worst. You get a feeling in your gut that tells you something is wrong and yet you cannot exactly 'place' or identify that fear. That does not make it any the less frightening.'

At this point Gabriélle picked up the note from the coffee table in front of them and re-examined it briefly.

'He says here that he 'knew for a fact' that the missing men had not left on 'urgent business'. He does not say *how* he knows that but it is said with some conviction. That knowledge, whatever it was, fuelled his fears. Moreover, there must have been other reasons why he had become so scared. Our problem is that we cannot know *when* exactly he 'left' without alerting the McBanes to our suspicions, vague as they are at this stage. If Mitchell was right and that at least two others have disappeared - 'mysteriously' is the word he uses in his note - then we are dealing with something far more serious than incest or even child-abuse. We are possibly dealing with cold-blooded murder and not just one murder but several, by all accounts.'

For a moment all four of them pondered the enormity of the situation that now faced them. It was during this silence that Gabriélle looked at Elspeth, as if for guidance. Elspeth, discerning immediately her lover's unspoken entreaty, nodded reassuringly.

It was, therefore, Gabriélle who spoke next.

'John, because of this new development and because I have information that supports Mitchell's suspicions and fears, I think it is time that I told you that I am not a journalist but a French police officer.'

There was a stunned silence at this announcement. Poppy's jaw was seen to drop visibly. Elspeth merely looked sheepish.

'My name is indeed Gabriélle Fourés but I am *Lieutenant* Fourés with the Direction centrale de la police judiciaire (DCPJ) in Paris. My presence here is official. Although I am concerned with both incest and possible child-abuse, I am primarily investigating a number of disappearances of EU citizens linked to this hotel.

Mitchell's note confirms my worst fears. I am also investigating Ronald McBane's possible connection with the murder and mutilation of a young Swiss national in 2007. All the missing people on our files stayed here, at this specific hotel. None have been found since - either dead or alive. Perhaps Charles Mitchell should now be added to that list.'

* * *

Supper that evening was a subdued affair for Detective Chief Inspector White and his wife. They occupied their usual seat in the far corner of the large baronial hall. They ordered their meal and a bottle of Sauvignon Blanc. The restaurant was full. Outside, it was still snowing.

The choices for main course that evening included seared foie gras, cloutie dumpling and ginger wine; king scallop with calamari, cauliflower risotto, caper and ink sauce; Comrie shitake feuilleté with beetroot purée; Scottish lobster (grilled) with garlic butter; lamb cutlets or Scotch beef on the bone served with pont-neuf potatoes, grill garni and béarnaise. All the main dishes were served with a choice of fresh vegetables. These included broccoli hollandaise; cauliflower mornay; honeyed carrots; buttered Heritage potatoes; hand-cut chips; French fries; spinach nature or spinach à la crëme.

They both chose the Comrie shitake feuilleté with beetroot purée.

Surprisingly, John was not particularly angry with Gabriélle for not telling him from the beginning the true reason for her unexpected arrival and presence that weekend at the Rannoch Moor hotel.

This was partly because he had thought something was not quite right from the start. Had the phones not gone down he could have found out fairly easily from Police HQ in Inverness who Gabriélle really was and what she was doing on Rannoch Moor. If she was in the UK on official police business, the French police would have been obliged to inform the UK authorities - if only as a matter of courtesy. Even though hers was a *preliminary* investigation - discretely gathering evidence that may or may not lead to a full investigation later - it would be necessary also to inform the regional constabulary in Pitlochry since Rannoch Moor was technically their patch.

He was not even angry that Elspeth had, to some extent, knowingly gone along with Gabriélle's little journalistic charade. She may have damaged her professional credibility but in the end, as soon as she knew who Gabriélle really was, she had persuaded her lover to reveal all. Mitchell's note had been the opportunity to do just that. Indeed, it later transpired that it was only that morning that Gabriélle finally confessed to Elspeth herself. Elspeth's mistake was to fall for a convincing and extremely attractive French 'journalist'.

No, Gabriélle's presence there was not what worried him. What worried him was that all four of them were in the middle of a situation in which they were not only outnumbered - and therefore in no position to arrest anyone - but in possible danger themselves.

'Darling, your food is getting cold.'

'Yes, sorry! Lots to think about. Did Elspeth say that she was going to join us for supper tonight?'

'No. I think they decided to eat in their room this evening. She said Gabriélle was feeling really bad about deceiving you. I should think so too!'

'Don't blame her, darling. She was not to know that we would pop up in the middle of her investigation. I'm a bit pissed off with Elspeth, though. She could have dropped me a hint or too instead of going along with the 'documentary' story. She never quite believed that either - or so she now claims. I would have expected better of her than to accept unquestionably that cock-and-bull tale about a 'documentary on incest in the Scottish Highlands'. She's patently in love with the woman and that, for once, clouded her judgement. She may rue the day that that happened. She still believes that her love for Gabriélle is reciprocated so I guess we must accept that Gabriélle is not 'using' Elspeth as blatantly as it might appear now to us.'

'What are you going to do then?'

'Not much we can do without proper support. Moreover, I am in no position to charge anyone with anything on the evidence we have thus far. Trapped here, unable to reach the outside world, I think our best plan is to discretely gather as much evidence as we can but without giving the McBanes the slightest hint of what we are doing. We should then pool our information with Gabriélle and Elspeth and pray for a break in the weather so that we can call in the troops. It will not come as any surprise to Inverness. They already have contingency plans for a mass arrest here on Rannoch Moor - but for child-abuse, not murder. That puts a whole new slant on their investigation. This is no longer a Social Services issue but a fully-fledged murder enquiry. The problem is that the police themselves in Inverness do not know that yet. My problem is that I have no means of warning them of the dangers they might now face.'

'Wow! Who though a wedding anniversary could be so exciting!'

'Quite. One thing we are definitely NOT doing is going out on those moors alone - even if the weather breaks. We - or rather you, my darling - are staying right here, in the middle of this crowd. You can eat yourself to death if you want but I am not having any degenerate psychopath getting anywhere near my lovely wife, especially as I am even now looking forward to celebrating out *nineteenth* wedding anniversary.'

'Yes, but *not* here please!' said Poppy. 'Let's celebrate the next one at home or at Mario's where we at least know we are safe! Of maybe the Bahamas? After all these little deceits you might just owe me a trip to Jamaica, my darling Chief Inspector Plod!'

* * *

Cecelia spent the larger part of that afternoon in the arms of her lover. Mind you, he was a little drunk after a morning imbibing with his cronies in the saloon bar but a light lunch sobered him up somewhat, even if it did not dampen his evident, rather uninhibited ardour.

They therefore skipped coffee, quickly took the lift back to their room and tumbled into bed. Frantically removing each other's clothes, almost helpless with laughter, they then set to with an enthusiasm that was remarkable considering that Cecelia had that morning finally resolved to run away with Erik and leave Miles Ballard and his astonishing wealth for good.

She was not entirely sure how she had arrived at this decision. Hours of anguished deliberation that morning and some doubts over lunch turned into determination and resolution over desert. That very evening, at eleven o'clock, she would meet up with Erik and take off with him into the night, hurtling across the wild wastes of Rannoch Moor to safety and freedom on a quad-bike. It seemed a fitting way to quit one life in order to start another.

Her love-making that afternoon was, however, genuine - tender, loving and even inventive. It was, for her at least, a last gesture of affection and gratitude to the man who had supported and nourished her for two, somewhat frantic and emotionally fraught years.

She was sure that Miles loved her, even though he seldom managed to express that love in ways that satisfied her. Like many rich men, he showed his gratitude and affection with material objects when a kind word or some small encouragement or gesture might have mean far more to her often shaky self-esteem. He was not good at articulating his feelings so jewellery, fur coats and expensive holidays became his chosen method of expressing what he probably felt in his heart yet dared not say out loud. He was a good man - despite his ruthlessness and frequent insensitivity towards her emotional needs or deeper feelings.

He had however managed yesterday to ask her who Erik was, explaining that he had seen them together walking from the station.

She had given him a noncommittal answer, saying that he was a young man she had met in the gift shop. She added that she knew nothing about him (which was true) but that he seemed rather shy. If Miles suspected that her relationship with Erik was anything more than a brief encounter, meaning nothing to either of them then he never said as much nor did he ever mention Erik again. Besides, his pride was such that the mere idea that she might prove unfaithful to him had never really crossed his mind. His status and wealth made him impermeable to jealousy of that kind. He lived in his own bubble of self-confidence, bordering on arrogance.

She could not, would not ever leave him - or so he imagined.

After making love that afternoon they both fell asleep in each other's arms. At five o'clock Cecelia slipped out of bed and had a shower. She washed her hair and let it dry naturally as she re-varnished her nails and completed her makeup.

When Sir Miles woke up she was dressed and ready for their evening meal - their last meal together.

She wore that evening his favourite dress - an original evening gown from 1938 by Elsa Schiaparelli. She looked absolutely beautiful. It clung naturally to her slim figure and perfectly matched her elfin looks, large eyes and pale complexion. Sir Miles was enchanted and accompanied her down to supper with a huge beam on his face. Even the loud bagpipe music of young Stewart did not dampen his mood. He entered the dining room on the arm of his lovely young companion as if he owned the place - which he probably could if he put his mind to it .

The choice of gourmet food that evening was even better than usual. Head Chef Moray McBane was clearly trying to outdo himself with a truly memorable meal.

Soups were either spiced pumpkin with basil yoghurt and garlic croutons; langoustine bisque with crab wontons and coriander foam; or chicken consommé.

Fish choices included Hebridean salmon with scallop tatin, sweet potato cake with sorrel and spinach sauce; halibut fillet with red wine fumé, herb crust and truffle mousseline; Dover sole, grilled or pan fried; langoustines flambéed in Pernod with mushrooms and cream.

The meat dishes included rack of lamb with boulangère potatoes or corn-fed chicken with foie gras and puy lentils with tarragon.

Deserts included Morello cherry soufflé with marzipan ice cream and almond wafer; apple 'tarte tatin' with Calvados anglaise and clotted cream ice cream; banana bombe Alaska with chocolate sauce or crèpes suzette.

They ordered their food and sipped Champagne.

'Here's to you, my darling. You look wonderful tonight. Really beautiful!'

'Why, thank you Miles. I feel beautiful!'

The clinked glasses. Teddy and Olympia were nowhere to be seen. Cecelia was glad. She did not want her last meal with Miles to be shared with anyone else, especially Olympia Garland.

They had both chosen fish as their main course. Cecelia had salmon and Miles Dover sole. The food was tremendous, the atmosphere in the room - entirely lit that evening with candles and paper lanterns - was enchanting and Sir Miles was on wicked form, telling her a stream of jokes that made her genuinely laugh - even if some of them were rather rude.

After supper they retreated to the saloon bar for a whiskey or two. Some of Miles' hunting cronies were there so Cecelia soon made her excuses and slipped away, pleading a slight headache after so much Champagne. She left Sir Miles propping up the bar and regaling his friends with more jokes. He loved company, particularly male company, and she knew that he was now in his element. It was now ten o'clock in the evening.

As she left the bar, she waved good night and blew Miles a kiss.

She then turned on her heels and stepped into the hotel foyer. At that precise moment she realised that this might be the last time she would ever see him. It was a sad thought but a new life beckoned and it was one she was now utterly determined to embrace. She did not look back but took the lift to the second floor and entered her room, eager now to change into clothes more suitable for a night on Rannoch Moor.

* * *

'Dr Thomas Neep' had thoroughly enjoyed his meal. He had chosen for his main course halibut fillet with red wine fumé, herb crust and truffle mousseline. It was perfection. Quite the best that he had ever tasted.

Thomas (whose real name was Bartholomew Trickett) now stood in front of his mirror in his underpants and vest staring at his reflection. He ran a hand over his tummy. He was starting to put on weight, he noticed. This of course was an occupational hazard with Michelin Guide Inspectors but so far he had managed to balance indulgence with exercise. As soon as the weather improved, he would take himself off for a stiff walk across the moors.

He undressed, stepped into his striped pyjamas, cleaned his teeth and slid into bed. The maid had already put his hot-water-bottle under the covers. He felt for it with his bare toes, then wrapped his feet around it.

He felt happy and content. It had been an exceptional meal although he would have liked to have tried the rack of lamb with boulangère potatoes. That looked delicious. For desert he had chosen the Morello cherry soufflé with marzipan ice cream and almond wafer.

It was with the taste of that dish still lingering on his palette, like some benevolent ghost, that Bartholomew Trickett, alias 'Thomas Neep', slid gently into a deep, contented sleep.

20

It took Cecelia a matter of minutes to slip out of her expensive dress, put thermal underwear over her silk bra and knickers and step into woollen slacks and a roll-neck, lamb's-wool sweater.

She had rehearsed these actions frequently in her imagination. The reality took even less time than she had thought it might. She hung her Schiaparelli dress in the wardrobe, giving her mink coat an affectionate farewell stroke with one hand as she did so. She would miss that. She then took off her diamond ring - the most expensive gift Miles had ever given her - and placed it in the envelope she had prepared earlier. She was not mercenary.

She slipped her mobile phone into her pocket, even though it was useless on Rannoch Moor - she could not part with that since it contained all her contact numbers. She stuffed her passport, bank book and credit cards into her hip pocket, together with the paperback with Tait's signature in it. She then chose a sensible pair of sturdy, flat shoes - but not walking shoes. She did not want anyone downstairs to think for one moment that she was about to go for a night's stroll on the moors.

She looked once more the note she had secretly written earlier that evening for Miles. It read:

'Dearest Miles, Erik and I have escaped. By the time you read this we should be far away. There are dreadful things going on in this hotel. We will tell the police and perhaps, if we succeed, they will come and rescue you all. Take care my darling and thank you for two wonderful years. I will never forget you. Your affectionate Cecelia.'

She put her note in its envelope with the diamond ring and sealed it. On impulse, she pressed her lips to the back of the envelope, leaving a clear outline of lipstick across which she wrote S.W.A.L.K - 'sealed with a loving kiss'. Miles would like that, she thought. She had done that when she had first written to him at their hotel in Monaco; the night she had taken him into her bed.

She slipped the envelope into the inside pocket of his brown suit. She did not want him to find it this evening and create a fuss. He would find it in good time for that was the suit he always wore when travelling.

She then placed a second note on the bedside table. It read:

'Darling Miles, unable to sleep. Have gone in search of a book in the Library. Do not wait up. Love, Cissy.'

She took one last look around the room then stepped into the corridor. It was empty. It was now ten-twenty. She had forty minutes before she had arranged to meet Erik below the station.

She got to the head of the stairs and looked down. The lobby was indeed empty. There were some people still up but by the sound of it they were mostly in the bar. She descended the stairs with as much confidence as she could muster, trying to look casual although her heart was thumping. If she met anyone she knew she would stick to her 'can't sleep, need book' story. If she met Miles she was not sure what she might do but then 'he who dares, wins'. Anyway, that is what she kept telling herself.

The lobby was indeed empty although there was a light on in Marie's office. Here the noise of men's voices coming from the saloon bar was much louder. Cecelia even convinced herself that she could discern Miles' particularly raucous laughter but that may have been her imagination.

It was as she was heading for the library that she noticed that the dining room door was ajar. On impulse she looked in. There, on the far side of the room and directly facing her, was the dumb-waiter that brought food from the basement and, presumably, the kitchen.

It was at that precise moment that Cecelia had the notion of climbing into that dumb-waiter and descending into the basement. There she would find the evidence both she and Erik badly needed.

It was a crazy idea but then, desperate measures sometimes call for desperate means! She glanced at her watch (thirty-five minutes, that should be enough for a quick exploration), then stepped into the dining room, quietly closing the door behind her. It was now ten-twenty-five. Since dinner had finished at about nine-thirty, the waiters had cleared the tables and had set for breakfast. By now, or so Cecelia hoped, most of them and the kitchen staff will have gone home. There was a good chance that the basement was now empty.

This indeed might be her only chance!

She was fairly confident that Erik would not approve of her taking such a risk but if they badly needed evidence then perhaps she might find something down there, in the bowls of the building. Erik would be proud of her, even if he might not relish what she was about to do. A quick look round and then back up the dumb-waiter, before anyone noticed that she had disappeared. Piece of cake or, as Miles would say, a 'walk in the park'!

The dining room itself was dark. There were no lights on anywhere but dying embers from the great fireplace gave the large room a warm glow.

She opened the doors of the dumb-waiter and climbed in, her heart beating hard enough to burst. She was slightly built and the cupboard-like space was large, certainly large enough for the banquets it regularly brought up from the kitchens below. Once in, with her knees up under her chin, she reached for the electric button and managed to close the doors before the dumb-waiter descended shakily to the cellars below.

On reaching the basement, Cecelia peered through the crack in the doors of the dumb-waiter and was relieved to see that the servery was empty. She opened the hatch and climbed out, then tiptoed towards the swing doors that she guessed led to the kitchen itself. She was right. She slowly pushed them open and stepped into the main kitchen area.

It too was empty. She was in luck!

Moray McBane's enormous kitchen was unlike anything Cecelia had ever seen. It was windowless, dark and somewhat baronial in appearance. From the ceiling hung strange cogs and wheels, designed to turn enormous haunches of beef above the fires below. Great marble slabs covered the centre of the room, on which were piled a veritable feast of raw vegetables, rich fruit, bread, cakes, scones, as well as jars and countless other containers - all piled high in riotous confusion. The room itself was bathed in steam, with water running down the tiled walls onto a floor covered in bloodstained sawdust. The only light came from florescent lighting in the ceiling - a flat, ugly light that cast a gloomy pall over this large 'medieval' kitchen.

It was more like a charnel house than a kitchen.

At the far end, on the largest stove, there stood an enormous stock pot simmering away over an open, gas flame. When Cecelia cautiously lifted the lid and peeped in she saw, to her horror, bubbling away in a froth of foam and grease, the decomposing head of Paula Leamington.

* * *

Erik carefully packed his rucksack, taking only the most essential belongings - his laptop, camera, torch, passport, mobile-phone and wallet. He added a spare sweater, gloves, woolly hat and ski goggles. He agonised over taking his Norwegian skis but decided that they would be too much of a hindrance on the quad-bike. In the end he left them behind.

He lit the small kerosene lamp and turned it low. He then stuffed his sleeping bag with all the rest of his clothes. He placed it and the lamp in the middle of his tent, crawled outside then closed the zip. From the outside it looked as if the tent was still occupied. If the McBanes decided to check his whereabouts it might fool them for a while - unless they actually opened the tent and saw that he was gone. He stepped back, checked his handiwork, then slipped away into the dark wood behind the tent.

This route, which he had discovered earlier that afternoon, brought him round the back of the stables, thereby avoiding the need to cross the exposed courtyard. He had heard the kitchen staff leave at about nine-thirty. The back of the hotel was now quiet but still fully lit.

The night staff had gone in to start their shift. All was now quiet.

The garage lay at the back of the stables and was reached by a narrow track that led to the service road behind the hotel. It was not locked since the doors were in a bad state of repair. Even if it had been locked, it would not have taken much strength to knock them down or even lift them of their hinges.

Erik opened the doors and entered the garage.

The quad-bike was a Yamaha, hitched to a small, two-wheel cart. The quad-bike itself was not particularly new but these were, Erik knew, reliable vehicles. He had often driven one on his father's farm back in Norway. The key was still in the ignition. He was not sure what he would have done had it not been there but farmers generally leave keys in vehicles like this one, for convenience and so that any of the estate staff can use it when required. Sure enough, it was there. The quad-bike itself even had chains on its wheels. Erik then looked around for fuel. He had seen several fuel cans when he had found the garage on his initial recce. They too were still there and, moreover, were full.

He unhitched the trailer.

Erik spent the next few minutes topping up the quad-bike's fuel tank and planning, in his head, how he was going to get the quad from the garage to the track below the station unseen.

The mere thought of this part of the evening's escapade made his heart thump and his skin sweat, despite the freezing conditions. Outside it had begun to snow but only lightly. That was good, he thought. It would reduce visibility somewhat but it would also help cover any tracks. That might prove important if they came after them in their Land Rovers. If he could find the two Land Rovers he knew the estate possessed, he might be able to damage them in some way. That might just give them valuable time to make good their escape.

With that thought in mind he left the garage, closed the doors behind him and set off to find the two Land Rovers, one of which he remembered seeing parked to the right of the stables.

* * *

Cecelia must have feinted but when she woke up she discovered to her horror that she was naked, gagged-and-bound and lying on the floor - with Moray McBane looming over her.

Moray said nothing but simply grinned down at her, prodding her with the tip of his boot. Cecelia, absolutely terrified, cowed away from him as best she could but so tight were her ankles tied and her arms bound behind her back that she could barely move. She began to cry, sobbing uncontrollably behind the gaffer tape round her mouth. She heard a door slam shut. Perhaps someone else had been there. She was acutely conscious of her nakedness but that was as nothing to the deadly danger she now felt herself to be in.

Moray leaned down, grabbed her by her bound ankles with one hand and dragged her across the sawdust-covered floor of his kitchen and into the next room, at the far end of which was a huge, walk-in cold store. With his free hand he opened the vast metal door. Cecelia immediately felt a cold blast of air on her naked body. She had stopped crying as the full horror of her situation began to dawn on her. She was going to die, not by a knife handled by a deranged Chef, but from hypothermia in a cold-store.

It was then that she fainted once more.

* * *

Erik found one of the Land Rovers. It was parked close to the stables and in a pool of light from one of the lamps attached to the stable roof. It was with some trepidation, therefore, that he stepped out into that pool of light, crouched down in the shadows away from the light, and let down both tyres on that side. He threw the screw nuts away into the snow.

He spent the next ten minutes or so looking for the second vehicle. He eventually found it but it was parked in full view of the hotel entrance. It was too risky to approach that one so he slipped once more into the shadows and made his way back to the garage. It was now ten-forty. He had twenty minutes to get the quad-bike out of the garage and down to their arranged meeting place, just below the station. This was the most dangerous part.

* * *

When she came round Cecelia discovered that she was now totally encased in a long, semi-transparent plastic bag and hanging from the ceiling of the cold-store by her ankles.

It was pitch black and very cold. At first she though that she would suffocate and began to bite frantically at the plastic to try to tear open a hole so that she might breathe. The plastic was too thick but after a moment of two she realised that she could breathe. There must be a gap somewhere, probably by her feet, that allowed air in. No, she would not die of suffocation. If she was going to die then it would be from the intense cold in this darkened room.

How long, she wondered, did she have?

She lay still, trying to preserve her energy and not use up too much air. She surprised herself at how calm she had become. Perhaps, since she knew now for sure that she was going to die, somehow her brain had accepted the inevitable. It also gave her time to think.

In this position, with her head hanging down towards the floor, she was bound to pass out sooner or later - if the cold did not do for her first. That meant that she needed to lift herself up - but to what end? Her arms were tied behind her back and her whole body sealed in the plastic bag. Even if she could bend upwards, using her stomach muscles, there was nothing she could do to release her ankles. It was utterly hopeless!

She closed her eyes and tried to breath slowly and calmly. If she was going to die in this horrible way then she would at least try and do it with some dignity.

21

Sir Miles and Teddy left their three cronies in the bar and headed upstairs to their respective bedrooms.

They had had an enjoyable evening, chewing the cud. Their talk was mostly business since the three guests they had struck up an acquaintance with were also professional men. Two of his drinking chums Miles had met on the shooting range that afternoon. Both were in textiles; indeed, the elder of the two he had actually met before - at some conference in Manchester two or three years previously. The third was a policeman. Decent chap, thought Sir Miles, but an unlikely person to be at a hotel like the Rannoch Moor. Fish out of water. Still, he had a few good yarns to tell which had amused the others.

White. Detective Chief Inspector John White he was called. Very attractive wife. Bloody pity she had gone to bed earlier.

Miles and Teddy wished each other good night and parted on the landing. Sir Miles was not surprised to find Cecelia's note. Cecelia had of late taken to sitting and reading in the resident's lounge at all hours. Indeed, she was turning into a moody bitch and not much fun to be with of late. Maybe her time was running out. Maybe he should tell her to buck up, change her ways or fuck off. Yes, he would talk to her in the morning. Time she was reminded which side her bread was buttered, the sulky little bitch!

Sir Miles, undressed, brushed his teeth and climbed into bed. He was not worried about Cecelia. She would turn up sooner or later. He yawned, turned over in bed and within minutes was fast asleep.

* * *

Erik had managed to wheel the quad-bike out of the garage and down the access path to the service road.

There had been a frightening moment when, quite unexpectedly, Head Chef Moray McBane had left the back entrance of the hotel and headed down the lane to his cottage. Erik immediately crouched low in the shadows. Fortunately Moray did not look in his direction or see the quad-bike parked conspicuously at the side of the road. That might have been the end of the night's adventures and all hope of escape. Instead, clearly lost in his own thoughts, the tall man walked on by and eventually disappeared into his cottage.

Erik crouched there for a few minutes, allowing Moray to close the curtains of the cottage and settle down to whatever he did at night. Erik had often seen his lights on well into the night. Perhaps he was an insomniac. Either way, he still presented something of a problem for it was past that cottage that Erik now had to wheel the quad-bike in order to get to the meeting place. There was fifteen minutes left before the rendezvous time he had agreed with Cecelia.

He looked in both directions to make sure the road was clear then silently pushed the quad-bike out into the open and down the lane.

The large rubber types - even with chains - were pretty quiet and there was sufficient snow on the ground to soften any sound. It was still snowing lightly. The street lighting here was minimal, just two lamp posts, which meant that it was fairly dark. Light spilled from Moray's cottage onto the road so it was with a beating heart that Erik edged his way past but, thankfully, he was soon back in the shadows again.

So far so good, he thought.

He reached the crossing and parked the bike beneath a tree. There was no street lighting here and with the snow falling gently it was pretty dark. The distant lights from the front of the hotel were clearly visible but most of the cottages were now in darkness - all except the one belonging to Moray McBane. There were no lights on in the railway station. All was quiet.

Erik at last felt safe - for the moment, anyway. It was now ten-fifty. Where was Cecelia?

* * *

Poppy had gone to bed early that night. She had enjoyed their evening meal but she did not particularly like Sir Miles - they had met once or twice in the bar on previous days so when John joined him and his friends for a nightcap, she had slipped away - to enjoy a long, relaxing bath before getting into to bed an settling down for a while with her book:

Tales of Odd - twelve short stories by an author she had not come across before. Bit like Roald Dahl's *Tales of the Unexpected* but darker. Much darker! Her favourite thus far was called 'The werewolf of Bethnal Green'.

* * *

Much to his surprise John was enjoying his chat with Sir Miles and his cronies back down in the saloon bar.

He was somewhat out of his element when it came to talk about business but when they discovered that he was the arresting officer in the celebrated Ledbetter case then it was his turn to shine in their company. He also found Ballard's stories very funny - even if the man became more incoherent as the evening went on.

It was, in fact, when John briefly left the bar to go to the toilet that he saw Cecelia enter the dinning room and close the door carefully behind her. Knowing that the dinning room was now empty, Detective Chief Superintendent White was intrigued. Since there was no one in the lobby at the time, he opened the dinning room door sufficiently to peep in.

It was then that he saw Cecelia climb into the dumb-waiter, press the button and close the door behind her. By the time he had crossed the room she had vanished. He opened the doors and peered down into the darkness. All he could see was the box-like top of the lift. Some light spilled from the room into which the dumb-waiter had descended but beyond that he could see absolutely nothing.

He was intrigued and not a little alarmed for her safety. The question is, what was she up to? Moreover, what should *he* do next? She was clearly up to some mischief. But what?

John left the dining room, returned to the bar and made his excuses. He wished his new friends goodnight and returned to the lobby. He noticed that Marie was not in her office, although the door was open. He peered in, just to make sure. No, it was empty. She must be in some other part of the hotel. The light was still on and it was likely that she would return soon enough. It was now or never! John seized his chance and rapidly descended the staff staircase to the basement. He arrived at a large door clearly leading to the kitchen. He was about to open it when he heard voices from inside the room.

He cautiously opened the door an inch or so. When he put his eye to the crack he was horrified to see Marie McBane bending over a prostrate Cecelia and rapidly pulling the girl's clothes off - watched by Moray McBane. John was in two minds as to whether to intervene or not. In the end he chose the latter and instead watched carefully as Moray tied the now naked girl's ankles with rope and bound her hands behind her back.

They then stood back and admired their handiwork.

'What now?' asked Marie.

'Cold store. That'll finish her. You get back upstairs. I'll manage. Say nothing to the others. If she is missed tonight say that you have not seen her all night. We'll concoct a story in the morning. Now get back up there - and act normal.'

It was at this point that John suddenly realised that he was about to be discovered by Marie so he dived into a dark corner behind the large door and waited until she had passed him on the stairs and had returned to her office.

When he looked once more he saw that Moray was now dragging

Cecelia by the ankles towards a large metal door in the adjacent room. The cold store. Moray opened the huge, metal door and hauled Cecelia into the room. He could feel the blast of cold air even from the far side of the kitchen where he stood, watching these bizarre and horrifying events through the crack in the door.

Cecelia began to struggle. If she had fainted or been knocked unconscious she was now coming to.

At least, thought John, she is still alive.

From his position behind the door he could not see into the cold store but after a few minutes Moray closed the door behind him, crossed the kitchen and left by another door, turning the lights out as he did so. John then heard the back door click shut - then silence.

He waited a moment or two then hurried across the kitchen. The only light came from the gas still burning beneath the huge stock-pot. It cast a creepy light into the otherwise pitch black, windowless kitchen. The air in the kitchen was fetid, with a smell that he could not 'place'. He resisted the temptation to look in the stock-pot and instead groped his way to the cold-store and wrenched open the door. The light came on automatically - a lurid, florescent light that hurt his eyes after the darkness of Moray's bizarre kitchen.

John was utterly horrified at what he then saw.

Suspended from the ceiling were at least five, long plastic bags in each of which hung a naked, human body. He could just make out their faces through the thick yet partially opaque plastic sheeting. He touched one cautiously - they were rock solid, completely frozen. Two of the bodies appeared to be headless.

John fell to his hands and knees, trying hard not to gag or throw up. He had seen some horrible sights in his time but this was by far the worst.

It was when the bag nearest to him began to move and that he suddenly remembered that he had to save Cecelia.

She was clearly biting the plastic, desperately trying to get out.

John stood up, looked about him wildly for some means to release Cecelia then threw his arms round her and lifted her in an attempt to unhook her from the large metal hook to which the rope securing her ankles was attached.

It worked, she came loose and together they fell to the floor. By now Cecelia was struggling like a wild cat. John took from his pocket his penknife and, with shaking hands, slit open the plastic. Cecelia, beside herself with panic and fear, suddenly stopped moving and stared in utter astonishment at John now rapidly cutting the plastic sheeting away. He turned her over and untied her arms. She suddenly began to thrash about wildly, desperately trying to escape from the claustrophobic plastic sheeting that still largely covered her.

'Cecelia, stay still. You are safe now. I am a policeman. Stay still and I will unfasten your feet. Stay still.'

Her panic abruptly subsided. She lay still, face down but sobbing uncontrollably. John cut the rope form her ankles and sat back on his haunches, breathless and exhausted. Cecelia began to try and struggle to her feet but she was still disorientated and dizzy from having been suspended head down for at least ten minutes. She fell back onto the floor, shaking violently. John then picked her up and stepped out of the cold-store into the relative warmth of the kitchen. He sat her gently in a chair and looked around for something to put over her, to keep her warm and to cover her nakedness.

'Erik. Where is Erik?' murmured Cecelia. She is now shaking even more violently and hugging her arms about her slim body. Her pale skin has turned blue in places and her breathing become laboured.

'Erik? Who is Erik and what on earth were you doing down here?'

'This place is evil. They murder people. They cook people. They are cannibals. The McBanes are cannibals. Erik and I must escape. Must tell someone.'

John had now found the girl's clothes - on the floor, partly hidden beneath the large metal table that filled the centre of the kitchen. The McBanes must have forgotten about them.

He picked them up and helped Cecelia dress. She was shivering so violently now that it was with difficulty that she finally pulled on her slacks, sweater and shoes.

'Where is Erik now?'

'By the railways station. We are going to escape on their quad-bike and cut across the moor. We have evidence. Burnt bones. Erik has a route. We are going to tell the police at Crianlarich. I have all the evidence we need. I must get to Erik. What's the time?'

'Eleven. Why?'

'I must get to Erik. We arranged to meet at eleven. By the station. Will you help me? Please, please help me!'

'Of course. Do you have your mobile on you?'

'Yes, but it will not work....'

'I know. Give it to me, quickly.'

Cecelia reached into her pocket and took out her mobile phone. John took it, ran to the cold-store and took three or four photographs. He then returned the mobile to Cecelia.

'Here, take your phone. There's all the evidence you need. Now, do you think you can you walk?'

'Yes.'

'Right, then follow me.'

John led the way to the back door - the way Moray had left ten minutes before. He opened it cautiously, then led Cecelia out into the yard. They crossed the cobbled courtyard and ran towards the cottages close to the railway line. It was now very dark for the street lamps had gone off and even the lights in Moray's cottage were off and his shutters closed.

Erik was astonished to see Cecelia, accompanied by some man, running towards him. For a moment he thought that perhaps Cecelia had been captured but when she ran up to him and threw her arms round him he immediately saw that she was safe.

'Explanations later,' said John, before Erik could speak. 'Get the hell out of here before they realise that Cecelia has escaped.'

Erik could see that Cecelia was in a state of shock and shivering violently. He took his spare sweater from his rucksack and pulled it down over her head. He then put his woolly hat on her head and gave her the spare gloves.

'What happened, Cecelia? Where have you been? Who is this man?'

'She can explain later, Erik. She is lucky to be alive,' said John. 'I found her in the kitchens. They were going to freeze her to death. She has all the evidence you need on her mobile camera. Now hurry. When you get to Crianlarich give the police this. This is my card. Tell them 'Security Code Five'. Can you remember that? Security Code Five. They will know what to do. Now, for God's sake get going you two, and good luck!'

Erik fired up the quad-bike while Cecelia threw her arms round John and gave him a huge hug. She then clambered onto the back of the bike, grabbed Erik round his waist and hung on for dear life as the quad-bike roared off into the night.

John then hurried back towards the hotel. Instead of going on to the hotel he made his way quickly to railway station. The lights were now off and all was plunged in darkness. He could hear the quad-bike disappearing rapidly across the moor on the far side of the railway track, moving fast towards the forest.

He stepped onto the platform and made his way cautiously to the signal box, hugging the shadows all the time.

What he had in mind, as he got closer and closer to that signal box, was a little breaking-and-entry.

Fifteen minutes later John entered the hotel by the front doors and headed for the lift. There was no one in reception. If Marie was back in her office then she saw or heard nothing for John was able to get into the lift unseen and retreat to the safety of his bedroom.

He opened the door cautiously then tip-toed across the room. Poppy was fast asleep. John turned off the bedside lamp and crossed to the window, parted the curtains and peered out.

He was there just in time to see four armed men clamber into a Land Rover near the forecourt, start the engine and drive off at speed into the night.

22

It was one of the night porters who alerted Marie to the theft of the quad-bike. He just happened to be in one of the empty bedrooms on the second floor - helping himself to a miniature vodka from the hospitality fridge - when he glanced out of the window and saw the quad-bike careering across the snow, away from the railway station. He picked up the internal telephone and immediately called the front desk.

When she heard this disturbing news Marie panicked but then rang Jamie McBane. It took a while for him to come to the telephone. While the landline to the outside world was still down, the hotel had its own internal telephone system.

'What the hell do you want?'

Jamie was clearly not please to be woken up at this hour of the night - certainly not after a evening of drinking with his pals.

'Someone has just driven off on the quad-bike. I thought you should know!'

'Fuck! Tell the others to meet me in front of the hotel. Now! Tell them to meet in the forecourt. Bring guns and ammunition. Do it Marie!'

He emerged from his cottage minutes later.

He met three of his ghillies in the forecourt and clambered into the Land Rover. It was these men that John had seen from his bedroom window, although he knew nothing at that time of the panic that had spread like wild-fire amongst the McBanes. All three ghillies were armed, as was Jamie himself.

One of the men had already discovered that the second Land Rover had been tampered with. There was no time to fix it so it was decided to use just the one vehicle. The quad-bike had a good fifteen minutes start on them. It was going to be difficult to catch them up before the track ran out - if, as it was assumed -

they were taking the road through the forest.

The tracks, clearly visible on the far side of the railway line, suggested that that indeed was the route the thief was taking. As yet they had no idea who he was but they were determined to pursue him at all costs. Apart from the need to silence this thief, to punish him for his audacity, the McBanes delighted in the hunt. It was for them the ultimate thrill - to chase another human being across the wild moor they knew so well and to gun him down in cold blood.

They could not have hoped for better sport than if they had organised it themselves!

Back in Detective Chief Inspector White's bedroom his wife stirred. John was still peering into the darkness through a crack in the curtains. It had begun to snow again. The forecourt was now silent and the hotel quiet.

'John? What time is it?'

'Go back to sleep, Poppy. I'm sorry if I disturbed you, my darling. I am just coming to bed. Go to sleep.'

Poppy turned over and was soon fast asleep, unaware that outside - on the cold, desolate wastes of Rannoch Moor - a life-and-death struggle was rapidly unfolding.

* * *

When Marie told her father - Ronald McBane - his only words were 'Check the cold store. I'll fetch Moray. Meet you there.'

Marie hurried downstairs into the kitchen, switched on the lights and saw to her horror that not only was the cold-store door wide open but that the latest addition to the McBanes' macabre 'larder' was missing. The plastic body bag lay on the floor in shreds, together with the cut ropes. The bird had well and truly flown.

'Who the hell got her out?', asked Ronald, on seeing the evidence for himself. 'She must have had help. But who, for God's sake? And how did they know she was down here?'

'Well, if there are two of them on that quad-bike that will slow them down. Jamie will catch them, I'm sure of it', said Moray.

'Well, let's hope so', added Ronald. 'If not, and they get away, then we are done for. All of us. Completely fucked! Do you hear that, Moray? Well and truly fucked!'

* * *

The forest to the west of the Rannoch Moor Hotel starts at the head of Loch Laidon and stretches nearly four miles, hugging the northern side of this fine stretch of water.

From the far side of the railway station a rough track leads across a patch of open moor-land then on into the forest itself, past Cruiach Cottage. This track, used by Forestry Commission wardens as a fire-break and to access the forest itself, eventually reaches the wild wastes of Rannoch Moor. In the forest this track is entirely suitable for vehicles so Cecelia and Erik made good progress along its length. There was less snow on the ground too, which meant that while the quad-bike's minimal suspension took a hammering - largely because of the chains affixed to its rear wheels - it did not slide about so alarmingly as on open land covered in snow and ice.

Cecelia clung to Erik's waist. She was still very cold but her shaking was less from the cold than from the aftershock of her close encounter with death in Moray McBane's kitchen. She drew warmth and comfort from Erik's solid body and clung to him with a mixture of fear and desire. He would save her! He would take her away from this terrible nightmare into which she had walked and which, but for John White's timely intervention, might well have cost her her life.

She had a lot to be grateful for.

Erik used the quad-bike's lights during this part of the journey, despite the fact that the track was straight and, even with a slight covering of snow, clearly defined. He had no idea how much of a head-start he had but if they were already after them, then it could not be more than fifteen minutes or so. He knew also that a Land Rover was much faster than a quad-bike so that if he was going to take advantage of this track then he needed to go as fast as possible now - hence the lights. He could feel Cecelia against his back. She was still trembling. He had no idea what she had been up to but whatever it was the dynamic of their planned escape had changed dramatically - and not for the better!

It was Cecelia who first raised the alarm.

It was not that she could see even the lights of the pursuing Land Rover, nor indeed hear the roar of its powerful engine. No, it was music that she could hear!

'What the hell....?'

Erik had heard it too. It was Wagner. 'The Ride of the Valkyries', to be exact - played very loudly and getting louder every minute!

'Oh my God, they *are* mad!', cried Cecelia, peering back down the dark track behind her.

'Can you see them?' asked Erik, shouting over his shoulder.

The quad-bike had no wing mirrors so Erik was unable to see anything behind him without looking back over his shoulder. At the speed they were now going that was not, perhaps, a good idea!

'Yes, but only a flash of headlights now and then.'

'How far away do you reckon?'

'A mile, perhaps. Maybe more. The headlights are only tiny spots of light but the music seems to come and go. What are they doing?'

'Trying to frighten us.'

'Well', cried Cecelia, gripping Erik even tighter round his waist, 'Its certainly working as far as I am concerned!'

* * *

John White did not go to bed but sat in an armchair in his darkened bedroom wondering what to do next. He needed to tell Elspeth and yet what could they do between them? He had grounds enough to arrest the McBanes but even with her help and that of Gabriélle he was both unarmed and hopelessly out-numbered. Who knew what the McBanes might do if cornered or threatened. He had Poppy to think of too, let alone the safety of the rest of the hotel's residents now asleep in their beds and entirely unaware of the deteriorating situation.

If Erik and Cecelia make it to safety and fetched help, what then? What, though, if they fail? What if the McBanes capture them or, worse still, kill them in cold blood. It would seem that they were quite capable of that. What happens then? Will Ronald and Marie McBane pretend that nothing has happened and try and cover it up - as they have clearly done on previous occasions?

The possible consequences were too horrible to think about. But something had to be done and it was up to him, the only serving police officer present, to decide what exactly!

Then there were the bodies hanging in that cold-store. Why? It was evidence of murder. Why leave the evidence for all to see? Cecelia had said that they were 'cannibals'. Could that be true? Incest, serial-killings and child-abuse but cannibals as well? Surely not! There has to be some other explanation for those bodies frozen solid in that ghastly basement. But what, for God's sake? What were the McBanes up to? Apart from murder, that is!

* * *

The four men in the Land Rover were in a state of high

excitement. It had been Neil's idea to play the tape. With Alec at the wheel, that left Jamie free to pull back the canvas covering and stand up on his back seat with his head through the roof. The two others steadied his legs, enabling him to raise his rifle and prepare to let off a few shots once in sight of the quad-bike. They were too far away as yet but if they kept gaining at their current rate Jamie should surely get a clear shot or two before the track left the forest and continued on into open ground.

The music was exhilarating. All four men, bouncing on their seats, sang along with it at the tops of their lungs.

The excitement of the chase had grabbed each of them by the throat, the music stirring their emotions to even greater heights. Blood lust had descended on them, like a red cloud. Years of repression and guilt needed an atavistic outlet and the hunting of human flesh gave them just that. That and revenge for the crimes committed in the past by others on their ancient tribe. Revenge that was as enduring as that still found in Spain or Sicily or other primitive cultures where one insult had to be countered with another and in which the knife or gun despatched its own cruel yet ineluctable justice.

Meanwhile, Erik had decided to turn off the quad-bike's lights and hug the side of the road, thereby reducing their visibility. Against the black trees it would be almost impossible for their pursuers to see them - or so he hoped.

The risk, of course, was to misjudge the edge of the track and end up in a ditch or wrapped round a tree. He closed his mind to either possibility and pressed his foot down even harder on the accelerator.

When Cecelia next looked back over her shoulder she saw that the Defender was gaining on them and that its lights were now far more than tiny spots but well defined beams. They were clearly gaining on them - and fast. Even above the music she could now hear the roar of its 2.5 litre, turbo diesel engine. Cecelia knew nothing about cars, let alone four-wheel drive Land Rovers, but even she could tell that it was a powerful vehicle.

More importantly, it was getting closer every minute.

Erik could now see the end of the forest looming up ahead. Here the track continued for several more miles but the trees on either side would soon fall away, leaving them exposed on open ground. To their left and below them was Loch Laidon stretching away to the west. There was also a line of electricity pylons that roughly followed the forest track but then took off across Rannoch - a stretch of open moor with the huge shapes of the Black Corries looming out of the darkness to their right.

Erik's plan was to follow the line of the loch but stay high, to avoid deep snow. If the Defender was going to catch them, then this part of the Moor would be the best place to do so. It would also be the McBane's best chance to take a shot at them, especially when the quad-bike became visible against the skyline. It was still pretty dark, with the occasional swirl of wind-blown snow, but the next ten or fifteen minutes could make the difference between success and failure. Erik, who had planned his route carefully, knew that it was now or never. If they got beyond the end of the track safely and onto rough terrain, then the advantage in speed that the Defender had over them would quickly vanish.

Then it would then be a matter of who fared best on rocky terrain, steering an erratic course between treacherous bogs and snow-covered lochans.

Meanwhile, back in the Defender, Jamie was loading his gun and preparing to take his first shot at the couple on the quad-bike.

'Turn that fucking music off!' he shouted. 'I canna hear meself think. And drive steady, Alec. I'll no hit them if you wave all over the fucking road like some piss artist rally driver. As soon as they quit the forest they will be visible on the horizon. The track rises there. That's my best chance. OK?'

The others nodded in agreement. With the music off the silence of the forest struck them, although the roar of the Defender's powerful engine now echoed back from the mountains looming behind the trees. There were flurries of snow but most of it just light stuff blown from tree tops by sudden gusts of wind. As they approached the end of the forest, now clearly visible ahead of them, the light improved.

'Neil', growled Jaime, 'turn the searchlight on. I can see them. Hurry man, this might be my best chance!'

Neil opened the window on his side and adjusted the lamp that was situated on the offside bonnet but within reach of anyone in the passenger seat. He threw a switch and a great beam of light cut through the darkness like a knife. There, ahead of them, was the quad-bike, clearly caught in its beam.

'Steady now, lads. Steady!' yelled Jamie above the noise of the engine. 'Steady, Alec. Slow down, man. Slower! Right, you little bastards!'

Jamie McBane pulled the trigger once, quickly took aim again, then fired a second time. The explosive sounds of his high-velocity rifle stunned those sitting close to it in the Defender. Alec, startled by the noise so near to his head, roared in pain, causing the Defender to swerve across the track alarmingly. It took him a moment of two to regain control of his vehicle. Neil, still trying to angle the search-light, immediately let go and put both hands to his ears. Jamie was the worst affected as he was standing on the back passenger seat with his head through the roof. He was thrown violently to one side, then back to the other, nearly dropping his gun in the process.

The bullets had passed so close to Cecelia and Erik's heads that they had actually felt the air stir. There was no noise but both bullets crashed into trees ahead of then, shattering one small branch as it did so. In the stunned silence that followed, Cecelia clung to Erik's torso and began to sob uncontrollably, pressing her face hard into his jacket.

23

They were now in open countryside. The cover of the forest had vanished abruptly. The track was still there but it was now pitted with holes and criss-crossed with countless streams running south from the Black Corries, down towards the loch. This meant that every thirty or forty yards or so they would encounter a water-filled dip in the road over which they bounced alarmingly. Some were deeper than others. Occasionally they came across a ford made of rough stones covering a sunken drain-pipe of sorts. These were even worse for at the speed they were going the quad-bike would literally take off and fly through the air, landing with a sickening jolt a few yards further on.

'Hang on, Cecelia. Its going to get rougher. Hang on with all your strength. They missed us. There's hope yet.'

His words fell on deaf ears. Although it was his way of trying to cheer her up it did not work. Cecelia was truly terrified. This was far worse than she had imagined. To be shot at in that way was itself really frightening. Now, with a good chance of either being shot again or thrown into a ditch it was almost too much for her to cope with. She closed her eyes, clung to Erik's back for dear life and prayed for this nightmare to end - one way or another.

The Defender was also encountering difficulties on the track. It had been forced to slow down - to lessen the danger of breaking an axle or careering off into a deep ditch on either side of the road. Still, they were slowly gaining on the quad-bike and in open countryside they stood an even better chance of another clear shot or two - even if they might not be able to overtake them.

'He's heading for Menzie's Stone', said Jamie, now sitting down in the back of the Land Rover and nursing a bruised elbow or two. 'He must be aiming for Lorn, north of Lochan Gaineamhach. There's no way he can cross before that. If he wants to reach the A82 he will have to go north of the lochan then drop south. There's still plenty time to get em. Now, put yer foot down, for fuck's sake Alec, and dinna dump us in some cauld ditch!'

It is one thing to see Rannoch moor in all its magnificence in full daylight but quite another to see it in the dead of night.

There was no moon but the vast expanse of snow-covered moorland now opening up before them, dotted with numerous lochans and streams, had a beauty that was quite breathtaking. Erik had known such landscapes all his life. He had driven quad-bikes over countryside as desolate and as dangerous as this one clearly was. His father's farm in the remote north of Norway was not unlike this vast moor. If they failed this night it would not be for lack of courage or knowledge of a terrain that to some would appear inhospitable and impassable.

Erik knew that this was not the case. Besides, he had a devious plan that might just save them!

* * *

Detective Chief Inspector John White did not sleep well that night. In fact he hardly slept at all. He lay in bed beside Poppy, staring blankly at the ceiling.

He had decided not to wake Elspeth and Gabriélle and tell them about the horrors he and Cecelia had found in the cellar earlier that evening. His best plan was to say or do nothing at this stage. If Erik and Cecelia survived the night then arrests would follow. What was essential now was that the McBanes thought that only the two young people on the quad-bike knew of their dreadful secret. If they suspected anyone else was 'in the know', then every innocent guest in the hotel was at risk. If these people were as deranged and as dangerous as Elspeth said they were, then who knows what they might do if cornered or exposed.

His little expedition to the signal box had been surprisingly successful but it was only 'insurance' and might still not work. No, everything now hung on Erik's courage and knowledge of the moor to get he and Cecelia to safety and, hopefully, to inform the police at Crianlarich.

There were other concerns.

He had no idea what Cecelia had said or done concerning her partner, Sir Miles Ballard. John had spent most of the evening in his company and had formed a clear opinion as to his character.

If Cecelia had dumped him that night then he was not going to take it lying down - especially if there was a good-looking young Norwegian involved. John's bet was that so far Miles knew nothing. He would, by now, have discovered that Cecelia was not in their bedroom. Perhaps she even told him of her plans. More likely, perhaps, she left some kind of diversionary note. He was pretty drunk when John had parted company with him and his cronies earlier. Perhaps, since there had been no shouting in the corridor or noisy altercation at reception, Sir Miles had simply fallen asleep - naturally assuming that Cecelia would return to their bed in due course.

Who can tell with irascible, inebriated millionaires from Sunderland!

John spent another hour or two exploring all these issues in his head before eventually tiredness and nervous exhaustion overcame him and he fell fast asleep.

* * *

Jamie McBane's theory was right - Erik and Cecelia were indeed heading for Menzie's Stone, on a route that closely followed the line of electricity pylons that extended due west. What he did not, could not know, was that this somewhat predictable route was part of Erik's devious plan; a plan that he hoped might give them an edge over his pursuers.

Here the terrain was very rough indeed. So far, though, Erik was following the exact route he had mapped out the previous day when he had spent nearly ten hours on the moor planning their escape. He tried to stay high, skirting the slopes leading to the summits of the Stob an Armailte, Stob na Cruaiche and Stob nan Losgann on their immediate right. Here the snow was thin, having been largely blown away. Occasionally they encountered a snowdrift that had not been there yesterday but most times he was able to skirt around such hazards without losing too much ground.

The Defender was not exactly gaining on them but, on the other hand, nor was it falling behind - as he had hoped. So far, though, the McBanes had not fired any more shots. The ground here was extremely rough and they would need to stop if they stood any chance at that distance of hitting them. If the Defender stopped Erik knew that gunshots would quickly follow. This is what he now feared the most. It was for that reason that he sometimes took a somewhat erratic route so that he could look sideways, back at the McBanes, without alarming his passenger.

Cecelia had fallen very quite now. The aftershock of her close encounters with death - first in Moray's kitchen and more recently here on the moor - had started to really impact on her frail nerves. She had hardly stopped sobbing since the McBanes had fired on them. As there was nothing Erik could do to comfort her, other than secure a successful escape for both of them, he had just pressed on, occasionally giving her a reassuring pat on her hands desperately clasping his waist. Since Cecelia was almost beyond caring it did little to comfort her but at least it made him feel a little better.

They had now reached a remote part of the moor called Tom da Chloiche. The small lochan was directly ahead of them. From its dark, glassy waters flowed a broad stream, heading south down the hillside towards the lower end of Loch Laidon where the great loch divided into two separate forks.

Erik stopped, turned off his engine and looked back over his shoulder. They were partly screened by a large rock but it did not afford complete cover. He needed to stop to get his exact bearings. It was still very dark and with the odd flurry of snow it was not always easy to see where they were on his mental map. Erik, seasoned explorer that he was, had one of those memories whereby he can 'see' a map in his mind's eye. He had no need to consult an actual map but he occasionally needed to get his exact bearings from the landscape itself.

It was just then that a shot rang out. Erik immediately dived for cover, dragging Cecelia with him, pulling her off the back of the quad-bike in the process. They lay on the frozen ground, their bodies pressed as flat as they could. Cecelia had stopped sobbing but Erik could feel her shaking violently. Suddenly, another shot rang out and a splinter of rock ricocheted from the boulder immediately above their heads. It was clear that whoever was shooting at them had not only spotted their exact position but had found the correct range.

Erik realised at once that if they stayed put they were in extreme danger. From behind their rock he could just make out the shape of the Defender parked some seven hundred meters away. Suddenly the powerful search-light came on and raked the hillside above and below them. After a moment or two it settled, illuminating the rock behind which they were crouching. Almost immediately a third shot rang out, the bullet cascading into the ground only a meter or so from their faces.

It was then that the McBanes did exactly what Erik had hoped they would do. Rather than keep their prey pinned down, the McBanes decided to move in for the kill. Erik heard the engine start up and the Defender move off towards them. He immediately hauled Cecelia to her feet, shoved her onto the quad-bike behind him and fired up the engine. For a terrifying moment or two it refused to ignite but then let out its familiar roar. Then, instead of proceeding on along the track past the lochan, Erik turned an abrupt ninety-degrees left and pointed the quad-bike directly down the hill towards the loch.

'Hang on, Cecelia. We are in for a rough ride. Don't fall off! I do *not* want to lose you just when we are winning!'

He then revved up the engine and hurtled down the steep hillside at an alarming rate - straight for boggy ground due south of them.

Back in the Defender, Jamie was the first to realise what was happening.

'Look! Look what he's doing? He's left the track and is heading down the hillside, the daft bugger! We have him now lads! He'll get no further than the narrow lochan and then get stuck. He'll be a sitting duck. Follow him, Alec. Follow the young bastard!'

Alec took a deep breath and turned the Defender off the track and pointed its bonnet down the hillside. It was really steep here and covered in ice so he drove with understandable caution.

'Faster, ye stupid bugger. We canna lose them now. Faster, Alec. Faster!'

Below them, some five hundred meters away, the quad-bike continued to hurtle down the hillside at an alarming rate, scattering rocks and shingle in its path. The ground here was covered in snow and ice so it was more a controlled slide than an actual drive. Erik loved this kind of terrain. This was Norway's answer to off-road racing and he was a dab hand at it.

The Defender fared less well. Alec was not used to this kind of off-road racing, certainly not in these conditions. They were starting to lose ground, despite the angry shouts from Jamie in the back seat.

It took less that fifteen minutes for Erik to quit the rocky hillside and reach flatter, boggy ground on either side of Allt Lochan Ghaineamhaich. This was a long, thin waterway that left the northern fork of Loch Laidon and joined Loch Ghaineamhaich itself, nearly three miles to the west. Normally, the wet ground on both banks of this narrow loch would be impassable for vehicles but on his recce yesterday Erik had seen that the ground here was so frozen that he was sure that it would stand the weight of the quad-bike, even with two people on it. Anyway, that was his theory.

Whether it would also stand the weight of a Land Rover was, of course, another matter altogether!

Alec was the first to sense the danger. The weight of the Defender, with four people in it, was possibly too much for the terrain they were now entering. Even at the start of this stretch of land, the wheels of their vehicle occasionally spun as it broke the crusty, frozen surface and momentarily hit soft mud.

'Its nay good, Jamie. Its too soft here. We canna follow them much further!'

'Wheesht, man! Yer bums's oot the windae! We have ta follow them. Once they get to the loch they are trapped. They canna go no place. Sitting ducks, I tell ye!. Sitting ducks! Keep thee heid, man, and press on.'

Meanwhile, Erik and Cecelia were making good progress, drawing nearer and nearer to the thin expanse of water straight ahead of them. The ground here was decidedly boggy but the quad-bike - as Erik had predicted - was able to skid across its surface without too much trouble.

Glancing back occasionally over his shoulder Erik could see, even at that distance, that the Defender was struggling. The roar of its engine gave the game away even if, in the darkness, he could not see its actual struggles with the mud and ice. It was the sound of an engine desperately fighting to drag its wheels free of mud and ice and snow.

To Erik's ears it was a lovely sound.

Cecelia was not sure at all what was going on. She was clinging so hard to Erik's waist that her arms had grown numb. She cared little if at all for their progress and had, in effect, mentally withdrawn from the whole, ghastly process. Erik could sense her bleak mood, even with his back to her. He now tried increasingly to reanimate her. He needed her complete concentration if they were to succeed in the next and extremely dangerous part of his plan.

'Cecelia, stay with me. I need you to stay with me. We are nearly done. Once across that water we are safe. They cannot follow us once we cross the loch but you have to cling even tighter to me and stay low. They may fire on us again when they realise what we are up to. Just stay low - and pray for us!'

Behind them and to their right the Land Rover plunged on, slipping and sliding, its wheels spinning and its engine roaring. The men inside were battered and bruised from constantly being flung from one side of the vehicle to the other. They now realised that there was a distinct danger that they would soon end up stuck in the mud. Their only consolation was that the two young people on that quad-bike were equally trapped. If necessary they would pursue them across the bog on foot and finish the business.

Erik and Cecelia were now within a few yards of the narrow loch. In places it was at least thirty meters wide. Erik paused for a moment to get his bearings then turned left, back towards the Land Rover.

'What are you doing, Erik?', screamed Cecelia when she saw what was happening.

'Trust me but hang on.'

It was then that a shot rang out. If passed in front of them, as if the gunman was trying to arrest their progress. Erik ignored the shot and pressed on.

'Erik! Not that way! Turn back. Not that way. They will kill us!' cried Cecelia, her panic rising by the moment.

In the dark it was difficult to see what had happened to the Defender but when the search light came on it was clear that the vehicle was well and truly stuck. Two of the four men were out, trying to push it out of the mud. The driver was revving the engine while the fourth, standing to one side, was now firing at them. His shots were getting closer and closer but since there was no one to adjust the search-light he was shooting into the dark - more by instinct than at what he could actually see.

That alone, thought Erik, might just save their lives.

It now became apparent why Erik had moved towards his pursuers rather than away from them. He was looking for a particularly narrow part of the waterway. He had now reached it and with a sharp swerve to his right plunged off the bog and straight onto the surface of the frozen loch.

Jamie McBane, reloading his gun as quickly as he could, stared in astonishment as the quad-bike skidded onto the surface of the loch.

Ice! It had never occurred to him that the narrow loch might be frozen over. He never for one moment thought that that would be their means of escape. Clever! Very clever! He had to admire that young man's courage and originality. He must have *known* that that part of the loch was frozen solid! That's why he came back towards them. That's why he had stopped. He was looking for his chosen crossing place. Clever young bastard.

All the more reason why he must now die!

Jamie McBane fired again and again at the quad-bike as it slithered and slid across that treacherous ice. Erik could feel the frozen surface starting to give way as they reached the centre of the loch but he pressed on. The groaning of that ice was actually more frightening than the bullets that whistled about their ears, some bouncing off the ice on either side of them. Cecelia, more frightened than she had ever been in her short life, clung on for dear life, longing for this nightmare to be over - whatever its outcome.

Death might be better that this protracted agony, she reasoned.

She was startled out of her mental state by a great cry of triumph from Erik as the quad-bike bounced up the bank on the far side of the lock and hit frozen mud once more.

'Yipeeeee!' he yelled, at the top of his voice.

It was not over yer, however, for a hail of bullets followed them as they careered across the bog. All four men were now firing at them.

They had only gone about two hundred meters when Erik felt a searing pain in his left shoulder. He had been hit. For a moment he panicked but when he realised that it was only a flesh wound and that nothing was broken he pressed his foot even further down on the accelerator and hurtled across the bog, deliberately taking an erratic course, swerving from one side to another.

Soon the shots from behind them became fewer and fewer until, eventually they stopped altogether. Silence fell about them like a great blanket. Only the sound of the quad-bike's engine troubled the great void above them.

A break in the clouds revealed a galaxy of stars, shining down on them. It was a sign, though Erik. They were safe at last!

On his left was a small loch and on his right a narrow stream. He saw exactly where they were. It was his route. If he followed this stream, keeping it on his right, it would take them directly to the A82. That was the route he had planned and it had worked!

Cecelia had not at first realised that Erik had been hit. It was not until she felt that his sleeve was wet with blood that she knew what had happened.

'Erik, we must stop. You have been hit, my darling. Stop. Let me fix your arm. I can drive this thing. Please stop.'

'No. We are nearly there. The main road is straight ahead. Another mile or so and we are safe. I am fine. Let's get to the main road then we can stop and have a look. Its only a graze, I'm sure.'

It took them a further ten minutes to reach the main road. Erik crashed straight through a wooden gate in his excitement, skidded to a halt, turned the quad-bike south and set off at speed down the main road.

The road itself was still covered in deep snow but was flat and clearly defined with wooden posts marking both sides of the road at regular intervals.

'Erik', cried Cecelia above the roar of their engine, 'what about you arm? Please let me fix it.'

'No, I'm fine. Let's press on. We need to get to Tyndrum. If there are police there they might even be able to catch those bastards back on the moor. It did not look as if they were going anywhere after I lured them into that bog. How are you feeling now?'

'Much better, thank you. You are definitely my hero. Sorry I was such a wet back there. Its not every night that one gets strung up naked in a plastic bag in a deep freezer than shot at in the dark.'

'What? I cannot hear you? What did you say about being naked?'

'Nothing. I'll tell you all about it later!'

They were just rounding a corner when the road ahead of them was suddenly and rather unexpectedly flooded in a great pool light - as if a massive searchlight was being shone straight into their faces. Erik barely had time to skid to a halt, stopping only yards away from the front end of an enormous snow-plough being driven by a huge tractor that now seemed to tower above them.

On the tractor's cabin roof was an array of lights that flooded the entire road and a large part of the countryside beyond.

Cecelia slipped of the seat of the quad-bike and ran forward, gesticulating wildly at the astonished young man dressed entirely in yellow who was even then climbing down from his cabin.

'Please help us', cried Cecelia. 'Erik has been shot. He is wounded. He needs help. Urgent help.'

When she looked round to point back towards the quad-bike she saw that Erik had fallen off the saddle onto the road and was now lying unconscious in a pool of blood.

24
Thursday, 24th October

John was not the first to hear that distinctive sound perhaps but he was probably the first to recognise its significance.

It was now five in the morning on Thursday, 24th October. Rannoch Moor was as dark and as ominous as ever but there were subtle indications in the east of a new dawn creeping up over the mountains towards Loch Rannoch.

Detective Chief Inspector John White had risen early, probably nearer four o'clock that morning. He was now dressed and fully awake. He had, however, slept extremely badly; a troubled sleep full of dreams and terrifying images of headless, frozen bodies hanging from the ceiling of his bedroom. Poppy was still blissfully asleep. Like most of the other residents still in their beds that morning, she had absolutely no idea what was about to happen.

Nor indeed did John but the sound of three or four helicopters rapidly approaching the hotel was enough to give him a good indication of what was to follow.

* * *

None of the McBanes had slept much that night either. The discovery that the blonde girl had somehow escaped from the cold-store and that she and the young Norwegian camper had set off across the moor on the estate's one and only quad-bike was not an encouraging start to their day. When, much later, in the very early hours of the morning, Jamie and three exhausted ghillies walked back into the hotel, then a kind of deep despondency descended upon the McBanes - at least those who were awake that morning.

Jamie McBane's devastating news that the two runaways had eluded them and were even now probably well on their way to Crianlarich filled Ronald, Moray and Marie McBane with absolute panic.

There followed a frantic hour or two as all seven of them emptied the cold-store and carted the five or so frozen bodies they had been storing there to the furnace, flinging them into the flames. Moray, meanwhile, went through his other fridges removing liver, brains, kidneys and other choice cuts of human meat - not forgetting Paula Leamington's still-bubbling head in its greasy stock-pot. These too were consigned to the flames in a desperate effort to destroy the evidence of widespread, persistent cannibalism.

It was because of this frantic and all-consuming activity that Ronald, Moray and Marie - plus the four ghillies helping them - were slow to realise that there were now three police helicopters hovering low over the roof of their hotel. From each helicopter armed police officers wearing helmets and body-armour rapidly descended on lines falling to the ground.

It all happened in less than two minutes.

Once on the ground, the three SWAT teams spread out. One occupied the hotel itself, the second surrounded the kitchens, stables and furnace room and the third took up positions on the outer perimeter of the hamlet - to round up any of the McBanes now slowly emerging from their cottages.

The team entering the hotel quickly gathered together the night staff, some of whom were still unaware of what exactly was happening. Two of the night porters had spotted the helicopters from a distance and had panicked, trying to hide in the attic. They too were soon discovered and apprehended, as were the two cleaners hiding in a cupboard on the second floor. By this time a number of frightened guests had appeared on the landing in their dressing-gowns, demanding to know what was going on. They were politely but firmly told to return to their bedrooms and wait there until called.

John White had also appeared on the landing. He showed his warrant card to the team leader and was immediately taken to the officer in overall charge.

'Well sir, I'm not sure I care much for your choice of hotel!' he said, after they had introduced themselves and shaken hands.

'Indeed, Inspector. Its not one I would now recommend - even to my enemies. The man you want most is Ronald McBane. He's the Manager. Be careful though, the four or five professional ghillies here are up to their necks in it all and armed. Tell your men to take care. One called Jamie McBane is the ring-leader. He is probably the most dangerous.'

'Thank you sir. I'll catch up with you later. I suggest you return to your room. We can handle this. Might be safer anyway, if there is any shooting.'

John did as he was told and retuned to his bedroom where Poppy was peering out of their bedroom window anxiously. The moment she saw him she ran into his arms and hugged him.

'Oh John, I thought you had been hurt. Where were you when I woke up? Did you know this was going to happen?'

'Yes and no, darling. Anyway, come away from the window. We have been told to stay here. There might be some shooting. Its all under control but still dangerous, do you understand?'
At that point Elspeth and Gabriélle appeared at their bedroom door.

'Come in, quickly you two. It looks, Gabriélle, as if your case has been blown wide open. There are three SWAT teams here to arrest the entire McBane family. About bloody time too, I say!'

'What?' exclaimed Gabriélle. 'How? Why? Who called them in? Was it you, John? Tell me at once.'

She was clearly very angry. It took both Poppy and Elspeth a while to calm her down. Eventually she sat on the bed, staring angrily at the carpet.

'I'm not sure who did call them in, Gabriélle, but they are here and there is nothing we can do about it. Now, if all three of you will sit down quietly on the bed I will tell you *why* they are here. I must warn you, though, that it is not good news - for any of us.'

* * *

Moray McBane was discovered in his kitchen with his hands in a large bowl of something that looked like human lungs. He was caught, therefore, literally red-handed.

Marie was apprehended in her office, desperately trying to burn (in her waste-paper basket) several plastic containers she had clearly taken from her safe for its door was still open and other papers lay scattered on the carpet. She was immediately apprehended, the flames extinguished and the half-burned evidence bagged. Her computer's hard-drive was also taken and placed for security in one of the helicopters.

She was then handcuffed and taken to the resident's lounge where she and the others so far arrested were being held under armed guard. She was in tears at this stage and as pale as a ghost.

Neil and Alec were arrested and disarmed behind the furnace room where they were found hiding under a tarpaulin. It was an ignominious end to their long career of murder and mayhem but they surrendered quietly enough. They too were handcuffed but this time they were both taken to one of the helicopters where they were placed under armed guard.

Ronald and Jamie had disappeared but tracks leading from behind the furnace room suggested that one of them at least had taken off across the fields at the back of the hotel. A team of three armed officers was immediately despatched to track him down and apprehend him.

It was Ronald McBane who had chosen to run off into the dark. It was easy enough to follow his footsteps in the snow but the officers moved cautiously, not knowing if he was armed or not.

They eventually found him cowering in a storm-drain at the edge of the estate. He was lying, curled up in a tight ball in a pool of muddy water and sobbing loudly. He was a pathetic sight but it was with extreme caution that the police officers dragged him out by his feet and made him stand upright while they searched him for weapons. He stood there, shivering, pale as a ghost. His blue eyes had lost their lustre. He looked like an utterly broken man. The police had to almost carry him back to the helicopter where he was handcuffed and his feet secured with plastic ties. He was then placed under armed guard in the back of one of the helicopters.

Through all this he said absolutely nothing, merely sobbed and took great gulps of air, as if he were suffering a huge and devastating panic attack - as well he might have been.

The younger members of the McBane family were gathered together and put in the dining room under guard but accompanied by the only WPC on the SWAT team. She tried to calm them down then started taking preliminary statements from several of the older children. There were no women present - they were being held under armed guard in the Library.

The one missing man - Jamie McBane - proved the most illusive of all.

He had last been seen, according to Neil McBane, behind the stables but had now vanished. The search for him involved at least ten armed officers. They began by searching all the outhouses, then spread out beyond the staff cottages and towards the railway station. It was here, at the far end of the platform, that a police officer spotted tracks heading north, along the railway line itself. If it was Jamie McBane then it was clear that he had a good head-start on them, for while his tracks clearly disappeared off into the distance the man himself was nowhere to be seen.

It was decided immediately to utilise one of the helicopters. Four officers clambered aboard and the helicopter took off in a swirl of snow. It rose rapidly into the air then dipped its nose and headed north, following the railway line that leads, eventually, to Fort William.

Police helicopters have, as part of their equipment, thermal imaging detectors. These cameras can spot heat emissions. A human, on the run for examples, emits a 'trail' of heat that the camera in a helicopter can pick up at some distance. It was this device that within minutes of the police helicopter taking off, spotted someone running through a wood adjacent to the railway line. It was, by all accounts, a single individual moving fast on foot.

The moving figure appeared to be running parallel with the line, using the wood for cover. The helicopter pilot decided to keep his distance and see what happened.

Instructions from back at the hotel had warned the officers on board that this man could be Jamie McBane and that he was almost certainly armed and dangerous.

Suddenly, and quite unexpectedly, the thermal image disappeared off the computer screen. It was as if the man had completely vanished! At first the police officers were puzzled but close examination of their map showed that ahead lay a snow tunnel, through which the line passed. It was just possible that their fugitive was hiding in that tunnel - a place impervious to their thermal tracking device. The order came back from the hotel to land and investigate.

The helicopter moved closer to the snow tunnel and hovered as lines were dropped and all four officers slid down to the ground. The helicopter immediately rose high, to act as an observation platform, just in case the fugitive made a dash for it from the far end of the tunnel. The men on the ground then spread out and moved cautiously on foot to the entrance of the tunnel. The police used hand signals only. The coordinated move forward into position at the entrance to the tunnel was thus done in complete silence.

Here the railway line did indeed disappear into a low 'tunnel' made of curved sheets of concrete designed merely to protect the track from snow drifts. It was unlit, since there were no trains running. The officers approached the tunnel and peered into the darkness. Some had night vision visors.

Suddenly a shot rang out and a policeman, struck full in the chest, was propelled backwards onto his back. A second and a third shot rang out. By this time all the policemen had either taken cover to one side of the tunnel entrance or were lying flat on the snow. Two of the injured man's colleagues crawled forward and pulled him to safety. His body armour had probably saved his life but he was badly winded. He lay there groaning in agony while one of the officers removed the man's flack jacket to check for other possible injury.

The officer in charge then spoke rapidly into his radio and gave a prearranged hand signal to his men. In the process he singled out two individual officers - both marksmen - to assume their firing positions. They both wore dark visors on their helmets, completely covering their faces.

It was then that something rather dramatic happened.

There was a roar of engines and the helicopter suddenly appeared at the far end of the tunnel, hovering only feet above the track. It was facing directly into the tunnel entrance. It then turned on its search lights - to reveal Jamie McBane standing upright in the tunnel, his gun to his shoulder. He was now silhouetted starkly against the helicopter's powerful lights.

'Police. Armed police. Lay down your gun.'

Jamie spun round to see what was happening but then immediately turned back the way he had been facing moments before and fired off two rapid shots towards the policeman who had shouted.

Immediately two police shots rang out.

The first struck Jamie on the shoulder, knocking him sideways.

The second shot struck him on the calf, forcing him to drop to his knees.

'Lay down your gun. Armed police! Lay down your gun immediately!'

The call echoed once more in the tunnel but Jamie ignored it. He immediately let out a great cry of pain and anger and staggered to his feet, firing rapidly straight at the police now advancing towards him.

A third shot, this time fatal, struck him in the chest, propelling him backwards. He lay on the floor of the tunnel in a rapidly spreading pool of blood.

Thus it was that the professional hunter (murderer and psychopath) was hunted down and shot - just as he had done to countless of his innocent victims.

25

You can image the confusion at the Rannoch Moor Hotel following that dawn raid by three helicopters containing SWAT teams of armed policemen.

It took all the efforts of the police that morning to calm down distraught residents, all of whom were demanding explanations and assurances that it was now safe to leave the security of their bedrooms. For several hours the police deliberately prevented residents from leaving their rooms, just so that they could process the large number of arrests and complete the preliminary questioning that they had to attend to, unimpeded by angry, confused or simply frightened guests.

There was, however, some relief when the snowploughs from Kinloch Rannoch finally arrived. The road out off the moor was now open and those guests who wanted to leave immediately were free to do so. They left in their droves, but not before the police had taken names and addresses.

Amongst the first to leave was Teddy Bosenquet and his bride-to-be, Lady Olympia Garland. Teddy fired up his Bugatti and sped down the drive as fast as he could go. He was followed by many others - or at least, those who had cars. The railway line was still closed so guests who had arrived by train either had to arrange alternative transport out of Rannoch Moor or wait for the coaches that had been booked to take railway passengers by road either to Crianlarich, where the railway line south was now clear, or north to Fort William and beyond.

These coaches arrived later that afternoon so that by tea-time almost all the guests had left.

* * *

John had left his wife and friends in a state of deep shock that morning, soon after the raid had begun.

While inbreeding, incest and now murder were very much on the cards, none of the four had suspected cannibalism amongst the McBanes. Not for one minute had any of them ever though that Moray and his staff would be serving up human meat to their guests. The thought that all four of them had now eaten human flesh unwittingly was something they were each finding difficult to come to terms with. That alone, apart from the horrors of Moray McBane's cold store or the missing guests, assumed dead, would take them all a long time to get over.

When Poppy had been told earlier that morning, she had rushed to the bathroom and thrown up in the sink. Elspeth too had felt extremely queasy and had had to lie down on Poppy's bed.

'Is there no end to what these beats are capable of?' asked Poppy, when she had recovered sufficiently.

'Clearly not', said Gabriélle. 'The fact is, though, they must have been doing it for years. Apart from their own insatiable needs it was also a neat way to dispose of the bodies of their victims. What they could not recycle as food they cremated, thereby destroying the evidence and heating their greenhouse at the same time. It may be bizarre and indescribably horrible but when you think about it it does make economic sense!'

Elspeth and Gabriélle left later that morning in Gabriélle's hired car. Before she left, John introduced her to the Investigating Officer - Detective Inspector Tom Palmer from Aberdeen. He was the man who had led the SWAT teams earlier that morning. He was delighted to meet such an attractive police officer and agreed to co-operate fully with the French police in the months leading up to the inevitable trial. He apologised for moving in on her case but the evidence produced by Erik Bergman and Cecelia Arnold left them no alternative than to move in quickly, before anyone else died.

'OK, you two', said John as they bid Gabriélle and Elspeth goodbye in the hotel forecourt. 'Let's meet up soon, in Dunkeld this time. I have had my fill of expensive hotels, especially where the food is of such dubious quality. I need to stay here for a few more hours but Poppy and I will be going home later this afternoon.'

'Goodbye, John', said Gabriélle. 'I'm sorry I did not come the clean earlier on but, well, you understand why.'

'I understand perfectly. I will let you both know what happens over the next few weeks. I suspect that you will both be involved in the lead up to the trial. All your research will not have been in vain, Gabriélle.'

They kissed each other, then Gabriélle threw their suitcases into the boot of the hired car. Poppy and John watched as they drove off.

* * *

The hotel, now almost totally devoid of staff, was taken over later that afternoon by a Manager brought in from Pitlochry. He was given the responsibility of maintaining health and safety for the few guest still at the hotel. In time, the hotel would be closed but for the moment it was one huge crime-scene.

The kitchens, cottages and outbuildings were therefore cordoned off and the public ordered to stay away. That afternoon, a large team from the Forensic Laboratories in Aberdeen arrived in four white vans and began the long and meticulous task of examining each of those areas where it was thought human bodies had either been butchered or stored. It was a grisly business and even hardened Forensic scientist and technicians were disturbed by the extent of human remains found on the estate.

Indeed, the furnaces were alight when the SWAT team had first arrived on the scene. The officer in charge had the presence of mind to put the fire out. Even if the contents of that furnace were now a pile of very wet ashes, his prompt action preserved at least three of the bodies the McBanes had tried to destroy.

It was there that the Forensic team began its detailed examinations.

Also that afternoon, several police vehicles and coaches arrived to take away those who had been arrested, pending further investigation. There were, in total, forty-seven, including women and children.

The children were separated from the female adults and taken in a separate coach to a local authority Care Home near Pitlochry. The slow, careful process of examination and questioning of these children - most of whom who it was thought had been subject to sexual abuse - would begin here. It was a delicate process and one that would take many months.

Ronald, Moray, Marie and the three ghillies were taken in a custodial police van, first to Police HQ in Perth where, over the next day or so they were questioned and charged. They were then taken to HR Prison, Perth where they were to remain on remand, pending further investigations and trial.

* * *

'Tell me, Inspector Palmer, who called in your SWAT teams? Someone must have acted decisively. Who actually gave the call?'

Detective Chief Inspector John White and Investigating Officer Detective Inspector Tom Palmer were having coffee in the Library after what had been a very hectic afternoon. It was the first chance the two most senior officers there had had a chance to talk.

'You did, sir.'

'Me? Really? You mean my Morse code message got through? Wow!'

'It not only got through, it was passed onto us within minutes of the railway people at Crianlarich getting it. They were somewhat surprised, however. That telegraph system had not been used in living memory. When it suddenly rattled into life late Wednesday night, the duty signalman nearly wet himself. Mind you, you were dead lucky. If that lad had not been a Sea Scout in his youth your message might have fallen on deaf ears. Still, he not only deciphered your message but immediately sent it on by FAX to the Police in Perth. The rest, they say, is history.'

'But what about young Erik and that girl, Cecelia? I assume that they escaped but did their message get passed on as well?'

'Not immediately, as far as I understand. The lad had been shot so their priority was to get him to hospital in Crianlarich. However, the moment they saw those images you had taken on the girl's mobile phone, the local police emailed them straight through to Aberdeen. They had been dithering somewhat, I suspect but when the girl then showed the police your card and mentioned Security Code Five, Management pulled finger and called in the troops. Since we had no means of contacting you or anyone else on site, we assumed the worst and sent in three armed SWAT teams - just in case. That Norwegian lad nearly died of loss of blood from his gunshot wound. If that's what the McBanes could do to their guests, then God knows what else was going on.'

* * *

Poppy White was packed and ready when John eventually got back to their room. She was sitting on the bed looking decidedly queasy.

John sat on the bed beside her and gave her a hug. She smiled weakly, laid her head on his shoulder and began to cry.

It took half-an-hour for her to stop crying. John felt decidedly guilty at having left her alone so long in her room but there was much to do downstairs and as the most senior officer on site he knew where his official duty lay that day. Still, he had clearly underestimated the impact that day's events had had on Poppy. That, together with the shocking news about the food they had all been eating for the last week, had clearly had a profound effect on his emotionally fragile wife. The sooner he got her home, the better.

Eventually, she recovered sufficiently for them to gather together their belongings and move down to the foyer.

'Thank you Tom for your splendid work today. Excellent operation. Pity we lost Jamie McBane. I would like to have seen that degenerate bastard in the dock. Still, you have plenty of other McBanes to get your teeth into. Call me if you think I can be of any help over the next few months.'

The two police officers shook hands. Poppy, who had stepped into the ladies to powder her nose, them followed John into the forecourt where he had begun to load the car.

'Well, my darling', said John as they drove off, 'I think we can safely say that that this is one wedding anniversary we will never forget!'

* * *

Later that afternoon, three police officers inspected the rooms throughout the hotel, to ensure that all the guests had departed.

They were anxious to close down the hotel, make it secure and send the troops home. A night watchman and two policemen would ensure that the property remained secure and that none of the crime scenes were tampered until Forensic had completed its painstaking work. Otherwise, there was no reason to remain in this desolate spot, particularly in the light of all the horrible things that had gone on here in recent weeks.

They were surprised, therefore, to find one of the rooms still occupied. They assumed it was occupied for from inside they could hear muffled sobbing.

Cautiously they opened the bedroom door. It was dark but when they switched on the light they saw a middle-aged man lying on the bed in his vest and pants. He was extremely distraught and appeared to clutching his bed cover as if it were some kind of security blanket.

'Sir, are you alright? Police. Can we help? What are you doing here? The hotel is deserted. Its time to go home. Sir?'

The man said nothing but simply turned his face to the wall and sobbed even louder. The police officers stepped into the room and drew closer to the bed which, they noticed, was strewn with menus. There were notebooks on the floor and a laptop on the bedside table.

'Sir, what's your name? We need to close the hotel. You have to leave. Can we help you? You seem very upset. What's the matter?'

'What's the matter, young man? What's the matter? Everything. Absolutely everything! I'm ruined. Utterly ruined.'

He had now sat up on the bed and appeared suddenly animated. The officers were somewhat startled at this abrupt transformation. They stepped back slightly, their hands automatically moving to their batons hanging on their belts. Perhaps he was mad. Dangerous even?

'My name is, was, Dr Thomas Neep. I am, young man, a Michelin Guide Food Inspector. For the last week I have been eating human flesh. And do you know what, young man, not only could I not tell the difference from ordinary meat but I actually enjoyed it!'

Epilogue

Dunkeld, Perthshire. The pretty, riverside cottage where Poppy and John White live is covered in snow but inside it is warm and cosy.

It is three days before Christmas. There is a small, decorated Christmas tree in one corner of the room and holly above the fireplace. Elspeth and Gabriélle are sitting in the lounge warming their toes before a roaring, log fire. They are drinking a rather fine Chardonnay from John's cellar (much enlarged since his promotion to Detective Chief Inspector) and nibbling home-made cheese straws, biscuits and paté.

Poppy, who had been bustling about in the kitchen, now enters and takes charge of the proceedings.

It would be something of a generalisation to claim that the wives of senior police officers are of a similar disposition when it comes to 'tying up loose ends' but Poppy had read enough detective fiction to know that a get-together of the key players in the arrest in October of the entire McBane tribe was absolutely necessary if she, above all, was to make sense of this somewhat sensational case. Fourteen McBane adults have been arrested, some for murder. Eleven children have been taken into care by the local authorities and the trial is scheduled for early next year. The Rannoch Moor Hotel is now closed. It was time, therefore, to give this remarkable case some closure too.

To that end Poppy has invited Elspeth and her French lover to stay at Dunkeld for the weekend. She has booked a table for four at Mario's Italian restaurant in the village and it is there that they are heading later this evening. Meanwhile, with the troops thus gathered, it is time to begin what Agatha Christie, celebrated author of classic detective fiction and creator of Miss Marple and Hercule Poirot, used to call the *dénouement*.

'Cheers everyone! Happy Christmas.'

They raised their glasses and sipped their Chardonnay.

'Now', said Poppy, with a determination that John recognised all too readily, 'I think Gabriélle should begin. Are we all sitting comfortably? Good. Gabriélle, tell us absolutely everything!'

Gabriélle took another long sip of her wine. She badly needed a cigarette but had already been told off (nicely, though) for lighting up on arrival earlier that afternoon. Still, Elspeth - another serial smoker - was also suffering in silence so that was some consolation. Elspeth, who was sitting next to her on the sofa, gave Gabriélle's knee a friendly squeeze and smiled encouragingly.

Gabriélle took a deep breath and began.

'It all started when two French citizens, quite unconnected with each other, disappeared mysteriously after staying at the now infamous Rannoch Moor Hotel. Both disappearances took place within a two year period. One was an Alpinist from Grenoble, the other a gourmet from Nantes. Their individual cases were investigated by officers of the National Gendarmerie in their respective communes but their cases remain unsolved. Neither man has ever been found, dead or alive.'

'I assume', asked John, 'that Marie McBane could prove that each man had paid his bill and checked out of the hotel?'

'Yes, their credit card records confirmed this. What was even more confusing was that both cards had been used *subsequent* to their departure from Rannoch Moor in the areas where they each came from. Each 'missing' person had used an ATM machine in their local area from which small amounts of cash had been taken. This threw us completely.'

'How do you explain that?' ask John. 'That surely put the McBanes in the clear, did it not?'

'Perhaps. The only explanation we could come up with was that someone had visited these two areas and deliberately used the cards to distance both men even further from the Rannoch Moor Hotel. Maybe at trial we will learn how they did this. Perhaps they had an agent in Europe or a relative living abroad? We have yet to find anyone like that. Whatever the explanation, there was nothing, on paper at least, to connect these disappearances with Rannoch Moor. Since there was no communication between either investigating officer in their respective regional areas, no one spotted that both missing individuals had disappeared immediately after staying at the *same* hotel - or so it seemed.'

'So what happened next?'

'What happened next was that we identified a *third* missing person, a woman this time. She was from Perpignan, in the south-west corner of France. The local representative of the *police judiciaire* ran her name through the missing persons list on the French police database and immediately spotted a connection with our two other missing French citizens - The Rannoch Moor Hotel. He was the first one to 'join up the dot.''

'Dots, darling. Its 'dots', not dot.' added Elspeth helpfully. She gave Gabriélle another encouraging squeeze on the knee.

'So Gabriélle, when did you become involved?', asked Poppy.

'I became involved in June of this year. I was at that time with the Direction centrale de la police judiciaire (DCPJ) in Paris. At this stage it was merely a preliminary investigation. If I thought there was a case to answer my evidence would be presented to a Judge who would then authorise a full police investigation, probably involving Interpol. In less than a week, with the use of Interpol's database, I was able to identify no less than five EU citizens who had disappeared over a seven-year period. All were lone individuals with interests in sport or food. Every one of them had stayed, unaccompanied in most cases, at the Rannoch Moor Hotel. None came home.'

'What did you then know about the McBanes?', asked John.

'Very little at that stage. We ran a background check on Ronald McBane. He was now listed as Manager. He seemed the best place to start but he was as clean as the whistle, I think you say.'

Gabriélle glanced nervously at Elspeth - who smiled and nodded encouragingly.

'OK, so you linked the suspicious disappearances of five individuals to the Rannoch Moor Hotel but where on earth did the idea of cannibalism come from? Its one thing to *suspect* possible abduction or even murder but quite another to suppose that these poor folk had been eaten!'

'I know, John. It sounds incredible. None of my colleagues believed me - not until I stumbled on something that happened near Leysin, in Switzerland in 2007. I had been looking into the McBane family history, concentrating on Ronald McBane. I had no idea at that stage that the entire family was involved in running the hotel and its estate. I soon discovered, however, that none of the McBanes had ever travelled abroad. The one exception was Ronald. For eighteen months he studied in Switzerland at the Swiss Hotel Management School in Leysin. He never completed his course. In fact, he left Switzerland somewhat abruptly, in November, 2007'.

'Did you find out why?' asked Poppy.

'No, but earlier that month a teenager had died in mysterious circumstances. The boy's body was found in a climbing hut three miles from the mountain village of Feyday. He had been strangled and sexually assaulted. His assailant left no DNA however, none that we could find. The really disturbing element in this case was that he had also been mutilated. Sections of flesh had been cut from his buttocks and thighs. At first it was assumed that this was just mutilation by a deranged killer but our Forensic people came up with the bizarre idea that this could have been the act of someone with cannibalistic tendencies.'

'Was this an isolated case or were there more?' asked John. 'I have a horrible feeling that you are going to tell us that there were more!

Gabriélle took another sip of her wine. Her hand was trembling slightly. Elspeth, seeing that she was upset, gently stroked her back.

'Yes, you are right. When we started collating the evidence we came across an alarming number of cases involving cannibalism in France. Nicolas Cocaigne in 2007 and Nicolas Claux in 1994 are too of the better-know examples. Claux was convicted of the murder of thirty-four-year-old Thierry Bissonier. Then there was the infamous case of Japanese student, Issei Sagawa. One day he propositioned a Dutch friend only to have his advances rejected. Sagawa shot and killed her and then sexually assaulted her corpse. He carved away pieces of his victim's body, including her breasts and buttocks, and consumed them. He was arrested in France in 1981 but never stood trial. He was held in a mental institution for a year or so before being returned to Japan, where he rapidly acquired celebrity status.'

'How terrible! What about other cases, outside France?', asked Poppy.

'Helsinki, Finland. In 1999 two men and a teenage girl were sent to prison for the torture, murder and cannibalism of a twenty-three-year-old man. In 1999, Dmitry Dyomin and two other accomplices abducted a fifteen-year-old girl in Kiev. The girl was eventually murdered and her tongue was removed and eaten by Dyomin. He and his accomplices decapitated the girl and kept the skull as a trophy. The difference between Dyomin and Ronald and Moray McBane is that our men used human heads to make meat stock!'

'Going back to the boy in Switzerland, was there anything to connect Ronald McBane with his murder?'

'Not really, Poppy. Although Ronald had been living only seventeen miles from where that boy was strangled and had left the country soon afterwards - and without finishing his management training course - he was never a suspect for that boy's murder. Why not? Because, again, no one made the obvious connection. No one had any reason to suspect a trainee hotel manager from Scotland with the murder of a Swiss boy in some remote mountain hut. No one, except me, that is - but then I was the only police officer in Europe actually *looking* for Ronald McBane.'

'So what did you do?'

'We decided to merely note the possible connection and reinvestigate that killing later. My immediate priority was to link Ronald McBane or others at that hotel with the disappearance of at least five EU citizens. However, I found the cannibalism issue fascinating, not least because it might just explain these possible murders. I consulted an American expert, Dr. Clancy McKenzie. He is a psychology professor at Capital University in Washington. He was too busy to help but he recommended Elspeth whom he had met at a conference in New York a year or so ago. He knew that she lived in Edinburgh but often worked in Oxford and was familiar with the subject. It was now October. I decided to see if she could help me. I immediately took a flight to London, hired a car and drove up to Oxford and for the next three days stalked her!'

'You stalked her?'

'Yes, well, I was already feeling way out of the depths so I thought I would approach her gradually, rather than barge in.'

'She started by attending one of my lectures at Oxford', added Elspeth. 'She then followed me back to 'Arse Holes' (All Souls) and accosted me in the street. Over drinks in the Turf Tavern she told me nothing about who she was or why she had been stalking me, other than that she needed my professional help. I thought she was just trying to pick me up. However, the more time we spent together that evening, the more we became attracted to each other. Anyway, we ended up in bed at the Randolph that night. The following morning I persuaded her to come back to Edinburgh with me. It was on the journey north that she spun me 'I am a journalist making a documentary about incest' story - the little minx! There was no talk of cannibalism at this stage, least of all murder. She only told me all about that later. I am still not entirely sure why she was so secretive at this stage. Anyway, we set off for Rannoch Moor the following morning.'

'And who said Romance was dead', quipped John, with a wicked grin and a wink at Elspeth.

Since this appeared to be a natural break in the *dénouement*, John fetched another bottle of Chardonnay from his fridge and refreshed everyone's glasses. Meanwhile, Poppy disappeared briefly into the kitchen, returning with a plate of salmon and cream-cheese *vol-au-vent*.

'So, Elspeth...', said Poppy, as she resumed her seat, 'you were now part of Gabriélle's investigation. When did she tell you what her 'documentary' was really about?'

'Never, really - as far as the 'missing persons, possibly murdered' scenario was concerned. I only knew about that - as did you two - when the Mitchell letter surfaced and Gabriélle eventually came clean that she was a French detective involved in a murder hunt. As far as I was concerned her 'documentary' was entirely about incest. However, in bed that night in my flat in Edinburgh she casually mentioned the possibility also of cannibalism. It was quite a shock, I must say. I'm not sure that I believed her at first but later, once we were at the hotel on Rannoch Moor, the more convinced I became that she was on to something. Anyway, that night in Edinburgh she told me what she knew about Ronald McBane. It was not much to go on but I agreed to help her in any way I could, not for money but because it was an exciting challenge. We decided there and then to visit the hotel and stay for a long weekend, just to check them out. Gabriélle was planning to do that anyway but with me along it meant we could double our efforts. Once we checked in and met Ronald and his ghastly family it all fell into place rather quickly, I must say. You could see immediately that the entire tribe was the product of interbreeding. As I later told John, distal renal tubular acidosis was the most obvious symptom.'

'What's that?' asked Poppy.

'Poor renal excretion. This leads to acidemia, which causes

osteomalacia. In other words, weak proximal muscles resulting in poor posture, bad backs and even rickets. The McBanes also showed below-average height and frequent facial asymmetry. It was soon clear to me that we were dealing with a far more complex situation than even Gabriélle had anticipated. If we could prove inbreeding, then incest and possible child-abuse naturally followed. At this stage I had, as I said earlier, no idea that Gabriélle was primarily investigating possible murder. What was clear, however, was that someone needed to expose the McBanes for what they were - murderous, incestuous cannibals.'

'At what point, John, did the Scottish police become involved. Presumably their interest in the McBanes predates Gabriélle's?'

'Yes, by some five months. We had been tipped off that there was possible child- abuse on that estate. Undercover officers and social workers had visited the hotel on a number of occasions. We had no scientific evidence of inbreeding but it did not take much expertise to see that the McBanes were an extremely odd bunch. At that stage we had no idea that cannibalism was also taking place and absolutely no idea that the McBanes were possibly killing their guests, either for sport or to stock their ghastly larders.'

'My primary aim', added Gabriélle, 'was to try and find out what had happened to those European citizens who had vanished. Incest, child-abuse and even cannibalism were of secondary concern to me at that stage, although they provided a ready excuse for my documentary 'cover'.'

'But why did you not tell Elspeth the *real* purpose of your investigation, let alone that you were working for the French police?'

'I wanted Elspeth to see what was going on scientifically - not as a possible murder investigation but as a place where, because of the peculiar psychological character and perverse nature of the McBanes, a number of atrocities were possible - incest, child-abuse *and* even murder perhaps. I wanted her objective observations, professional insights or intuitions - *not* forensic proof. That was my job. Besides, if Elspeth knew that I was on a murder investigation she would have been obliged to inform the local police at once. I could not risk that at this stage. I had no idea that the Scottish police were remotely involved already. Had I known that from the start I might have played it entirely differently. I admit that it was wrong to deceived Elspeth, even though I am still not convinced that she ever fell for my deceit. She's far too intelligent to be taken in by a so-called 'journalist'. Why did she call you at Dunkeld if she was not already suspicious?'

'Indeed. But tell us more about what you found at Rannoch - particularly in those first few days.' It was John who asked this question.

'Once I saw how the hotel was run I could see how easy it could be for Ronald or his brothers to pick off vulnerable guests. Those travelling alone, without partners would be prime subjects. How they died was also relatively easy to guess. These individuals often went walking alone or hunting with McBane's staff. It would be easy to kill them on the open moor, far from anyone else and then dispose of their bodies. I also discovered the large furnace behind the hotel. You could cremate a body in there and nobody would be much the wiser. And that, so it subsequently proved, was exactly how they disposed of unwanted 'evidence'. The rest you and I - all of us at that hotel - ate!'

A voluntary shudder went round the room. Elspeth, caught reaching for the paté, rapidly withdrew her hand - somewhat sheepishly.

'Why *did* you call me, Elspeth?'

'I was worried. I wanted to help Gabriélle. For a Criminologist, a combination of inbreeding, incest and possible child-abuse is something of a Godsend - for research purposes, that is. The trouble was that I was not entirely convinced by Gabriélle's claim that she was a journalist. My worry was that, whoever she was, she might interfere with ongoing police investigations. I had no idea at what stage they might be but to cover my back I called you in Dunkeld. I told you everything I knew at that stage. I assumed that you would then tell Inverness, just so that they were aware that was someone else on their case. I never imagined that the following day *you* of all people would turn up at the hotel in Rannoch Moor, least of all with your gorgeous wife. Gabriélle immediately assumed that you were there officially, as a spy but then what kind of spy gives their full name and rank to reception. Besides, you are probably the best-known copper in Scotland, after the publicity that attended the Ledbetter case. The McBanes naturally knew who you were the moment you stepped through their front door. As far as you were concerned they were probably already on their best behaviour. With you here it seemed best, for the moment at least, for Gabriélle to stick to her journalist 'cover - even though I was myself was never entirely convinced by it.'

'Yes, but….'

'When the telephone lines disappeared because of the weather, Gabriélle and I were frankly relieved. It meant that she could keep her secret since you, presumably, had no way of finding out who she really was. I'm sorry to have lied to you John but there was a lot at stake. We needed to explain what we were doing with the McBanes without giving you a reason to arrest the lot of them or even interfere with Gabriélle's own investigation. It was a tricky situation. What was true was that Gabriélle did indeed have a hidden camera. She was secretly recording as much of the McBanes as she could, together with the layout of their estate. She never told me this at the time but she even managed to get a shot inside the furnace room and a bag of ashes. She would need that evidence to convince Interpol that there was a case to answer. At this stage, however, she still did not have any real, solid evidence - only alarming suspicions that grew worse and worse each day that we were here.'

'OK. I can see the need for secrecy although there was little I could have done to either help or hinder you. That's by-the-by. What I do *not* understand is how you made the cannibalism link to the McBanes. Where on earth did that come from?'

At this point an involuntary shudder ran round the room as each one present contemplated the enormity of their unwitting part in that horror. Each one of them had almost certainly eaten human flesh at that hotel - on the assumption, shared by hundreds of other guests over the years - that it was fresh food of the highest quality and cooked to perfection by a Master Chef. It was something that none of them would ever forget.

It was John who broke that awkward silence.

'As far as I can see, apart from a tenuous link with some mutilated lad in Switzerland, you had absolutely no evidence then that Ronald and his lot were actually eating their guests themselves, let alone serving them up as gourmet food! Is that not so, Elspeth?'

'Indeed. No proof whatsoever. That was what was so frustrating. We had always assumed that Ronald McBane was a lone serial-killer using the hotel as a way to target vulnerable guests. The idea that the entire family was involved in some way only occurred to us gradually. The incestuous nature of that family, their medical condition and ease of access to likely targets did suggest to me that we were dealing with a disturbed group of individuals, acting together. My own research into cannibalism had always concentrated on abnormal individuals, acting alone. The idea that these murders - if that is what they were - was a *team* effort was a startling idea and one which, eminent Profiler that I am, I had not even anticipated at that stage.'

'The break-though came', added Gabriélle, 'when I discovered that the McBane family name had disappeared abruptly from historical records, sometime in the early 18th Century. My *assistante de recherché* in Paris - working in association with the National Museum of Scotland - traced McBane as far back as 1750 but then, nothing! The record simply stops. One possible explanation was that they had *adopted* the name McBane at that time, changing it from something else. The question is: why would they have done that? It was then that Elspeth made a startling proposal. Elspeth, you tell them. I am so proud of you!'

Elspeth visibly glowed with pride, gave Gabriélle a kiss on the cheek and leant back comfortably into the cushions of the sofa.

'I know, I know!' she purred.

'Well go on then, Elspeth. Prove it!' said Poppy with a grin and a glance at John. John just smiled and raised his eyebrows as if to say - 'Well, Poppy, you know what's she's like!'

Elspeth took a large sip of her wine, placed it carefully on the table in front of her, and resumed her story.

'If McBane was not their original name then I assumed, naturally enough, that sometime in the past they had deliberately changed it from something else, some other clan name. Why would they have done that? To conceal the past? To make a clean break? To hide from some momentous event that had taken place from which they wished to be disassociated? It was only then that I had one of those wild, serendipitous moments. Since all the McBanes probably ate human flesh, it suddenly occurred to me that perhaps their real, *original* name was 'Beane'. This name is notorious in Scottish history. At the very beginning of the 17th Century the Beane family - and it was a very large one, almost a complete clan - lived on the remote Galloway coast, in sea-caves below Bennane Head. They stayed there hidden all through the day, emerging only at night to seize unwary travellers on the lonely road above the cliffs.'

'So they were robbers? Highwaymen?' said Poppy.

'Yes. Not uncommon in that area or in those times but these were robbers with a difference. A terrible difference! Their leader and patriarch was one 'Sawney Beane' - a man who raised eight sons, six daughters, eighteen grandsons and fourteen grand-daughters - on human flesh. Not only were they robbers they were also cannibals.'

There was a general intake of breath from Poppy and John. Gabriélle gazed lovingly at her mentor and lover as if Elspeth had just invented the internet or had solved the Poincaré conjecture. Elspeth, having paused for dramatic effect - which was duly noted by her rapt listeners - then continued with her account of their great 'break-through'.

'The Sawney Beane tribe was eventually captured - sometime in 1602 - after an extensive search by local militia. Their secret hideaway was discovered by chance one night by a fisherman. Inside, soldiers found a sea-cave littered with human bones and a family of some forty-eight or so individuals, including numerous children, all living in indescribably squalid conditions.'

'Incest?', asked John.

'Indeed. Incest was how that family had grown in such secrecy. Diseased, inbred and degenerate, they were unique - even for those barbaric times. Cornered and trapped in their squalid cave, the entire family was arrested and carried by boat to the harbour at Bute Wynd and then on to Edinburgh by horse-and-cart. The soldiers guarding the carts struggled hard to keep the irate country folk from stringing the entire family up there-and-then or stoning them to death at the roadside.'

'What eventually happened to them?' asked Poppy.

'There was no trial as such but their punishment was extreme. The men were dismembered and left to bleed to death in front of their women and children, who themselves were then burned alive. All this was watched by thousands of people who had come from all parts of Scotland to witness the gory end of Sawney Beane and his grotesque family.'

'That is terrible but can you prove that the McBanes are related to these historic cannibals? If they were effectively wiped out in 1602, well, that's over four hundred years ago!'

'I agree. We have no DNA from the Sawney Beanes so we cannot establish that blood line. Our theory though is that some of the original Sawney Beanes either escaped or were never captured in the first place. Somehow they survived and remained undetected over the years, even as practising cannibals. Gabriélle's subsequent research has collated a large number of recorded cases of cannibalism, between 1650 and the late 19th Century in Scotland. Some were even in the Fife area. These are all isolated cases of course but there have been few, if any, arrests. In other words, I think the Sawney Beanes survived, changed their name to McBane, prospered and multiplied and ended up running the hotel on Rannoch Moor where, unfortunately, we have all partaken of the excellent food. What part of that was of human origin, only Moray McBane can tell us but I for one will not be eating there again!'

'A horrible yet fascinating story', said Poppy, getting up from her chair. 'I think now we should go and have something to eat. It's eight and Mario is expecting us.'

'Elspeth has told me that Mario's is an excellent restaurant', said Gabriélle, 'but does he have a vegetarian option?'

Footnote

The McBane trial took place in Edinburgh early the following year. Five of the McBanes were eventually convicted of murder, on thirteen counts. Two further counts of murder were dropped for lack of evidence. Ronald McBane and Moray McBane were both given live imprisonment and are currently receiving psychiatric treatment at The State Hospital for Scotland and Northern Ireland, Carstairs. Ronald McBane has not been charged with the murder in Switzerland but Interpol are intending to re-open that case soon.

Neil and Alec McBane and their five sons were convicted of murder on nine counts and are all serving life imprisonment in various prisons in Scotland, including Barlinnie. Marie McBane, who was both eldest daughter and 'wife' to Ronald McBane, is serving a ten-year prison sentence in the Cornton Vale Women's Prison, Stirling.

Jamie McBane - had he survived - would have been charged with the attempted murder of Cecelia Arnold and Erik Bergman and grievous bodily harm against four police officers when resisting arrest on the morning of October 24th. He was, instead, quickly cremated and his ashes scattered secretly somewhere on Rannoch Moor. It is thought that over the years he was directly responsible for at least eleven murders.

Five McBane women were charged with cannibalism and systematic child-abuse or unlawful sexual relationships with siblings. Four of the original five women thus charged are serving various custodial sentences at Cornton Vale and undergoing extensive psychiatric treatment. The fifth - Angie McBane - committed suicide in her prison cell soon after sentences had been passed.

Marie's youngest sister, Bridget McBane - then living in Castelnaudary, France - is charged with assisting her sister in covering up the murders. She is thought to have been the person abroad who further disassociated the Rannoch Moor Hotel from 'missing' guests by using the credit cards of its victims in Europe, thereby making it look as if they were still alive. She was last seen in Paris and is currently being sought by both the French police and by Interpol.

Of the eleven children belonging to the McBane tribe, all were found to have been regularly abused by their relatives, including blood parents. All of the seven children under the age of sixteen have been taken into care by Child Protection Agencies in several parts of Scotland. The three male teenagers, including Stewart McBane, were each sentenced to a period of imprisonment for physical violence or attempted murder. All three are currently serving their sentences in Scotland's only male Young Offenders Institution, in Polmont. The two female teenagers are undergoing psychiatric treatment at HM Prison and Young Offenders Institution, Cornton Vale.

During the seven-week trial in Edinburgh the press made much of what was surely Scotland's most complex case, involving no less than twenty-seven family members. Apart from the murders themselves, evidence of widespread incest and cannibalism hit every tabloid paper and TV station across the globe. It was a sensational story and many papers picked up the connection with the Sawney Beane story from the 17th Century. Although the prosecution made much of these historical connections, no actual evidence was produced to establish this link, least of all DNA proof, so it was dismissed by the Judge. That did not stop the press from enjoying what remains to this day a fascinating possibility. The McBanes themselves denied any such links with the past.

Lieutenant Gabriélle Fourés was highly praised for her research into the McBane case and preliminary investigation. She was seconded to the Scottish police and the Scottish Prosecution Service for a further three months in the lead-up to the trial itself. After the McBane trial in Edinburgh she returned to Paris and resumed her normal duties. Two months later she was promoted Capitaine and is currently attached to the French equivalent of the Drug Squad, working out of Marseilles.

During the period up to and including the trial Gabriélle lived with Elspeth Grant in Edinburgh but since returning to France it would seem that they have lost contact with each other.

Erik Bergman and Cecelia Arnold did not become a couple. Cecelia stayed with Erik in hospital until he recovered from his wounds. He then returned to Norway alone - to resume his duties as a serving officer in the Norwegian army. Cecelia did not sell her jewellery or cash in her 'rainy day nest egg'. Some months after her escape from Rannoch Moor she took up with an elderly but rich industrialist from Russia whom she had met in Paris. She is now thought to have become his mistress and is living in Nice, in the south of France.

Sir Miles Ballard was not surprised to learn that Cecelia had left that night with Erik Bergman. When he later learned of her part in exposing the McBanes, he was rather proud of her and dined out on her story for several months thereafter. He now has another mistress.

When eventually Cecelia returned to her flat in Mayfair she discovered that not only had Sir Miles assigned to her the lease on the flat but had returned her clothes left at Rannoch and put them back in her wardrobe - including the mink coat. He thus remained generous to the end. Cecelia wrote to him to thank him but he never replied. Had she not sealed her letter 'with a loving kiss' who knows what might have happened. Cecelia immediately let the flat to a Saudi business man at nearly £1,000 a week.

Teddy Bosenquet and Lady Olympia Garland did not get married after all. They remain friends, however.

As for Michelin Guide Food Inspector 'Dr Thomas Neep', better known to his relatives as Bartholomew Trickett, well he was sacked by his bosses in Paris and is no longer an official food inspector for them. This upset him no end but he understands why. He recognised that he had not only failed them but had failed himself - badly. He is now, incidentally, a vegetarian.

THE END

If you enjoyed this book then why not try the others in this series

Volume 1
But who killed Caroline?
By
Mike Healey

Volume 2
The beasts of Rannoch Moor
By
Mike Healey

Volume 3
Cri de Coeur
By
Mike Healey

Also by Mike Healey

Tales of Odd
Twelve short stories similar to Roald Dahl's celebrated 'Tales of the Unexpected' but darker. Much darker!

Printed in Great Britain
by Amazon